D0561887

# ADVENTURE THROUGH WORLD WAR II

# OPERATION CARTWHEEL
## THE FINAL COUNTDOWN TO V-J DAY

### BY LAWRENCE CORTESI

**ZEBRA BOOKS**
**KENSINGTON PUBLISHING CORP.**

ZEBRA BOOKS

are published by

KENSINGTON PUBLISHING CORP.
475 Park Avenue South
New York, N.Y. 10016

Printed in the United States of America

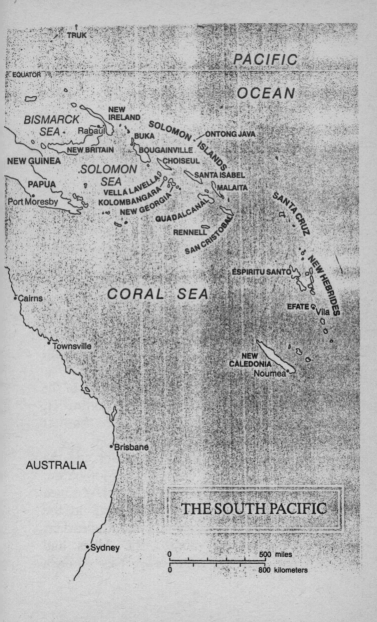

THE SOUTH PACIFIC

# Chapter One

Only two things were certain in the Southwest and South Pacific in October of 1943. The Japanese hoped to maintain their hold on the northern Solomons, New Britain, and western New Guinea, while the Allies hoped to dislodge the Japanese from their Southwest and South Pacific bases. Ever since the battle of Midway in June of 1942, Japanese and Allied military leaders conducted one or another military operation that often resulted in hard fought Pacific battles.

The American invasion of Bougainville in the northern Solomons, as part of plan Elkton III, triggered another vicious Pacific battle that left one side gasping for breath.

By the fall of 1943, both the Allies and the Japanese were looking for a new major battle. The harsh Papuan campaign in New Guinea and the severe Guadalcanal campaign in the Solomons had ended some nine months earlier. During the ensuing months the Allies had ousted the Japanese from other New Guinea bases and other Solomon islands. The Japanese, meanwhile, had carried out extensive air attacks on Allied airfields and harbors to stem the slow Allied advance.

Operation Cartwheel, the second phase of the Elkton III strategy, was a plan to neutralize Rabaul, Japan's super base in the Southwest Pacific. At the same time, the Japanese had readied Operation I-110, a plan for massive air and sea assaults on the American bases in both the Bismarck Archipelago and the Solomons Islands, to stop any further Allied advances in the Bismarck Archipelago.

In October of 1943, five major military strongholds dominated the Pacific battle area. The Japanese maintained an exceptionally strong naval base on the island of Truk in the Caroline Islands group and the Allies maintained a major naval base on the island of New Caledonia in the South Pacific. Closer to the battle fronts were the Japanese stronghold of Rabaul on New Britain and the major Allied bases of Port Moresby on New Guinea and Guadalcanal in the Solomons. If the Japanese could diminish the importance of these Allied bases by cutting off supply lines and destroying advance bases, the Allies could make no further incursions into the Japanese inner empire. Conversely, if the Allies could pulverize Rabaul and Truk, the Allies could move swiftly north from New Guinea and west from the Central Pacific to the Philippines.

"We would need large numbers of aircraft

and ships to carry out Operation I-one-ten," Admiral Junichi Kusaka, commander of the 11th Air Fleet, told reporters after the war. "But aircraft production in Japan had risen to about five hundred planes a month by mid-1943. By the fall, we had on hand almost a thousand operable aircraft between the Army and Navy Air Forces. As soon as the Japanese Combined Fleet had built up its warship strength, we planned to launch the one-ten operation. However, the Allied invasion of Bougainville forced us to alter these plans."

U.S. Adm. Bill Halsey, commander of the South Pacific Allied Forces, said after the Cartwheel campaign: "We still weren't that strong in the summer of 1943. The TF thirty-eight fleet included a mere two carriers with only about two hundred planes. Sure, we wanted to neutralize Rabaul so we could advance toward the Philippines. But I was uneasy about the invasion of Bougainville, only a couple hundred miles from Rabaul, because I suspected the Japanese would respond with a vicious, all out effort—and they sure did!"

In mid October, 1943, Adm. Mineichi Koga, CinC of the Japanese Combined Fleet, arrived in Rabaul via seaplane from his headquarters at Truk. The Japanese service troops at Rabaul, working at their chores along the shorelines, stopped their labors for a glimpse of this man who had replaced Isoroku Yamamoto, the former, almost worshipped CinC. Yamamoto had been killed a few months ago when

American P-38 pilots shot down the admiral's plane over Bougainville, killing Yamamoto and everyone else aboard.

The sailors on the shoreline were not impressed with this new Japanese Combined Fleet commander. He was quite short, with an obese frame and moon face, and small, dull eyes. He carried none of the stiff, confident posture of Yamamoto. Yamamoto had a muscular build, oval face, tall stature, and penetrating eyes—physical features that marked Yamamoto as a man deserving trust and respect. Still, the presence of Koga at Rabaul excited these working sailors of the Southeastern Fleet. Perhaps the admiral was here on an inspection tour and they might see the CinC close up and maybe even speak to him.

The shoreline work parties watched Admiral Koga get into a waiting car that whisked the admiral along the beach road to the bungalow of Gen. Hitoshi Imamura, commander of the 8th Area Forces in Rabaul.

Shortly after the shore-based sailors resumed their work, a second Emily seaplane alighted in Blanche Bay and pulled to a shoreline berth. Again, these service personnel on shore watched visitors get out of the plane. An entourage of officers respectfully escorted a central figure out of the Emily. He was a ruggedly built man, with a strong chiseled face, and deep, flashing eyes. Most of the men did not know this figure and some of them turned to their petty officer.

"Who is he?"

"A most impressive man," the petty officer answered. "He is Adm. Takeo Kurita of the Second Support Fleet."

The shoreline work crews studied the visitor more intently, for if they did not recognize him in person, they surely knew the reputation of Admiral Kurita. The admiral's heavy cruiser fleet had been the only bright spot in the Battle of Midway when the cruisers had bombarded the Americans at Midway Island and almost forced a U.S. evacuation of the island. Kurita's fleet had also been one of the successful units in the Solomons campaign, when his cruisers had successfully bombarded Henderson Field to allow a Japanese transport group to land the army's 2nd division on Tassafarongo. His fleet had also protected the 2nd Carrier Fleet during the Japanese naval victory at the Battle of Santa Cruz where one U.S. carrier had been sunk and another seriously damaged.

In fact, of all the admirals in the Combined Fleet, no officer had enjoyed more success during nearly two years of war against the Allies than had Kurita. Now, the esteemed admiral had come to Rabaul. Why?

"It appears," the Japanese petty officer told his shoreline work crews, "that our admirals intend to follow through with the I Operation prepared months ago by Admiral Yamamoto."

"Does that mean that more planes and ships will come to Rabaul?"

"Yes."

"But can we maintain more ships and aircraft

11

at Rabaul?''

"We can maintain every ship and aircraft in the Japanese Combined Fleet," the petty officer said. "No base in the Pacific is more formidable than Rabaul."

The petty officer spoke the truth, for the very name of Rabaul had become synonymous with the spirit and strength of the Japanese armed forces in the Pacific. Since the Japanese first occupied Rabaul in early 1942, more than one and a half years ago, the mere mention of this mighty fortress sent shivers through the Allied airmen, sailors, and soldiers of the Southwest and South Pacific. If Hitler had his Festung (Fortress) Europe, Japan had its Festung Rabaul in the Pacific.

The Rabaul complex, on the northeast tip of New Britain's Gazelle Peninsula, sat at the top of the Bismarck Archipelago. To the south lay New Guinea and Australia, and to the southeast was the Solomon Islands chain. The location of Rabaul assured its occupant of a strategic position to control the sea and air lanes from the Bismarck Archipelago and the Solomons to points north into the Central Pacific, East Indies, and the Philippine Islands. No military force could really move northward through the Carolines, Marianas, and Bonin Islands on the road to Japan as long as Rabaul remained a formidable military base.

Rabaul possessed the small Matupi Harbor and two large, well sheltered harbors. Simpson Harbor could anchor a hundred ships without

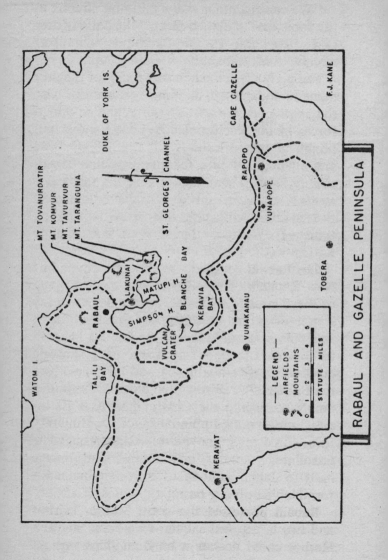

RABAUL AND GAZELLE PENINSULA

difficulty and Blanche Bay could anchor another hundred more. About the two harbors was an expanse of flat terrain that could accommodate every type of military facility, including airfields. And, since the Rabaul complex lay within a bowl-shaped semi-circle of high, volcanic hills, the Rabaul Bowl was inaccessible by any land army. The tallest hills, the volcanic ones, had been named the Mother, Two Daughters, and Vulcan.

The climate on the Gazelle Peninusla was quite pleasant compared to the steaming humidity of New Guinea and the Solomons, and men could work here without suffering the diseases and fatigue that prevailed in other Pacific areas.

The first white man to see Rabaul, Captain James Simpson of the Royal Navy, sailed into cozy Blanche Bay in 1781 and continued on into the even more sheltered Simpson Harbor. Captain Simpson at once claimed the Gazelle Peninsula for England. He named the outer harbor Blanche Bay after his flagship *Blanche,* and he named Simpson Harbor after himself. In time, more than 1,000 Europeans and several thousand Chinese came to Rabaul; government officials, traders, missionaries, laborers, and planters.

After World War I, all of New Britain came under the rule of Australia, a British commonwealth. The Australians, besides improving the Rabaul harbors, built two airports at Rabaul and the area became a major shipping and trade center in the Bismarck Archipelago.

When World War II began, Rabaul became a prime objective for Japan and she wasted no time in assaulting this strategic Gazelle Peninsula with a large landing force on January 22, 1942. The invaders easily overwhelmed the small Australian garrison. Some historians say the Japanese conducted a ruthless spree of murder against Australian prisoners, but the Japanese denied these charges. They claimed that such incidents were isolated and that those responsible for killing or mistreating prisoners had been severely punished.

"These were lies!" Col. Inoyu Kusunose told Allied interpreters after the war. Kusunose had been part of the Nankai Shitai force under Gen. Tomiru Horii which had captured Rabaul. "General Horii was an honorable man," Kusonose insisted. "He would never allow the mistreatment of prisoners." (Horii was later killed in the Papuan campaign in the fall of 1942.)

Once the Japanese had captured Rabaul, they worked feverishly to turn the Rabaul Bowl into the most formidable Japanese base in the Pacific. They improved the Australian airfields of Lakunai and Vunakanau, while they built three more airfields: Rapopo Drome, Tobera Field, and Keravat Field. All of the airdromes except Karavet had concrete all-weather runways, and each field contained revetments for from 80 to 100 planes, with miles of taxiways, ample supply depots, and plenty of service facilities. The Japanese had also improved existing roads and built miles of new roads on the Gazelle Peninsula.

By August of 1943, the Japanese housed permanently at Rabaul about 100 bombers and 150 fighters, most of them belonging to the navy's 11th Air Fleet under Adm. Junichi Kusaka. But some of the aircraft belonged to the army's 22nd Sentai Air Division.

Rabaul's harbor facilities included seven wharves and numerous piers that jutted into both Simpson Harbor and Blanche Bay. As a supplement, the Japanese also kept several floating cranes in these harbors. Further, the Japanese had built extensive repair, service, and supply buildings under the dense foliage of Lakunai Forest east of Simpson Harbor. At the smaller Matupi Harbor, the Japanese maintained a submarine berth.

The 8th Area Forces, under General Imamura, was headquartered at Rabaul. Imamura was in charge of all operations on land, sea and air throughout the South and Southwest Pacific. Under his command was the Southeastern Fleet, commanded by Adm. Tomushige Samejima and based at Rabaul; the 11th Air Fleet under Admiral Kusaka also based at Rabaul; the 17th Army under Gen. Haruyoshi Hyakutake that operated in the Solomons; and the 18th Army under Gen. Hatazo Adachi that operated in New Guinea.

In October, about a dozen warships and 15 or 20 transports and freighters were anchored in the Rabaul harbors, while some 175 naval planes and about 80 army planes were housed at the airdromes. Totally, some 22,000 navy personnel and 97,000 army personnel, including airmen, were stationed here. Finally, the 8th Area Forces had on hand about a six month inventory of supplies: food, medicine, ammunition, spare parts, and other necessities.

To protect this huge Gazelle Peninsula complex, the Japanese had installed some 43 coastal defense guns about the coastlines and hills of Rabaul Bowl. The Japanese also had some 367 anti-aircraft guns, 200 tanks, and 300 artillery pieces within the confines of the bowl. And, besides arms and men, Japan maintained several warning radar sets about Rabaul Bowl, with more radar sets at nearby Kavieng and Cape St. George. The radar could pick up Allied air formations or surface fleets at least 30 to 60 minutes before the potential assailants reached Rabaul Bowl. So fighter planes could be airborne in time to intercept enemy intruders.

Thus the Allies' Operation Cartwheel was a most ambitious plan. They would need plenty of muscle to reduce Rabaul into impotency.

On October 12, when Admirals Koga and Kurita reached Imamura's bungalow, Gen. Hitoshi Imamura himself greeted the visitors from Truk. The 8th Area Forces commander stood on the porch in his formal gray uniform. A colorful braid hung from his shoulder, a row of medals bristled on his chest, and the sword and scabbard at his side glistened in the morning sun. Next to Imamura was Admiral Kusaka of the 11th Air Fleet. He too stood stiffly on the porch. Medals bristled on his dark blue uniform while the oversize buttons on the front of his coat blinked in the sun.

As Admiral Koga came up the porch steps, Kusaka bowed. "Welcome to Rabaul, Honorable Koga. I offer humble greetings for myself and Admiral Samejima who is in the map room."

"I am glad to see you again, Junichi," Koga said.

"I also welcome you, Tokusaburo," Kasaka turned to Admiral Kurita.

General Imamura looked steadily at Admiral Koga, but did not bow because Imamura held the same high rank in the army as Koga did in the navy. Imamura merely nodded to the CinC of the Japanese Combined Fleet. "Let us hope we complete favorable plans to stop our enemies from creeping ever closer to our homeland."

"With good cooperation, we will do so," Koga answered.

Inside the bungalow, other officers were already present: Gen. Haruyoshi Hyakutake, commander of the 17th Army; Gen. Noburo Sasaki, commander of the 6th Division at Bougainville, Capt. Goro Furugori of the army's 22nd Sentai Air Division, and of course General Samejima of the Southeastern Fleet.

Aides served tea and cakes to the high ranking visitors and after the refreshments, the Japanese officers seated themselves around an oval table in the map room. Admiral Koga sat at the head of the table with General Imamura as aides passed about 8″ by 10″ maps that were miniatures of a large map on the wall behind Imamura's chair. After the officers studied the maps, Koga rose to his feet and spoke.

"Gentlemen, you can see from the maps the incursions the Americans have made since the unfortunate loss of Buna and Guadalcanal. In the past several months they have occupied the Russell Islands, Munda, Vella Lavella, and Barodoma in the Central Solomons. And only last month they captured Lae and Finchhaven in New Guinea to complete the conquest of Papua and take control of the Dampier Strait between the Bismarck and Solomon Seas. We cannot allow these encroachments to continue against the outer rim of our empire."

"Then we will initiate Operation I-one ten?" Admiral Kusaka asked.

"Yes," Koga answered. 'We now have more than five hundred aircraft available between the Eleventh Air Fleet and the Third Carrier Fleet. And, we have been promised more." He turned to Imamura. "General, do you know how many aircraft are available from the Twenty-second Sentai?"

"We have nearly one hundred aircraft at Rabaul and about another one hundred on our bases in the northern Solomons," Captain Furugori suddenly spoke.

"The army also has about one hundred aircraft in the Fifth Wing in New Guinea," General Imamura said.

"Then we can count on some eight hundred planes for the I operation?" Koga asked.

"So it appears," Imamura said.

"And what of army units?" Koga asked.

"The Eighteenth Army has some thirty thousand troops in various New Guinea encampments and the Seventeenth Army has more than twenty thousand troops at bases in the northern Solomons. We also have at least two divisions of reserves here in Rabaul." Then Imamura questioned Koga. "What about navy units?"

"We have built up our surface ship strength both here and at Truk," Admiral Koga said. "Admiral Kurita's Second Fleet now numbers seven heavy cruisers, four light cruisers and a dozen destroyers. Admiral Samejima has six cruisers and a dozen destroyers along with transport and freighter marus to carry men and supplies if necessary. Admiral Ozawa has his carrier fleet at Truk with more than three hundred aircraft. I believe we have ample resources to carry out the I operation."

"When will this operation begin?" Admiral Kusaka asked.

"By mid-November at the latest," Admiral Koga said. He took a pointer from an aide and turned to the wall map. "You may follow me with the maps in front of you. Here, at Lae and Finchhaven," he slapped the map, "the enemy is improving both the harbors and inland airfields. I will ask Admiral Samejima to sail through the Bismarck Sea with the Southeastern Fleet to conduct major naval bombardments of these New Guinea shore and harbor facilities." He looked at Imamura. "Is it possible that the Fifth Wing in New Guinea can support the Southeastern Fleet with air assaults?"

"Yes," General Imamura answered. "Between the Fifth Wing and the Twenty-second Sentai we can mount some two hundred army aircraft. We will conduct daily air strikes for as long as necessary."

"Excellent," Koga nodded. He then moved the pointer to the Central Solomons. "I will ask Admiral Kurita to sail southward from Truk with the Second Support Fleet to conduct a series of naval bombardments against the enemy's advanced bases in the Solomons: at Vella Lavella, Bunda, and New Georgia. The Eleventh Air Fleet, meanwhile, will conduct massive air assaults on these areas in conjunction with the surface ship bombardments. We will keep Admiral Ozawa's carrier fleet in reserve to make air strikes wherever they may be needed."

"The Second Fleet is prepared for combat," Kurita said, "and my sailors are most anxious to deal a blow to our enemies."

"With Admiral Kurita's cruiser fleet to aid our air units, we can strike hard," General Imamura said.

"It is important that we succeed in this endeavor," Admiral Koga gestured, "for if we allow the Americans to strengthen and expand their newly won bases, they will be encouraged to make more invasions."

"I agree with the honorable Koga," Imamura said. "If we do not stop the Americans soon, they may invade Bougainville, the Admiralties, or New Britain. They may even attempt to assault Rabaul itself."

Most of the officers grinned in amusement at this last suggestion. Invade Rabaul? Imamura was talking nonsense, for the Allies could not possibly capture or even reduce Rabaul. No, Imamura's reference to the loss or collapse of Rabaul was merely a dramatic gesture to impress upon those present the need to successfully carry out Operation I-110.

But the Americans had indeed intended to remove Rabaul as a threat to the Allies in the South and Southwest Pacific.

Noumea, New Caledonia had been the Allied South Pacific Force (COMSOPAC) headquarters since early 1942 when American and Australian forces simply occupied the island. Many French colonials here had protested the occupation, for they had regarded New Caledonia as the property of Vichy France which was now a neutral in World War II. But the Allies had simply taken the position that the island belonged to the French government in exile. Against American might, the Vichyites in New Caledonia could hardly resist. The U.S. immediately built New Caledonia into a major base of operations against the Japanese.

By the fall of 1943, New Caledonia was comparable to Rabaul in strength. Engineers had constructed two huge airdromes, Tontouta and Plaines de Caiacs outside of the city of Noumea. The fields could handle over 300 aircraft and in October the army's 7th Bomb Group, 44th Fighter Group, and the marine's Air Group 2 were housed here. Service squadrons on New Caledonia readied new aircraft from the states before these planes staged out to Air Force Solomons, COMAIRSOL, on the island of Guadalcanal.

Seabees had also improved and expanded Noumea Harbor that could now service and shelter a hundred surface ships at once. Row after row of repair, service, and warehouse facilities lined the shoreline, while inland, countless tons of supplies, ammunition, and arms lay in huge quonset huts.

The city of Noumea itself, populated by French, Chinese and native Polynesians, offered the only civilian diversion on New Caledonia. And, as more Allied servicemen came here, the price of everything from a meal to prostitutes had skyrocketed.

COMSOPAC headquarters included a dozen buildings on a five acre complex just beyond Noumea Harbor. Here, Adm. Bill Halsey with some 30 officers and 100 enlisted men, both army and navy, directed operations in the South Pacific. Army representatives were on Halsey's staff because army ground and air units were part of COMSOPAC. Halsey's worst problem had been with Gen. Douglas MacArthur, CinC of Allied Forces in the SWPA. MacArthur's wishes generally prevailed over those of Admiral Halsey, much to Halsey's irritation.

Fortunately, General MacArthur not only approved of Operation Cartwheel for the reduction of Rabaul, but he had encouraged the plan. Further, he was delighted with the plan to invade Bougainville. The SWPA commander promised Halsey any air and ground forces he could spare for the operation.

The Elkton plans had been on the drawing boards since the fall of 1942, as a series of military moves to return to the Philippines. Elkton I ended with the capture of Buna and Guadalcanal. Elkton II had dealt with the capture of Lae, Finchhaven, and the central Solomons. Now the Americans would launch Elkton III, Operation Cartwheel, to complete the ring around Rabaul and render this major Japanese base helpless.

"We were sure we had the resources to carry out Elkton III," said Gen. Nathan Twining, commander of COMAIRSOL. "We had plenty of planes in our Air Solomons command and Fifth Air Force had even more planes in New Guinea. We had ample surface ships, both warships and transports, and we did have a carrier group assigned to COMSOPAC, with another carrier group available if needed. We also had five divisions of army and marine troops to occupy important areas around Rabaul."

The key points to complete the ring around Rabal were the islands of Bougainville in the northern Solomons, the Admiralty Islands northwest of Rabaul, and Cape Gloucester on the southern tip of New Britain. Elkton III called for the invasion of Bougainville, then the seizure of New Britain in December of 1943, and finally the occupation of the Admiralties in February of 1944. In order to succeed in these operations, the Americans needed to neutralize Rabaul. In conjunction with the Bougainville invasion, American air power needed to pound the Japanese stronghold relentlessly and render the base useless. Then, the United States could move unmolested from New Guinea and the Central Pacific into the Philippines.

On October 17, only a few days after Admiral Koga's conference at Rabaul, Adm. William "Bull" Halsey called his own conference at COMSOPAC headquarters in Noumea, New Caledonia. He would discuss plans for the invasion of Bougainville and the reduction of Rabaul—Operation Cartwheel.

Halsey's own Pacific fleet was based at Noumea, and for the most part his naval units staged out of Noumea for operations in the South Pacific. His naval vessels escorted amphibious landing forces in the Solomons chain, or they supported ground operations already in progress, and they occasionally fought Japanese war fleets. The air arm of COMSOPAC, General Twining's COMAIRSOL, included six air groups: the U.S. Army's 18th Fighter

Group, 5th Heavy Bomb Group, 307th Heavy Bomb Group, 42nd Medium Bomb Group, the 24th Marine Air Group (MAG 24), and the New Zealand 18 Squadron.

Halsey also had ready for use two marine and two army infantry divisions.

Besides the land based air units of COMAIR-SOL, Halsey had on loan from the Pacific Fleet, the TF 38 carrier fleet for Operation Cartwheel. TF 38 under Adm. Fred Sherman was built around carriers USS *Princeton* and USS *Saratoga*.

Halsey had also been assured of air support from 5th U.S. Army Air Force of the SWPA command to join in this operation. 5th Air force, based in New Guinea, included three medium bomb groups, two heavy bomb groups, and four fighter groups, as well as an Australian air wing.

So if Adm. Mineichi Koga believed he had the resources to carry out Operation I-110, Adm. Bill Halsey felt equally confident that he could carry out Operation Cartwheel—invade Bougainville and then complete the ring around Rabaul.

A new major battle was shaping up in the Pacific war.

## Chapter Two

The American sailors who worked the docks and wharves about Noumea Harbor showed little concern when military VIPs arrived in port. But then admirals and generals from outlying bases came and left Noumea regularly for conferences at COMSOPAC headquarters. So the arrival of high military officers rarely stirred the working shore parties. The arrival of Gen. Nathan Twining from Guadalcanal to Tontouta Field on this October 17 day had gone unnoticed. Similarly, few men paid attention to the arrival of the deputy 5th Air Force commander, Gen. Ennis Whitehead, who had flown in from Port Moresby, although his arrival from a different command, the SWPA, should have drawn some curiosity.

The other commanders involved in Operation Cartwheel were already headquartered in Noumea: Adm. Stanton Merrill of TF 39, the cruiser-destroyer support fleet; Adm. Len Reifsnider, commander of the TF 31 amphibious troop transport force; and Gen. Allen

Turnage, commander of the 3rd Marine Division.

Admiral Halsey opened his conference at mid-morning, and like Admiral Koga, Halsey also distributed to those in attendance the maps for the Bougainville invasion. Halsey's aides also furnished photos so that the men at the conference table could better understand the Bougainville invasion site. After some refreshments of rolls and coffee, Admiral Halsey spoke to the assembled officers.

"As you can see," the COMSOPAC chief began, "We'll be invading Bougainville in the Empress Augusta Bay area and so by-pass the enemy's strong positions on the south coast of the island. We know they have about a division of troops entrenched around the Buin-Kahili area, and they have a back-up force of maybe regimental strength at nearby Kara. The southern coast is simply too strong to make a frontal assault.

"However," Halsey gestured, "our coast-watchers report that no more than two or three thousand Japanese troops are in the Empress Augusta Bay area, and we can easily handle them." Halsey gestured to his aide, Capt. Harry Barker.

"We've made a complete survey of the bay area," Captain Barker said. "Landing parties from the submarine USS *Guardfish* have reconnoitered the area. About fifteen miles from Cape Torokina. Here," Barker tapped a photo, "is a good flat area without swamps where we

28

can build good airfields. Cape Torokina itself has no obstructions so the beaches around the cape would be a good place to land."

"We also have another good reason for landing in the Cape Torokina area," Halsey said. "Torokina Bay has an excellent anchorage, about the only place along the entire west coast of Bougainville that does have a good anchorage."

Captain Barker now hung another photo on the wall. "The Japanese ground troops are quite scattered in thin units of no more than company strength along the coastal area of Empress Augusta Bay. You can see from these photos that we've seen few defenses and few troops. So we aren't likely to run into much opposition."

"The main body of Japanese is to the south," Halsey spoke again. "There's fifty miles of dense jungles and high mountains between their strongpoints on southern Bougainville and the Cape Torokina area. That means the bulk of Japanese troops cannot interfere with our landings."

"What about air power?" Admiral Reifsnider asked.

"That will be a problem," Halsey said. "The Japanese have about a hundred planes among their fields at Buin and Kahili in Bougainville and at Ballale in the Shortlands. They could also bring more planes down from Rabaul. So it's vital that we knock out these fields." He looked at Twining. "Well?"

General Twining, commander of the mixed bag of air units from COMAIRSOL, looked at some papers in his hands. "We'll begin air assaults tomorrow by hitting those airfields in the northern Solomons. We'll make sure they have no planes to fly out of those bases, and we'll also keep their fields chopped up so they can't bring in any more aircraft from Rabaul. I'm sure we'll have their airfields neutralized by the time the marines land at Cape Torokina."

The COMAIRSOL air force had been an offshoot of the old Cactus Air Force of the Guadalcanal campaign, where an array of planes from the army, marine, and New Zealand forces had furnished air units to operate against the Japanese. Now COMAIRSOL's six air groups totalled nearly 300 planes. Among the colorful personages in COMAIRSOL was Lt. Thomas Lamphier of the 18th Fighter Group who had shot down the Betty bomber carrying Adm. Isoroku Yamamoto, killing the commander of the Japanese Combined Fleet and most of his staff. Also assigned to COMAIRSOL was the famed Maj. Gregory "Pappy" Boyington and his Black Sheep 214 VMF squadron of MAG 24.

COMAIRSOL aircraft operated mostly out of Guadalcanal airfields and their primary work included the support of amphibious landings in the Central Solomons during the spring and summer of 1943; and COMAIRSOL aircraft bombed Japanese troop concentrations and land bases in the Solomons, or they attacked

Japanese war fleets and air formations. Now General Twining found himself with a most formidable task, since he could expect numerous Japanese fighter and bomber units from Rabaul to challenge his own air units when the U.S invaded Bougainville. Twining would need help and he turned to General Whitehead of the army's 5th Air Force.

"Well, General, can you knock out Rabaul?"

"We've got some heavy air strikes planned for Rabaul," General Whitehead said. "The Fifth Air Force has already carried out the biggest raid yet on Rabaul. We sent three hundred and forty aircraft of all types to Rabaul on October 12 and we cleaned out their airfields and harbors: damaged, destroyed or sank everything there."

The October 12 raid had come almost immediately after Admiral Koga's conference and the attack had totally shocked the Japanese Combined Fleet commander. The Americans, however, had exaggerated the results of this surprise raid, claiming the destruction or damage to 160 planes on the ground and 26 planes shot down. The 5th Air Force pilots had also claimed they had sunk or damaged three large merchant ships, three destroyers, and 70 other harbor vessels. The damage or destruction of aircraft had been quite accurate, but the Americans had only sunk a pair of 100 ton ships in the harbor, while damaging several more.

Still, the destruction had infurated General

Imamura and he had summarily relieved the radar commander of command, claiming he had been derelict in allowing the Americans to make the huge surprise raid on Rabaul. Imamura had then ordered radar crews to intensify their vigil, while he ordered all air commanders to keep fighter pilots on continual alert.

Now, here at Noumea, Admiral Halsey turned to Whitehead. "General, you'll need to fly into Rabaul every day from now until November first, L-Day for Bougainville. We can't afford to have the Japanese sending massive air formations or strong surface fleets down from Rabaul to chop up our invasion forces."

"Don't worry," Whitehead said. "I guarantee that Rabaul will be dead by November first." The ADVON 5th Air Force commander was that confident.

The ten air groups of 5th Air Force, based in New Guinea, Woodlark Island, and Kiriwina Island, numbered more than 600 planes of all types for use in Operation Cartwheel. Whitehead intended to use all of them in a series of air attacks on Rabaul, hoping to finish the job he started on October 12.

Admiral Halsey now looked at Adm. Stanton Merrill who commanded the TF 39 cruiser-destroyer fleet. "How many of your ships are available to escort the amphibious landing force?"

"All but two destroyers," Merrill answered. "We have our four cruisers and two desrons of four destroyers each. Unless the Japanese send down a large fleet from Truk, our TD thirty-nine should be adequate to defend the landing operations."

"I don't think the Japanese will commit any carrier groups or heavy warships to the Solomons again," Halsey said. "We've got too much air power now and they've got an obsessive fear of planes. Their big eighteen-inch battleships have been sitting in Truk for weeks and they apparently won't commit these ships anywhere."

Halsey now looked at Adm. Len Reifsnider who would lead the III Amphibious Force transports that would carry the 3rd U.S. Marine Division and the 2nd Raider Regiment under Gen. Allen Turnage. Because the U.S. Navy had been planning an invasion of the Marshalls in the Central Pacific, the III Amphibious Corps had limited transports: 12 APA's and AKA's along with a few LST's. The combat troops would be quite crowded and even the supply ships would be jammed. However, the trip to Empress Augusta Bay would stage out of Guadalcanal so the voyage would only take 24 hours in the sail up The Slot.

"Len," Halsey asked the transport commander, "are you ready to go?"

"We'll have all troops and supplies moved to Guadalcanal within a couple of weeks. We won't have any trouble leaving Guadal' on October thirty-first."

"Good," Halsey nodded. He then turned to

a map and pointed to the Treasury Islands group immediately south of Bougainville and the large Choiseul Island just southeast of Bougainville. "We'll be making our diversionary landings on Mono Island in the Treasury group and on Choiseul during the last week of October. We hope these landings will convince the Japanese that we're establishing a forward staging area to assail Bougainville on the south coast, right into the teeth of their defenses at Buin and Kahili. It's our hope that these landings will convince the Japanese to mass their troops for an invasion on southern Bougainville."

"We're reconnoitered the Treasury Island group quite thoroughly," Captain Barker said. "A party from submarine *Greenling* studied the island a few weeks ago and they say the best landing beach is on Mono Island. The only things the Nips have there is a radio station and a few troops, no more than platoon strength. We also sent a survey party to Choiseul and they say the best place to land is at Vozo on the Slot side of the island. The Japanese only have about a company of men in the area and they're lightly armed."

"We intend to land the Second Parachute Battalion and a New Zealand company on Mono and the First Marine Regiment at Vozo," Halsey said. "As soon as the AKA's and LST's discharge these troops and supplies, they'll return to Guadalcanal to load troops and equipment for the Augusta Bay landings." He looked once more at General Twining. "Can I suggest, General, that your COMAIRSOL units start hitting the landing sites on Mono and Choiseul immediately?"

"Yes," Twining nodded.

"Then you can start pounding those Japanese airfields at Buin and Kahili," Admiral Reifsnider said. "We may have enough trouble from Japanese air units out of Rabaul and we certainly don't want enemy air strikes from bases only fifty to sixty miles away from our invasion site."

General Nathan Twining nodded again.

"Does anyone else here have any questions?" Halsey asked.

None.

"Okay, let's get this show moving."

The very next day, COMAIRSOL air units began a series of aerial assaults to soften the landing sites on Mono in the Treasury Island group and at the Vozo landing site on Choiseul Island. The VMDB 232 dive bomber squadron and the VMTB 242 torpedo squadron of MAG 24 conducted a half dozen raids on West Cape at Choiseul, while the B-24s of the 5th and 307th Army Bomb Groups, along with B-25s from the army's 42nd Bomb Group pasted the landing areas.

The invasions on Mono came off on the morning of October 27, with troops of the 2nd Parachute Battalion, the New Zealand infantry company, and 3,870 tons of supplies. Against light resistance, the Allied troops occupied and secured Mono in the Treasury Islands group by nightfall of the 27th. The next morning, the 1st Marine Regiment landed on Choiseul, again with little opposition. The U.S. marines occupied and secured most of the Vozo area by nightfall.

The twin landings had affected the Japanese exactly as Halsey hoped. As soon as word reached Rabaul, General Imamura interpreted the Treasury and Choiseul landings as a prelude to an invasion of southern Bougainville. He immediately alerted Gen. Noburo Sasaki to strengthen his 6th Division defenses at Kahili and Kara. Sasaki quickly complied and he also brought in troops from the nearby Shortlands Islands until he had massed some 20,000 troops along the south coast of Bougainville to repel the expected American invasion attempt.

"You must not falter," Imamura told the 6th Infantry Division commander.

"We have strengthened all beach areas and improved the obstructions off the coast," Sasaki answered Imamura. "I can promise that we will push back any enemy invaders into the sea."

"Good, good," the 8th Area Forces commander said.

But on the afternoon of October 27, COMAIRSOL began its relentless attack against Japanese air bases on southern Bougainville. Col. Richard Mangrum, commander of MAG 24, led the 232 Squadron bombers himself, while Capt. Robert Smith led the marine group's 242 Squadron of torpedo bombers. MAG 24 would hit Japanese supply barges, airfields, and troop concentrations.

Dick Mangrum had been the CO of the famed marine Blue Devil VMSB 232 that had seen considerable action during the Guadalcanal campaign in 1942. His Blue Devils had been the first air unit to land on Guadalcanal, on August, 20, 1942, only a couple of weeks after the American invasion. The 232 Squadron had suffered the brunt of Japanese air counterattacks and by late October of 1942, only Mangrum was still unscathed among the Blue Devil pilots and gunners. Seven had been killed, four evacuated, the rest wounded.

For his aggressiveness around Guadalcanal, Mangrum had won both the Navy Cross and the DFC. By November of 1942, the Blue Devil Squadron had been totally spent and other air units had relieved the macerated VMSB 232. Mangrum had returned to the States to train new units, but he got restless for more combat. In August of 1943 he had returned to the Pacific to assume command of MAG 24 that included a refurbished VMSB 232, the VMTB 242, and two marine fighter squadrons. Mangrum and his MAG 24 bomber crews pounded southern Bougainville on the 28th, 29th, and 30th of October.

The army air groups, B-25s and B-24s of the 42nd, 5th and 307th, also pounded Japanese installations and airfields in the northern Solomons.

By the evening of October 31, the Japanese airfields on southern Bougainville lay in shambles, without a single operable plane. Further, the runways had been so devastated that no planes could come in from Rabaul to land on these fields. Admiral Halsey personally sent congratulations to Colonel Mangrum and MAG 24 for the excellent efforts by the groups VMSB 232 and VMTB 242 squadrons. Halsey also congratulated the army bomb groups of COMAIRSOL for their exceptional work. The COMAIRSOL units had effectively paved the way for the Bougainville invasion.

Meanwhile, Gen. Ennis Whitehead resumed his assault on Rabaul. He sent 5th Air Force bombers to Rabaul on the 18th and 28th of October when B-24 Liberators of the 90th and 43rd Bomb Groups struck the Rabaul airfields with fragmentation bomb clusters and 500 pound bombs. Also, B-25 medium bombers of the 5th Air Force's 3rd, 38th, and 345th Bomb Groups attacked shipping in Simpson Harbor and Blanche Bay. The 5th Air Force strikes destroyed more grounded planes, eroded runways, and sank or damaged more ships in the harbors.

But bad weather rolled over the Bismarck Archipelago by October 29th and the 5th Air Force could not conduct further raids on Rabaul. During the respite, the Japanese rapidly replaced wrecked planes, quickly repaired runways, and hastily prepared a warship fleet. Thus the cancelled 5th Air Force missions against the Japanese stronghold enabled General Imamura to prepare an ominous threat to any Allied invasion of Bougainville, only 210 miles from Rabaul.

By October 31, Admiral Koga had sent a swarm of new aircraft to Rabaul, aircraft from the 3rd Carrier Fleet in Truk. The reinforcements, the 26th Kokutai Wing under Cmdr. Minoru Genda, included 82 Zero fighters, 45 Val dive bombers, 40 Kate torpedo planes, and six recon planes—173 new aircraft to bolster the planes already at Rabaul in the 4th Navy Kokutai Wing and the 22nd Army Sentai.

Koga had also dispatched to Rabaul several freighters with new supplies for the Southeastern Fleet, the freighters escorted by cruisers and destroyers of Crudiv 5 under Adm. Sentaro Omori. Koga intended to send reinforcements to Bougainville in the event the Americans intended to invade this northern Solomons island.

When U.S. recon planes from COMAIRSOL reported these reinforcements on the way to Rabaul, Halsey refused to cancel the Bougainville invasion. "The landings will go off as scheduled," he told his COMSOPAC commanders.

But as the invasion force sailed up The Slot from Guadalcanal to Empress Augusta Bay, all eyes among the COMSOPAC sailors and combat marines looked apprehensively to the northwest—in the direction of Rabaul.

*  *  *

On October 30, Adm. Sentaro Omori arrived in Rabaul with his cruisers, destroyers, and the several maru freighters and transports. Omori had no intention of remaining in Rabaul with his Crudiv 5 warships, but had planned to return to Truk as soon as the freighters and transports had been safely delivered to the Japanese stronghold. However, before Omori left Rabaul, Admiral Samejima invited the Crudiv 5 commander to his bungalow for a noon meal. With Omori came his chief of staff, Capt. Usha Yamada, and his Desron 61 commander, Capt. Morikazi Osugi, with desron flag aboard light cruiser *Agano*.

Omori, a veteran naval officer, had been in the Solomons naval battles since the American invasion of Guadalcanal in August of 1942, and in early 1943 he had won command of Crudiv 5. With the impending Bougainville invasion, Omori was anxious to return to battle for he had not seen action since the I-90 operation in April of 1943. Omori's fleet had escorted carriers whose planes had made massive attacks in the Solomons, Oro Bay and New Guinea. He now felt disappointment when told he would return to Truk and miss the expected action around Bougainville.

"I am pleased to see you," Samejima told the Crudiv 5 commander. "I would like you and your officers to enjoy a good meal before you return to Truk."

Omori squeezed his face. "I cannot understand this order to return to Truk if the Americans are bringing an invasion fleet to Bougainville. I should be sailing to the northern Solomons to stop them."

"For the time being, our air units will deal with the Americans," Samejima said.

Captain Osugi and Captain Yamada exchanged disappointed glances. Both officers had hoped that Samejima would have taken full advantage of Crudiv 5 and request from Admiral Koga that Crudiv 5 sail for Bougainville to attack the American invasion fleet now sailing up The Slot from Guadalcanal.

"I am sure you have seen the disappointment on our faces, Honorable Samejima," Omori said. "We are now quite certain the Americans intend to land on Bougainville. Yet our cruiser fleet is scheduled to return to Truk. Should we not attempt to break up this possible enemy invasion attempt with naval gunfire?"

Samejima grinned. "The Sixth Division is well entrenched at Buin and Kahili where the Americans will attempt their invasion. They can surely repel the enemy. Besides, we have strengthened our air units at Rabaul and we will deal with the invaders with air power."

"I see," Omori answered.

However, by the time the officers of Crudiv 5 had completed their meal and prepared to return to their ships, a communication reached Samejima's bungalow from the commander of Combined Fleet, Adm. Mineichi Koga. "You will dispatch at once Admiral Omori's Crudiv 5 to attack the American war fleet now sailing up the Sealark Channel. This war fleet is apparently leading an invasion fleet toward Bougainville. You will also ask Adm. Matsuji Ijuin to join this attack with his Desron 27.''

Samejima was delightfully surprised by Koga's sudden change of instructions while Omori and his Crudiv 5 officers were elated. "You will leave tomorrow," Samejima told Omori, "and I will ask Admiral Ijuin to join you with his Desron 27. He is now reported nearing St. George's Channel after an escort mission to Buka above Bougainville. He should be here by late afternoon and you can certainly be aweigh by tomorrow morning.''

"Excellent,'' Omori said. The Crudiv 5 commander knew of Admiral Ijuin's high reputation as a destroyer group commander, and he was elated to have Ijuin join him on the mission to Bougainville.

Adm. Matsuji Ijuin of Desron 27 had become the new Tanaka the Tenacious of the Solomons Islands. As Tanaka had successfully carried to the Solomons or evacuated from these islands thousands of troops in his Tokyo Express, Ijuin had also landed or withdrawn thousands of reinforcements or trapped Japanese troops in the Central Solomons during 1943. Most recently, Ijuin had successfully evacuated 3,000 men from Vella Lavella after a nighttime engagement with a U.S. fleet in which he had thwarted the American attempt to stop the evacuation.

As soon as Admiral Ijuin arrived in Blanche

Bay with his Desron 27, the light cruiser *Sendai* and four destroyers, Samejima ordered him to a conference with Admiral Omoro, Capt. Usho Yamada, Captain Osugi, and himself. Ijuin assured Samejima that he only needed to refuel and take on a few supplies to move again. Samejima then turned to Omori.

"How soon can you leave?"

"At once," Omori answered. "Captain Yamada has worked swiftly to prepare this warship fleet for our sortie."

Samejima grinned at the Crudiv 5 chief of staff. "I am pleased, Captain. Admiral Omori is fortunate to have a man of your ability to aid him in planning."

"Thank you, Honorable Samejima."

Capt. Usho Yamada had been an aide or executive officer or chief of staff for most of his combat career in the navy, but he had never won a flag command. Yet he had been an indispensable help to Omori in recent months. Yamada, of course, hoped for a promotion and a command, but unfortunately Imperial Headquarters had considered him an administrator and not a leader. So Yamada found himself once more in the administrative role of a fleet officer's chief of staff.

The sailors aboard the warships of Crudiv 5, Desron 61, and Desron 27 were eager to resume battle against the Americans, and they worked hard and quickly to load stores and ammunition aboard their warships. In fact many of them worked throughout the night of October 30-31 to make certain they would be ready by morning.

On the morning of October 31 Admiral Samejima made a final check with Admiral Omori and Captain Yamada. "Are you ready to sail?"

"Yes, Honorable Samejima," Omori said.

"Our reconnaisance planes have identified the enemy ships as a cruiser fleet. (Merrill's U.S. TF 39) We can expect this American war fleet to be approaching Bougainville waters soon. I suggest therefore that you sail directly southeast when you leave St. George's Channel. The Yokoyama Wing out of Ballale Airfield in the Shortlands will attend to the enemy invasion fleet behind their war fleet."

So at 1000 hours, October 31, Omori's fleet got under way: heavy cruisers *Haguro* and *Myoko,* light cruisers *Agano* and *Sendai,* and six destroyers.

However, by heading toward the Shortlands, Omori missed the American cruiser fleet that had sailed straight north to pound the Japanese airfields at Buka above Bougainville on the afternoon of October 31. Meanwhile, Reifsnider's transports of the III Amphibious Force had not come anywhere near the south coast of Bougainville, but had steamed to Empress Augusta Bay on the west-central coast.

Not until 0230 hours, November 1, did Omori realize what happened. Japanese recon planes had spotted both Merrill's fleet around Buka and the invasion fleet near Empress

Augusta Bay. A messenger brought the report to Omori in the flag room of heavy cruiser *Myoko*. Omori read the reports in astonishment.

"Uncanny! The Americans intend to invade far above the south coast, and the enemy cruiser fleet is far to the north. We have made a useless sail."

"May I suggest, Admiral," Captain Yamada said, "that we return to Rabaul. I suspect that General Imamara will wish to reinforce the Empress Augusta Bay area and he will need us to escort such reinforcements."

"A wise suggestion," Omori nodded. "Issue orders to all ship commanders."

So, at 0230 hours, November 1, the Japanese Crudiv 5 made an about face and sailed back to Rabaul.

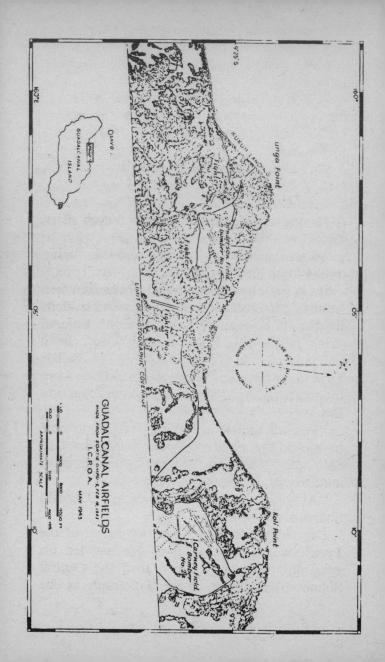

# Chapter Three

Having missed the American cruiser fleet, Omori now sailed back toward Rabaul while he awaited further orders. Meanwhile Adm. Junichi Kasaka of the 11th Air Fleet reacted swiftly to the news of an apparent invasion fleet heading for Empress Augusta Bay. After alerting the 4th Kokutai Wing and the 26th Kokutai Wing in Rabaul, Kusaka called Capt. Benji Shimada of the Yokoyama Wing at Ballale Field in the Shortlands, less than 100 miles from the expected invasion site at Empress Augusta Bay.

"You will muster as many aircraft as possible to attack the enemy invaders," Kusaka told Shimada. "It appears the enemy will attempt to land troops at Empress Augusta Bay."

"At once, Honorable Kusaka," Captain Shimada promised.

Captain Shimada had been a veteran of the Pacific war since early 1942. He had led his wing out of Rabaul, Buna, then the Central Solomons, and now in the Shortlands as the

Americans climbed the Solomons ladder. In September, after the Americans had ousted the Japanese from New Georgia, the wing had strengthened its base at Ballale Field, just across the Tonoge Strait from southern Bougainville.

The Yokoyama Wing had based some squadrons at the bases in southern Bougainville, on the island of Buka, and in the Treasuries as well as at Ballale. The late October Allied air assaults by COMAIRSOL's MAG 24, the army air units, and the New Zealand squadron had knocked out most of the wing's aircraft at the bases beyond the Shortlands. Now, the Wing numbered less than 50 operational planes, most at Ballale Field.

Shimada's air service crews had deftly filled bomb craters on both the Ballale runway and taxiways. By dawn of November 1, the day of the American invasion, the runway at Ballale had been repaired and Captain Shimada had ordered all available planes, 19 Vals and 22 Zeros, to prepare for attacks on the American invaders who were now reported inside Empress Augusta Bay. By 0600 hours, Shimada was briefing the Zero pilots and the two man Val dive bomber crews. Meanwhile, ground crews had loaded the Vals with four 500 pound bombs and the Zeros with two 500 pound bombs so they could be used as fighter-bombers.

"We will be the first to attack these invaders," Shimada told his fliers. He looked at Lt. Cmdr. Toyotara Iwami of the Zero units. "Toyotara, you will attack the enemy's landing barges with the Mitsubishi fighter bombers. We will attack the enemy vessels in the bay with the Aichi dive bombers.''

"But do we know when these enemy troops will assault the beaches?''

"Our intelligence at Empress Augusta Bay indicates the barge laden troops will leave their transports between oh-seven hundred and oh-seven-thirty hours to reach the beaches at about oh-eight hundred. We will plan our mission to reach this area at oh-seven-thirty-five hours.''

"I understand,'' Lt. Cmdr. Iwami said.

By 0645 hours, with Captain Shimada himself leading the Val dive bombers, the pilots and crews of the Yokoyama Wing boarded their aircraft and waited for take off signals. At 0655 hours Shimada and his wingman zoomed down the bumpy, hastily patched Ballale runway. Within a few minutes the other 39 aircraft also zoomed down the runway and took off. By 0705 the formations jelled into their standard 3 plane V's and headed north.

"Keep the formations tight, always tight,'' the wing commander cried into his radio. "And stay alert for enemy interceptors.''

"Yes, captain,'' Iwami answered.

Shimada looked at his watch: 0715. He would reach target in 20 minutes, for the Empress Augusta Bay area landing site lay only 75 miles from the Shortlands.

However, the Americans expected a Japanese reaction to the invasion at Cape Torokina and Halsey had instructed Twining to maintain combat air patrols over the invasion site, beginning at dawn. At 0400 hours, before daylight, Twining called both Col. Aaron Tyer of the Army Air Force's 18th Fighter Group and Col. Dick Mangrum of the marine's MAG 24. "We want CAPs up there by dawn. I'd like each of you to send out a squadron, so that we've got two units of covering fighter planes over the area at all times."

Colonel Tyer of the 18th Group called on Maj. Bob Westbrook, CO of the group's 44th Squadron to take the first CAP tour. Westbrook was probably one of the most aggressive squadron leaders in the Pacific. He had been acclaimed by both General Twining of COMAIRSOL and Gen. Millard Harmon of the 13th Air Force. Both agreed that Westbrook was a good man. The major was both stern in his discipline and compassionate with his airmen. He maintained a tight command, but he also showed flexibility when necessary. And no one doubted Westbrook's courage for he had never asked a pilot to do anything he would not do himself.

Westbrook had been an ROTC student in high school and he had then joined the California air national guard where he excelled in flying and aircraft maintenance. He then joined the Army Air Force in 1940 and at the onset of World War II he was a captain and served two combat tours in the Pacific. He returned to the Pacific in mid 1943 to assume command of the 18th's 44th Squadron.

The squadron leader, a native of Hollywood, California, could have easily passed for one of those handsome leading men in the movies: a classic square face, deep blue eyes, and a mop of light brown hair. In stature he stood 6' 2", with a muscular 190 pound weight to complement his height. The handsome pilot would fly 367 combat hours and down 20 Japanese planes before he finished his career.

At 0330 hours, Westbrook arrived at the 18th Fighter Group briefing tent on Guadalcanal's Fighter Strip #3 at the Tenaru River. Within 15 minutes, the pilots of the 44th Squadron had also arrived.

"We'll be flying out at oh-five hundred," Westbrook told his pilots. "General Twining is sure the Japanese will send planes down from Rabaul to attack the Bougainville invasion site and recon planes have already spotted a surface fleet of cruisers and destroyers sailing east. So we may have a busy day." He then gestured to an aide who pulled down a wall map.

"Here's where we maintain our CAP," Westbrook tapped the map, "right over the Cape Torokina landing site. We've pretty much eliminated the Japanese airfields in Bougainville and other islands in the northern Solomons, so we can expect all Japanese air strikes to come from Rabaul, either straight west or from the north. We'll be watching the northern approach."

"Who'll cover the western approach." Capt. Bill Harris asked.

"A squadron of Corsairs from MAG twenty-four."

"How long do we maintain CAP?"

"About three hours," Westbrook answered. "We'll be out in relays, with the Forty-fourth first. We'll be leaving at oh-five hundred to be up at Bougainville by oh-seven hundred. Our Twelfth Squadron will relieve at about ten-hundred hours, and the Seventieth will relieve at about thirteen hundred. Then we start over again."

"Will somebody hit that Japanese surface fleet?" another pilot asked.

"It's my guess that heavies and mediums from the three hundred and seventh and forty-second Groups will hit the surface ships," the major said, "and maybe the Avengers and Dauntlesses of MAG twenty-four. But we might be called on to escort." Westbrook then scanned his pilots before he spoke again. "If there are no more questions, the briefing is over."

Within a few minutes, the pilots of the 18th Fighter Group's 44th Squadron boarded jeeps for the ride to revetment areas where ground crews had pre-flighted eight P-38 and eight P-39 fighter planes. By 0500 hours, the first pair of P-38s zoomed down the runway for Guadalcanal's Fighter Strip #3 at the Tenaru River. By 0510, the 16 aircraft, with Maj. Bob Westbrook leading, were zooming north.

At the same 0330 hours, Maj. Gregory "Pappy" Boyington briefed his pilots of MAG 24's

VMF 214 Squadron. This unit, the Black Sheep Squadron, was an alleged squadron of malcontents, rebels, and misfits. But Mangrum considered the Black Sheep excellent pilots and he did not hesitate to call on Boyington for the first CAP tour over Bougainville.

No doubt, Gregory Boyington was among the most colorful American fighter pilots of World War II. No one had been as incorrigible as Boyington. The moon faced pilot with the sharp gray eyes was probably the most undisciplined, flamboyant, and rebellious U.S. fighter ace in the Pacific. But he ranked among the most courageous and he would finish his combat career with 28 air victories, more than any other marine pilot.

Boyington, a native of California, is a legend in American military history, ranking with men like Davy Crockett, Stonewall Jackson, or Sergeant York of World War I fame. He had joined the U.S. Marine Aviation Corps, but from the start he had been a problem—despite flying ability and leadership qualities. He drank heavily, exhibited a boisterous attitude, and he usually spoke obnoxiously to others. He had shown none of the officer and gentleman image that the marine aviation corps had sought in its men, and he had often embarrassed the corps because of his drinking and brashness.

"Talking to Boyington about discipline," one marine officer said, "was like taking a punch in the nose."

In early 1941, Boyington resigned from the

Marine Corps and joined the Flying Tigers in China. Some marine authorities had claimed the resignation was illegal and that Boyington had actually deserted the corps. However, Boyington did well with the AVG, downing six Japanese planes over China. But he had trouble with Chenault, the CO of AVG, and he returned to the U.S. Marine Aviation Corps. Authorities did not know whether to court martial him because he had left the corps to join the Flying Tigers, or to promote him because of his excellent combat record with the AVG in China.

They settled on assigning Boyington to the stifling, hostile jungles of Guadalcanal, placing him in charge of a group of undisciplined, rancorous, mutinous marine pilots—outcasts like himself. However, the pilots were good and they did an outstanding job under Boyington, who merely demanded courage, not discipline. By November of 1943, the Black Sheep had downed more than 200 Japanese planes.

Despite their notorious reputation, the VMF 214 had won respect in the SOPAC. So Col. Dick Mangrum felt no apprehensions when he ordered VMF 214 on the first CAP over Bougainville during the initial landings, when the Japanese might hit hard with aerial assaults. Mangrum instructed Boyington to maintain his CAP until 1000 hours, as would the army's 44th Squadron, and the VMF 214 commander readily agreed.

Boyington briefed his pilots at Guadalcanal's

Fighter Strip #1 at Henderson Field. "We maintain a CAP right here," the major tapped a map on the wall, "west of Empress Augusta Bay in the Solomon Sea. The army's Eighteenth Fighter Group will maintain the CAP over the Torokina Bay area. I don't know how many planes the Nips will send down from New Britain, but it's our business to stop them from reaching the invasion site."

"What about that Nip surface fleet we've been hearing about?" asked Capt. Bob McClurg, a flight leader.

"We have no orders about that," Boyington shrugged. "It's my guess that our Avengers and the army's bombers will take on those Japanese surface ships as soon as the ships come within range."

"How long do we maintain CAP?" Captain McClurg asked.

"Three hours," Boyington answered, "the same as the army's squadron. We should be over Bougainville by oh-seven hundred hours and VMF two-twenty-one will relieve us at about ten hundred hours." He scanned his pilots. "Any questions?" When no one answered, Boyington nodded. "Okay, I only ask that you stay with your wingmen; otherwise you're on your own."

By 0440 hours, Boyington and his 15 Black Sheep pilots left the briefing tent for the ride in personnel carriers to their waiting Corsairs on Fighter Strip #1. A slight chill hung in the air on this pre-dawn morning and the marine pilots appreciated the coolness, for within two hours the heat and humidity of the South Pacific jungles would again cause irritable discomfort to these Americans.

At 0510 hours, only ten minutes after Westbrook's 44th Squadron had left Fighter Strip #3 at the Tenaru River, Greg Boyington zoomed down Fighter Strip #1 with his wingman. Moments later, Boyington's other sixteen Corsairs had also taken off. The VMF 214 Squadron then jelled into formations of four diamonds and zoomed northward up The Slot toward Bougainville to await expected Japanese air strikes from Rabaul.

The Japanese would not disappoint Boyington. Cmdr. Benji Shimada was on his way to Empress Augusta Bay with his 19 Vals and 22 Zeros from the Ballale airfield in the Shortlands.

The island of Bougainville, 130 miles long and some 30 miles wide, lay at the top of the Solomon Islands chain, except for the small island of Buka. Empress Augusta Bay in the central area of the west coast of Bougainville lies a mere 210 miles from Rabaul. The island had been discovered by the Spaniards in the 16th century, but the small armada saw nothing of value and sailed away. Two centuries later, during a voyage around the world, a French sea captain, Sieur de Bougainville, rediscovered the island in 1767. Although Bougainville named the island after himself, he did not stay here long and he did not claim the island for France.

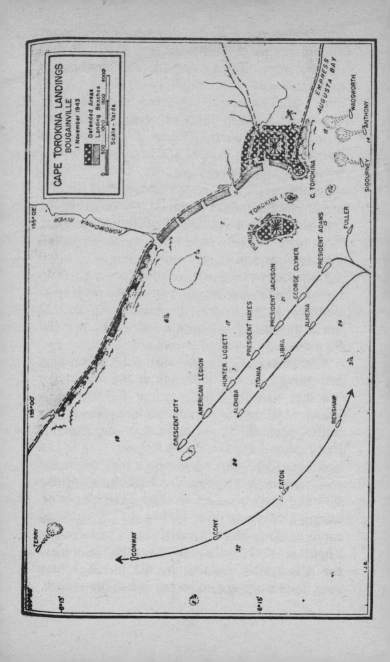

CAPE TOROKINA LANDINGS
BOUGAINVILLE
1 November 1943

Defended Areas
Landing Beaches

Scale - Yards
0   500   1000   1500   2000

Bougainville finally came under the control of Germany who after World War I gave up the island along with other Solomon Islands to the British. In 1919, the Commonwealth of Australia obtained a mandate over the Solomon Islands from the League of Nations, and the Australians occupied the island of Bougainville until the Japanese dislodged them during the early months of World War II.

The native population of the steaming, humid jungle island numbers about 42,000 Polynesians who live in small villages of 50 to 100 people. The island contains wide areas of swamps and brochide lagoons because of the heavy rainfall and only small, narrow, winding trails furnish the principal means of movement. However, the Australians developed a series of coconut groves on Bougainville and these groves became the principal source of income. The anchorage at Tonolei Harbor on the south coast prompted the Australians to build roads from Kara inland to Kahili and Buin on the shoreline. In fact, most of the native population lived along the south coast, the only developed area on the island.

Not surprisingly, therefore, the Japanese developed their air, land, and sea bases in the Buin-Kahili-Kara area on the south coast of Bougainville when they wrested the island from the Australians. Now, in late 1943, the Japanese waited alertly for the expected Allied invasion. The constant bombardment of airfields had convinced the Japanese that an invasion was imminent. Further, the recon aircraft sightings of the Allied fleets sailing north up The Slot from Guadalcanal had erased any lingering doubts.

The Americans had surprised the Japanese by by-passing the strong points on southern Bougainville and sailing into Empress Augusta Bay. Although an estimated 2,000 to 3,000 Japanese troops had been deployed along the Empress Augusta Bay shoreline, only 270 Japanese soldiers, with a single 75mm gun, defended the Cape Torokina area where the U.S. Marines would land.

At 0726 hours, November 1, 1943, the first wave of marines hit the beaches of Cape Torokina in landing barges. Radar men on picket destroyer USS *Conway* of Desron 45 picked up blips on their screens at almost the same 0726 hours. The radar men quickly called the destroyer's bridge.

"Bogies coming in! Bogies! Speed about two hundred knots, distance, twenty-five thousand yards; about fifty of them."

Cmdr. Ralph Earle, commander of *Conway,* was shocked by the report. "Bogies at twenty-five thousand yards? How the hell could they come this close to us from Rabaul already? Rabaul is a long way off."

"They're coming in at one-ninety degrees from the south," the radar man answered.

"The south?" Earle hissed. "Christ, they can't have a goddamn plane left to the south of us."

"They must have come from Ballale in the Shortlands," the *Conway* executive officer said. "We'd better notify CAP's, Sir."

Commander Earle nodded and then called Adm. Len Reifsnider of the III Amphibious Corps transport fleet. Reifsnider was maintaining his flag on transport USS *George Clymer*. "Sir, we've got enemy planes coming in from the south. They're only about twenty to twenty-five thousand yards off."

"Goddamn it," Reifsnider cursed. Then he sighed. "Okay, notify the CAP's at once. I'll have to get these transports the hell out of here in a hurry."

"Aye, Sir," Commander Earle answered.

Fortunately for Reifsnider, the bulk of the assault boats had been dropped from the transports, and the troop ships could quickly weigh anchor and scatter to avoid Japanese bombers. However, the hundreds of assault boats in the bay could be victims of Japanese bombs and strafing fire before the boats putted in to shore.

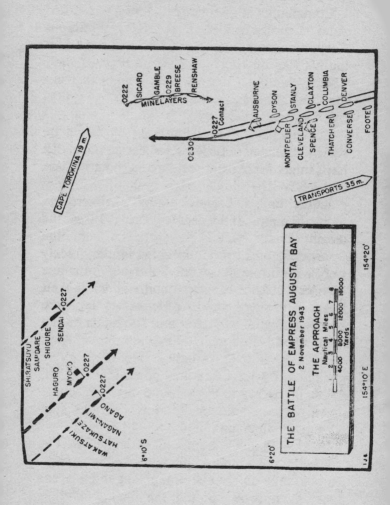

THE BATTLE OF EMPRESS AUGUSTA BAY
2 November 1943
THE APPROACH

Nautical Miles
1 2 3 4 5 6 7 8
Yards
4000 8000 12000 16000

154°10'E          154°20'

6°20'

6°10'S

CAPE TOROKINA 19 m.

TRANSPORTS 35 m.

SICARD  GAMBLE
0222    0229 BREESE
        RENSHAW
MINELAYERS

0227 Contact

0230

AUSBURNE
DYSON
MONTPELIER  STANLY
CLEVELAND  CLAXTON
SPENCE
THATCHER  COLUMBIA
CONVERSE  DENVER
FOOTE

WAKATSUKI
HATSUKAZE
NAGANAMI
AGANO
0227
MYOKO
0227
HAGURO
SHIGURE
SAMIDARE
SHIRATSUYU
SENDAI 0227

# Chapter Four

As soon as Earle finished talking to Reifsnider, he called the two airborne CAP units hovering north and west of Empress Augusta Bay. "Bogies coming in from the south on a one-ninety degree bearing. Please intercept."

"We've got them on our radar scopes," Maj. Bob Westbrook answered, "and we're on our way." The 44th Squadron commander looked in the bay where dozens of launch boats were carrying marines to the landing beaches. He then called his pilots. "Okay, let's move. Bandits coming in at one-ninety degrees and they've got an awful lot of targets down there. We'll climb to twenty-four thousand feet and come down on them. Stay with your wingman; stay with your wingman."

"Okay, Major," Capt. Bill Harris answered.

The 16 P-38s and P-39s then zoomed southward to take on the oncoming Japanese planes. Soon Westbrook spotted the enemy aircraft that were flying in their usual three plane V formations. He looked at his watch: 1735 hours. He looked once more at the Japanese air formations before he cried into his radio. "In pairs; attack in pairs! Those gyrenes are in a very vulnerable position right now because most of the launch barges are halfway between the transports and the shoreline."

Below and to the south, Cmdr. Benji Shimada first heard the whining echo of American planes and then saw the U.S. aircraft roaring down at his formation. He quickly picked up his radio phone and called his pilots. "Aichi dive bomber pilots will stay in tight formation; remain in tight formation. Fighter-bombers will also remain in tight formations and Mitsubishi fighters will attack enemy interceptors.

"I have heard your instructions, Commander," Lt. Cmdr. Toyotara Iwami said. "I will take our twelve fighter planes to stop the Americans from attacking our dive bombers and the ten Mitsubishi fighter-bombers." Then, Iwami called his pilots. "We will attack the enemy interceptors so that our dive bombers and fighter-bombers are not hampered from striking their targets. In pairs! Attack in pairs!"

The 12 Japanese fighter pilots rocketed upstairs to meet the American fighter pilots of the U.S. 44th Squadron. Maj. Bob Westbrook watched the Zeros come toward him while the Val dive bombers and Zero fighter-bombers continued on their tight, three plane V's. The major called Capt. Bill Harris.

"Captain, take Three and Four Flights and

get after those bombers. I'll stay upstairs with One and Three Flights to take on the escorts. As soon as we dispose of them, we'll join you."

"Yes, sir," Harris answered before he banked away with the eight P-39 Airo-cobras of Third and Fourth Flights to hit the Japanese dive and fighter bombers. Meanwhile Westbrook led his eight P-38 Lightnings towards the Zero escorts, 12 of them. But Westbrook and his fellow P-38 pilots would not take on the Japanese alone.

Immediately after Commander Earle of USS *Conway* called Westbrook, the destroyer skipper called Maj. Greg Boyington who had been maintaining CAP west of Empress Augusta Bay with his 16 Corsair fighter planes.

"Major, bogies; we've got bogies coming up from the south at one-ninety degrees to hit our ships and landing bases in Empress Augusta Bay. Our last radar report put those enemy planes at about twenty thousand yards from Cape Torokina. I've already notified the army CAP. You'd best get over here to help out."

"Will do," Boyington answered.

"We understand that Major Westbrook has sent two flights of P-thirty nines after the enemy bombers and he's taken his P-thirty eights to hit the Japanese escorts," Cmdr. Earle said.

"We'll do the same," Boyington answered. He then picked up his TBS and called his pilots. "Bandits coming in from the south. We'll intercept along with the army's Forty-Fourth Squadron."

"Yes, sir," Capt. Bob McClurg said.

The 18 Corsairs of VMF 214 then arched in a 90 degree turn and zoomed quickly eastward at a full 280 knots. They had roared on for a mere five minutes before Boyington got blips on his radar scope: enemy planes. He continued on for only two minutes more when he saw the darting arching planes high above him and to the northeast. Boyington quickly distinguished the twin fuselage P-38 U.S. army planes from the single fuselage Zero fighter planes. The Black Sheep Squadron leader picked up his TBS and called Capt. Bob McClurg.

"Bob, take your division and help out against those Nip bombers. I'll take the First Division to help out those P-thirty eights against the Zero escorts."

"Yes, sir," McClurg answered. Then he called his own pilots. "Enemy bombers at eleven o'clock after our gyrenes in the launch boats. Army fly boys are already after them. Let's help out." A few minutes later, McClurg spotted the P-39s diving on the Val dive bombers and Zero fighter bombers. He called the leader of the P-39s. "This is Baa Baa two; Baa Baa two; come in."

Capt. Bill Harris quickly answered McClurg. "This is Rostro two, Rostro two. We read you."

"We're coming in to help out."

"Okay, Baa Baa," Harris answered. "We can use the help. There's a hell of a lot of bandits after those landing boats."

Meanwhile, Maj. Bob Westbrook and his fellow P-38 pilots had played a cautious game with the 12 Japanese Zero fighter planes. Perhaps the P-38s were superior to the Japanese Zeros, but many of the Japanese pilots were good and the three to two odds were not very good. Westbrook was conducting more of a holding action than a dog fight, trying to keep the Zero fighter pilots occupied while the rest of the 44th Squadron took on the Japanese bombers. However, with the approach of the eight marine Corsairs that put the odds in the Americans' favor, Westbrook could show more aggressiveness.

"We got help from marine fly boys," the major cried into his radio phone. "Now we can go after them."

Meanwhile, Lt. Cmdr. Iwami gaped in awe when he saw the approaching Corsairs. He must now engage in a full dogfight. He picked up his radio phone. "More enemy interceptors coming in from the west. We must stop them or they will surely harass our bomber formations."

Thus began a dogfight southwest of Empress Augusta Bay as the U.S. Army and U.S. Marine fighter pilots waded into the Japanese Zeros. Chattering strafing fire echoed across the sky as did the whooshing rockets from American planes and the thumping 20mm cannon shells from Japanese planes. Aircraft arched across the sky, dove down on one another, chased each in straight runs, or zoomed upward after each other.

The dogfight seemingly continued - for an hour, but had actually lasted only five minutes. During this short period, the Japanese lost half of their Zero fighter planes. Mitsubishis went down in flames, exploded in mid air, or plummeted into the sea with trailing smoke. The six surviving Zero pilots, including Iwami, now saw no choice but to break off the fight. Iwami led his pilots quickly southward, leaving Captain Simada's dive bombers and fighter bombers without escorts.

Maj. Bob Westbrook got two Zeros himself, while Pappy Boyington of the marine VMF 214 unit also got two Japanese planes. The Americans had lost four planes but American destroyers from Desron 45 that had supported the III Amphibious Force had fished these pilots out of the sea.

"We're finished here, Baa Baa leader," Westbrook called Pappy Boyington. "Let's help out against those bombers."

"Lead the way, Rostro leader," Boyington answered.

But the Lightning and Corsair pilots who had just disposed of the Japanese escort planes found few pickings by the time they reached the enemy bombers. Capt. Bill Harris and Capt. Bob McClurg had enjoyed a field day of their own.

Benji Shimada had come within 20 miles of his target, the marine laden landing craft and the zigzagging transport ships, when Capt. Bill Harris and his fellow P-39 pilots pounced on

67

the nine Vals and ten Zero fighter-bombers. Shimada, when he saw the oncoming American fighter planes, quickly cried into his radio phone. "Enemy interceptors! Enemy interceptors! Maintain tight formation."

Fortunately for the Japanese, Shimada's pilots heeded instuctions and the American P-39 pilots ran into heavy fire from Val gunners and Zero pilots. Still the American P-39 pilots, in pass after pass through the tight Japanese formations, slowly whittled down the number of Japanese aircraft. Harris and his pilots shot down six planes from the enemy Vs as Shimada continued on towards Torokina Bay.

The Yokoyama Wing commander finally saw the dozen skimming invasion boats ahead. He grinned and started to call his pilots. But within a few minutes of target the Japanese air formations collided with VMF 214 Corsairs under Captain Bob McClurg. Once more the Japanese suffered losses as the Corsair pilots now hit the Japanese in pass after pass. Bob McClurg himself knocked down two Vals while Lt. Bob See of VMF 214 got his sixth kill of his combat career.

Shimada lost another six planes, while a half dozen more Japanese planes abandoned the mission and veered off to avoid destruction. Still Shimada continued on grimly with seven planes, as his own gunner knocked down one of the P-39s. Shimada led three Vals and four Zeros into the chugging barges, the beachhead at Cape Torokina, and the zigzagging transports and destroyers in the bay. Heavy anti-aircraft fire from both escorting American destroyers and from the transports themselves badly disrupted the Japanese air formations. The ack ack damaged two planes and shot down two.

The Japanese planes did make several hits on the supplies stacked along the shoreline. The explosions from 500 pound bombs started fires on the beaches. Zero strafing fire, meanwhile, had sunk two of the invasion boats, while killing or wounding a dozen Americans. And finally, a near miss on destroyer USS *Wadsworth* killed two men, wounded five, started heavy fires, and opened a hole in the hull to put the destroyer out of action.

This relatively minor damage had been the extent of the 41 plane effort by the Yokoyama Wing out of Ballale. Capt. Benji Shimada had lost 20 of his 41 planes and he now droned back to the Shortlands in disappointment. The American CAP fighter planes dared not pursue because other Japanese formations might arrive over the Cape Torokina area.

Adm. Len Reifsnider, meanwhile, angrily called Gen. Nathan Twining of COMAIRSOL at his headquarters on Guadalcanal. "General, we got hit by a swarm of Japanese planes out of the Shortlands. I thought your airmen knocked out Ballale Field?"

"Goddamn," Twining hissed. "I didn't think they could get a glider out of there. Okay, Admiral, we'll send out some heavies right away."

Within an hour a squadron of B-24s, 12 army air force heavy bombers of the 307th Bomb Group, were heading for the Shortlands. They arrived over Ballale only moments after Cmdr. Benji Shiamda had landed survivors from the Augusta Bay donnybrook. The Liberators punched a score of deep holes in the runway with thousand pound bombs. An hour later, 12 more B-24s from COMAIRSOL's 307th Heavy Bomb Group worked over the Ballale Field again with thousand pounders. The twin raids put the field out of commission.

At Empress Augusta Bay the VMF 214 Squadron under Pappy Boyington and the 44th Squadron under Bob Westbrook maintained their vigil with elated smugness. They had knocked down more than 20 enemy planes in less than a half hour, a quite succesful morning's work.

Thanks to the intercepting planes that had thwarted the Yokoyama Wing, the marine landing at Cape Torokina came off smoothly and speedily. Within 70 minutes, 64 LCVPs and 22 LCNs had carried the American troops and their supplies ashore. Within hours the marines moved more than four miles inland and established a perimeter more than six miles wide. Preliminary naval bombardment had knocked out the single 75mm gun and had killed or chased off the 270 Japanese troops defending the area. When the marine troops moved through the dense wooded areas to meet Japanese defenders from other points on Empress Augusta Bay, the marines had with them the 1st Dog Platoon.

The canines, mostly Doberman Pinschers that had been trained in Guadalcanal and New Caledonia, went forward along the trails with their handlers. The dogs proved invaluable in pointing out ambush and sniper positions. Thus the marines destroyed dozens of these ambush positions before the Japanese cut loose from their concealments against the American troops advancing on foot.

Adm. Len Reifsnider, fully aware that the Japanese might send more bombers to the Bougainville invasion site, did not loiter in Empress Augusta Bay once he had put ashore all troops and supplies, especially after the early morning air attack by the Yokoyama Wing. Reifsnider moved his transport ships and LSTs out of the bay before heading southward with his vessels. Meanwhile, Adm. Stanton "Tip" Merrill positioned his TF 39 cruiser-destroyer force in Empress Augusta Bay to meet the expected enemy cruiser fleet under Adm. Sentaro Omori, a fleet now designated the Torokina Interception Force.

Meanwhile, at Rabaul, Adm. Junichi Kusaka had ordered both Capt. Tokeo Shibata, the commander of the 4th Kokutai Wing, and Cmdr. Minoru Genda of the 26th Kokutai Wing to his headquarters.

"No doubt you have heard already of the American invasion at Bougainville only hours ago. The enemy operation was not unexpected.

71

Even now, Admiral Omori sails with his Torokina Interception Force to attack the enemy invaders. Since the Americans have now lodged themselves at Empress Augusta Bay as well as in the Treasury Islands and Choiseul Island, they have cut off the troops of General Sasaki. It is imperative, therefore, that we destroy the enemy on this new beachhead with our surface ships and air units."

Kusaka looked at Shibata. "You will mount at once Aichi dive bombers and G-four-M bombers (Betty heavy bombers) to attack the American invaders. Commander," he then looked at Genda, "you will escort Captain Shibata with two squadrons of Mitsubishi fighter planes from your Twenty-sixth Wing."

Genda nodded. "I have already briefed my pilots at the Vunakanau Field. It was my understanding that the Twenty-sixth Wing would escort bombers from Rabaul."

"The Yokoyama Wing in the Shortland Islands at this very hour has concluded an attack on the enemy at Bougainville," the 11th Air Fleet commander said. "They have caused considerable damage to American ships in the bay, destroyed their supplies on the beaches, and sunk dozens of landing barges. The bomber squadrons of the Fourth Wing will make further attacks while your mission, commander, will be to escort them. However, should the opportunity arise, you will be free to attack the Americans with strafing fire and twenty millimeter cannon."

"Yes, Honorable Kusaka," Genda said.

Within the hour, Genda gave his men a final briefing. Then, Lt. Takeo Tanimizu asked the 26th commander a final question. "When will we leave?"

"We are expected to eat an early mid-day meal, at eleven hundred hours, and leave Rabaul by twelve hundred hours so we can attack the enemy by early afternoon."

"Are we likely to meet interceptors?" Lieutenant Tanimizu asked.

"Without doubt," Genda answered. "We must be resolute in our determination to keep such interceptors away from the bombers of the Fourth Kokutai Wing, so they can conduct their bombing mission. I will personally lead One Squadron, and you, Lieutenant," he gestured to Tanimizu, "will lead Two Squadron."

"Yes, Honorable Genda," Tanimizu answered.

A few miles away, at Rapopo Drome, Capt. Takeo Shibata held his own final briefing with bomber crews of the 4th Wing. "The Yokoyama Wing has already made one successful aerial assault on the American invasion forces, and we shall make another aerial assault—a more intensive attack. Our service crews are now completing preparations on our heavy G-four-M bombers and Aichi dive bombers. We will eat an early meal and then leave Rabaul about noon."

"We will not fail you," answered Cmdr. Yasuho Izawa of the 4th Wing's Val dive bomber squadrons.

For the remainder of the morning, the ground crews at Rabaul worked on aircraft; fueling them, loading them with bombs and ammo, and checking out engines where necessary. The men worked in revetment areas or under trees where planes were sheltered from possible Allied air attacks.

The Japanese at Rabaul had been quite fortunate for the past few days because the poor weather over the Bismarck Archipelago had ruled out air attacks on the Japanese stronghold by 5th Air Force. By 1100 hours, when the combat airmen sat down for their early noonday meal, the ground crews had readied the aircraft of the 26th and 4th Kokutai Wings. And, by 1120 hours, 48 Zeros, 24 Vals, and 24 Bettys were zooming down the Vunakanau and Rapopo runways. By 1130 hours, the huge formations circled over St. George's Channel, jelled into the standard Japanese three plane V's, and then headed southeast.

At 1200 hours, November 1, new squadrons of CAPs were maintaining the vigil over and around Empress Augusta Bay: 16 P-38s and P-39s of the 18th Fighter Groups's 70th Squadron and 24 Corsairs from MAG 24's VMF 221. Again the army planes, under Capt. Tom Lamphier, patrolled over Torokina Bay, while the marine planes, under Capt. James Swett, patrolled to the west.

Capt. Tom Lamphier had gained notoriety in April as the pilot who had downed the Betty bomber that carried Adm. Isoroku Yamamoto, the commander of the Japanese Combined Fleet in the Pacific. American intelligence had learned that Yamamoto was flying down from Truk on an inspection tour of the Central and Northern Solomons. He and his Combined Fleet staff had come into Bougainville in two Bettys with an escort of eight Zeros. Capt. Tom Lamphier and five other P-38 pilots of the 70th Fighter Squadron had penetrated the Japanese fighter screen to shoot down the Betty bombers.

Both bombers carried naval staff. The plane carrying Adm. Matome Ugaki, the fleet's chief of staff, had successfully ditched in the sea and all hands had survived. The plane carrying Yamamoto had crashed in the jungle, exploded into fragments, and killed all aboard.

Lamphier would down four more Japanese planes to become an ace before he returned to the States.

No doubt every Japanese airman in the Pacific, from Commander Genda to the newest P/O would have relished the chance to kill Tom Lamphier and gain a measure of vengeance for the death of the highly respected and greatly admired Yamamoto. But no Japanese pilot would down Lamphier on this early afternoon of November 1, 1943.

Capt. Jim Swett of VMF 221 had been in the Pacific for about a year and on his first combat mission he had scored an astonishing victory. Swett had led a division of four Hellcats that had run into some 20 Japanese planes.

Although damaged in the air fights and with limited use of guns, he downed *seven* planes himself and chased off a dozen more. He managed to bring his damaged plane back to Guadalcanal, but was forced to ditch in Iron-bottom Sound, where a Higgins boat rescued him. For the next few months he continued to score and by November of 1943 he had downed over a dozen enemy planes. He would finish his combat career with 16 enemy kills and the Congressional Medal of Honor.

At 1250 hours, bogies once more showed up on the screens of picket destroyer USS *Conway*. "They're coming in again, sir," the radar man told Cmdr. Ralph Earle. "Two-seventy degree bearing, two hundred knots. They're about fifty miles out."

"How many planes?"

"An awful lot, sir; maybe as many as a hundred.'

"Okay," Earle said. He then called Capt. Tom Lamphier of the 18th Group's 70th Squadron and Capt. James Swett of the marine VMF 221. "Bogies coming in at two-seventy degrees at about two hundred knots. Radar thinks there may be as many as a hundred planes."

"We'll get out there," Captain Lamphier said.

"We're on our way," Jim Swett answered.

Moments later, the 40 American fighter planes roared westward to meet the oncoming Japanese planes. Soon the Americans spotted the huge formation of Vs and Lamphier called the VMF 221 leader. "This is Rostro leader; Rostro leader. We'll take the escorts. You gyrenes take the bombers."

"Will do, Rostro leader," Swett answered.

Soon enough, Capt. Tokeo Shibata saw the American fighter planes coming after his formations. He quickly spoke into his radio phone. "Enemy interceptors. Bomber pilots will maintain tight formations; fighters will attack interceptors."

"We will do so," Capt. Minoru Genda answered. Genda then led his fighter pilots of the 26th Wing after the American fighter planes.

Unfortunately for the Japanese, they could not have approached the target area at a worse time. Just as their formations approached Empress Augusta Bay, two squadrons from the U.S. Army Air Force's 347th Fighter Group, under fighter ace Capt. Murray Shubin, were arriving over Bougainville to relieve the 70th Squadron and VMF 221 on CAP.

Captain Lamphier quickly called Shubin. "This is Rostro leader. Please help out with enemy escort planes. The gyrene squadron is handling the enemy bombers. As soon as we dispose of their escort, we'll help out the marines against the Japanese bombers."

"We're on our way," Captain Shubin answered.

Now, three squadrons of P-38s came after Genda's Zero escorts.

In the subsequent darting, arcing, swirling dogfight high over Empress Augusta Bay, the rattle of machine guns, the whine of aircraft engines, and the thump of cannon and rocket fire thundered through the sky. Marines on shore looked up in delight, for they saw Zeros going down one by one, but few if any American planes. Within a few minutes, ten Zeros from the 26th Kokutai Wing were down and Genda quickly decided he could not handle this swarm of superior American planes and their capable pilots. He picked up his radio and called Captain Shibata.

"Captain, we find the task impossible. We cannot contain so many American fighter planes and we have already lost nearly a dozen of our fighter planes."

"What do you suggest?" Shimata asked.

"I believe we should abort this sortie and retire to Rabaul."

Captain Tokeo Shibata hesitated, but he soon saw the 24 Corsairs of VMF 221 under Capt. Jim Swett coming toward his bombers. Further, the other American fighter planes that had engaged the 26th Wing would soon be after his bombers. Shibata concluded that he'd best get his Vals and Bettys away from there, preferring discretion to valor. He could always attack the Bougainville invasion site tomorrow. He called Lt. Cmdr. Yasuho Izawa.

"Commander, we are aborting the mission and returning to Rabaul."

"Must we, Captain?" Izawa asked.

"There are too many enemy fighter planes."

The 24 Bettys and 24 Vals veered 180 degrees and roared back toward Rabaul. For part of the way, Capt. Jim Swett and his VMF 221 Corsair pilots sniped at the Japanese bomber formations, shooting down four of them. Swett ordered retirement as he was getting too far away from his base on Guadalcanal to go any further.

The American fighter pilots were elated. They had downed 14 of the Japanese planes without loss to themselves, while they had denied the Japanese the opportunity to drop a single bomb or fire a single round of strafing fire on the American beachhead. Captain Lamphier had downed a plane himself, while Captain Shubin of the 34th Fighter Group and Captain Swett of the VMF 221 Squadron had each downed two aircraft to raise their score of kills.

On shore the marines at Cape Torokina felt grateful. They had not suffered a second Japanese air attack and they would not likely suffer any more today.

# Chapter Five

While Adm. Junichi Kusaka had been busily sending out air formations to attack the invasion site at Bougainville, General Imamura had been making decisions of his own. As soon as he learned of the American landings at Cape Torokina, he called Admiral Samejima of the Southeastern Fleet. "Admiral, I would like to send reinforcements to Bougainville immediately. The Fourteenth Mountain Battalion, the Sixty-sixth Artillery Battery, and the Sixty-seventh Artillery Battery are prepared to leave at once. These forces would include some fifty artillery pieces, fourteen hundred men, and several tons of supplies. Can your marus carry all these men and supplies at once?"

"We have four freighter marus and six transport marus ready to sail," Samejima said. "I am sure we will have ample space. Meanwhile, I will ask Admiral Omori to return to Rabaul as quickly as possible so his fleet can escort these ground troop reinforcements."

"Excellent," General Imamura said.

At 0830 hours, long before the Japanese air units had attempted to attack Cape Torokina, Admiral Samejima sent a radio message to Admiral Omori, asking that he return to Rabaul so he could escort reinforcements to Bougainville. Capt. Usho Yamada had been correct in suggesting that the Torokina Interception Fleet return to the Gazelle Peninsula for possible escort duty. By the time Omori got the message from Admiral Samejima, the Torokina Interception Fleet had already reached St. George's Channel, a mere 60 miles from Rabaul Bowl.

Admiral Sentaro Omori sailed into Blanche Bay at 1100 hours on November 1 with his aborted Crudiv 5. He had no sooner anchored his fleet in the bay when Southeastern Fleet headquarters ordered him to report immediately to Samejima. As Omori and his staff putted toward shore in a harbor boat, Omori could see that shore crews were busy loading men, supplies, and guns aboard the transports and freighters in the harbor.

As the staff cars brought Omori and his officers to Samejima's bungalow, motor launches were still weaving among the freighters in Blanche Bay, carrying ammo, arms, supplies, food, medicine, clothing, and other necessities to the marus. The launches skimmed around the Vulcan Crater point to reach ships before floating cranes hoisted the supplies from the launches and lowered them into the holds, where barking petty officers urged the sailors to stack the stores quickly.

Other launches pulled away from jetties with the big guns, 75mm and 105mm artillery pieces as well as the 40mm and 5" antiaircraft guns, whose weight left the launches low in the water as the small boats putted toward the freighters. Then the cranes hauled the big guns to decks of the marus where sailors aboard the freighters chained the artillery to the decks. Not until the holds and decks of the freighters were crammed with supplies and guns would the loading stop.

More harbor boats carried men from the docks to the six transports in the harbor: troops of the 14th Mountain Battalion, the 66th Artillery Battery, and the 67th Artillery Battery. As troops rode to the anchored transports, other soldiers on shore moved about restlessly on the wharves as they waited their turn to board the ships. The battleclad soldiers jerked at the green belts that held their medical packs and ammo kits, or fingered their shiny tan helmets or yanked their wraparound leggings that covered the calves of their legs. These troops welcomed the opportunity to fight back against their enemies, hoping the big guns could blow the Americans off the invasion beaches.

The loading activities would continue throughout the morning and into the afternoon. The beehive of activity would end only after the 8th Naval Service Battalion had loaded more than 100 guns, 2800 tons of supplies and 1440 officers and men on the six transports and four freighters. Then, the weary service personnel would enjoy a rest, especially since the continuing bad weather had kept American bombers away from Rabaul again today.

At 1200 hours, Admiral Omori, Admiral Ijuin, Captain Osugi, and Captain Yamada sat down to a noonday meal with Admiral Samejima in his bungalow. "As you can see," Samejima said, "we have been loading the marus with guns, men, and supplies."

"You have acted swiftly," Omoti said.

"General Imamura is anxious to bring these reinforcements of men, artillery, and supplies to Bougainville to destroy the invaders and relieve General Sasaki's Sixth Division on the southern coast."

"We will sail as soon as possible," Admiral Omori said.

Samejima now looked at Admiral Ijuin. "I am glad to see you again, Matsuji," the Southeastern Fleet commander grinned. "Your duty this time will be somewhat different than your recent accustomed duties of evacuating troops. This time you will be bringing men into combat instead of carrying them away from combat."

"I will appreciate this opportunity to strike at our enemies instead of retreating from them," Ijuin said.

"And are the enemy invasion marus still lingering in Empress Augusta Bay?" Admiral Omori asked.

"No," Samejima said. "They have sailed south, perhaps to load more troops and supplies for the Empress Augusta Bay invasion site. We would like our own troops and guns at Cape Torokina before the Americans make further landings."

"Captain Yamada and myself have drawn up a tentative plan to expedite the landing of these troops and guns," Admiral Omori said.

Samejima now looked at Yamada. "I am sure you have planned well, Captain, as you have always shown great skill in organizing and planning."

"We have done our best, Honorable Samejima," Captain Yamada said. "If we are to bring these reinforcements to Bougainville, we must be certain they can be unloaded at once and without harassment from American aircraft."

"We will weigh anchor as soon as the marus are loaded and our warships have taken on fuel and supplies," Omori said.

"Good, good," Samejima nodded.

"We can expect to reach Cape Torokina at this time tomorrow," Omori said, "and by dark, we will have all men, supplies, and guns unloaded."

"General Sasaki and his troops of the Sixth Division will be delighted to get these reinforcements," Samejima said. He then looked at a slip of paper he had pulled from his pocket. "I was told by Admiral Kusaka that the Eleventh Air Fleet would furnish aerial escort for most of your voyage to Bougainville. Then, Captain Shimada of the Yokoyama Wing in the

Shortlands will furnish air cover for the remainder of your voyage to Bougainville."

"That is reassuring," Omori said.

"I must tell you, however," Samejima pointed, "that the enemy cruiser fleet still loiters in Bougainville waters. They are apparently intent on protecting the American invasion forces."

"Our sailors are eager and competent," Omori said, "and we will engage this enemy fleet with determined aggressiveness should the need arise."

"Perhaps we will be fortunate enough to meet them in a night action," Admiral Ijuin said.

"I suspect that a night action would delight you, Matsuji," Samejima grinned at the Desron 27 commander, "for you have enjoyed considerable success in night engagements against the enemy."

"I cannot take credit myself, Honorable Samejima," Ijuin said. "The credit belongs to the officers and men of Desron Twenty-seven who have shown such excellent ability and undaunted courage in fighting against our enemies."

"You are modest," Samejima said, "for we cannot discount your own ability to inspire the sailors of your command."

Admiral Ijuin did not answer.

"Let us enjoy our meal," the Southeastern Fleet commander continued, "and let us hope we will stop the enemy this time. Sentaro," he gestured to Omori, "I must warn again of this American cruiser fleet that accompanied the enemy invasion forces."

"I assure you, Tomushige," Omori said, "should we meet these enemy warships, the misfortunate will be theirs, not ours."

Admiral Samejima grinned. "I am pleased with your confidence, Sentaro. Confidence is quite important to succeed against the Americans."

After the fleet officers finished lunch, Admiral Samejima bid his guests goodbye and watched them drive over the winding Blanche Bay Road towards the bay's wharves. At 1700 hours, November 1, 1943, the signal flags went up on flag cruiser *Myoko*. "Away all ships!"

By 1730 hours, the four cruisers, six destroyers, and ten marus slid slowly out of Blanche Bay and sailed into the wide expanse of St. George's Channel. By this time tomorrow Omori expected to anchor his ships just north of Torokina on the west coast of Bougainville. Throughout the night, he would discharge his reinforcements of men, guns and supplies.

By the time the Torokina Interception Fleet had cleared St. George's Channel, Capt. Tokeo Shibata had returned from his aborted bombing mission to Empress Augusta Bay. Both Admiral Kusaka and General Imamura were shocked by the 4th Wing's failure to strike a second aerial blow at the American invaders. General Imamura called to his 8th Area Forces headquarters in Rabaul both Captain Shibata and

Commander Genda, along with Capt. Goro Furugori of the army's 22nd Sentai Air Division. Admiral Kusaka sat glumly and somewhat uneasily at Imamura's side.

"I cannot believe that you aborted this mission," Imamura glared at Shibata.

"There were too many American interceptors," the 4th Kokutai commander said. "Commander Genda, despite the aggressiveness of himself and his pilots, could not deal with the swarms of American fighter planes. He suggested that we abort the mission for fear of losing most of our bombers without making any telling strikes. I agreed with him."

Now, both Imamura and Admiral Kudaka glared at Cmdr. Minoru Genda.

"Were you certain that Captain Shibata could not carry out this mission?" Imamura asked the 26th Wing commander.

"I do not wish to appear cowardly, Honorable Imamura," Genda said, "nor do I wish to appear self-righteous. However, after a heavy air battle with American fighter planes, I was certain we could not stop these interceptors from causing heavy losses to Captain Shibata's bombers. It is my belief that we will need to use more than 48 fighter planes as escorts if we hope to contain American interceptors. Only by containing these enemy planes can our bombers make telling strikes on Cape Torokina with minimum losses."

Imamura now looked at Kusaka. "Can we furnish more escorts?"

"We have nearly two hundred aircraft of our Eleventh Air Fleet here at Rabaul," Kusaka said. He then looked at Captain Furugori. "What of the Twenty-second Sentai?"

"We have nearly one hundred aircraft," Furugori answered, "half of which are fighter aircraft."

"I would remind you, Commander," Imamura now looked harshly at Minoru Genda, "that your own commander of the Combined Fleet, Honorable Koga, has told all of us that we must spare no effort to relieve the Sixth Division troops on southern Bougainville. He believes as I do: we must destroy the American invasion forces." Imamura hastily pawed through some papers on his desk and yanked out a sheet. "In fact, the Honorable Koga has informed us that he is sending us Adm. Takeo Kurita and the powerful Second Fleet to join in the assault against the enemy invaders."

"As you know," Kusaka now spoke to the air commanders, "a reinforcement fleet has left Blanche Bay with troops and guns to join our beleaguered forces at Empress Augusta Bay. They will arrive there by tomorrow afternoon. We ourselves must plan new, massive air strikes against the enemy to protect these reinforcements. I want aircraft from both the Fourth and Twenty-sixth Kokutai Wings ready for sorties tomorrow morning." Kusaka then looked at Imamura. "With your permission, I would also like to include the Twenty-second Sentai in these sorties."

"Of course, of course," Imamura nodded vigorously.

"We must stop the enemy somewhere," Kusaka gestured emphatically, "and Bougainville is as good a place as any."

The American marines and sailors who had looked apprehensively toward Rabaul during the sail up The Slot to Bougainville had ample reason to stare uneasily to the northwest. The great enemy dragon at Rabaul was about to spit awesome fire.

At 1730 hours, November 1, 1943, Adm. Stanton "Tip" Merrill relaxed on the bridge of his flag cruiser USS *Montpelier*. The TF 39 commander leisurely sipped a cup of coffee and stared at the other ships of his fleet: fellow light cruisers USS *Cleveland, Columbia,* and *Denver;* and destroyers USS *Spence, Thatcher, Converse,* and *Foote* of Cmdr. Bob Austin's Desron 46. Merrill's other destroyer unit, Captain Arleigh "31 Knot" Burke's Desron 45, had gone to Hawthorne Strait in the Treasury Islands to refuel from a tanker. In the waning afternoon, Merrill was anchored in Vella Gulf off Vella Lavella, while he too waited to refuel and reload.

During the previous 24 hours, Merrill's fleet had been uncannily busy. Early yesterday evening, the fleet had pasted with 5″ and 6″ guns what was left of the Japanese airfields at Kahili and Buin on the south coast of Bougainville. The fleet had then scooted north at almost flank speed to the upper end of Bougainville, where shortly after midnight TF 39 had pounded the Japanese airfield at Buka with more 6″ and 5″ shells. Ironically while Merrill was busy at Buka, Admiral Omori's Torokina Interception Force had been sailing southward some distance to the westward, and so the Japanese fleet had completely missed Merrill's TF 39 fleet.

After pounding Buka, Merrill had reversed course and taken his four cruisers and eight destroyers into Empress Augusta Bay for a final bombardment of Cape Torokina before the U.S. marines had begun their invasion. Merrill's ships had also helped out with anti-aircraft fire against the Japanese planes from the Shortlands that had struck the American invasion forces at about 0730 hours this morning. His ships had then stood off shore for the remainder of the morning and into the afternoon to shell enemy positions for advancing marine combat troops who were moving inland.

By 1700 hours on this afternoon of the Bougainville invasion, TF 39 took a needed respite. The fleet's bluejackets were tired from a long 36 hours of activity and the ships were low on ammunition, fuel, and supplies.

As Merrill stared out at his anchored ships, his executive officer, Capt. Ralph Parker, came up to him. "Admiral, the service ships are on the way from Barakoma Bay. They should start refueling and rearming us within an hour. If we're lucky, they'll be finished by dark."

"Good," Merrill said. "What's the word on Burke?"

"I guess he didn't have enough fuel to get to the refueling station here in Vella Gulf," Parker said. "But he's almost refueled up in Hawthorne Strait and he'll join us here as soon as he's finished."

Merrill shook his head and grinned. Capt. Arleigh Burke had earned his tag of "31 Knot" Burke because the Desron 45 commander had an obsession to sail his destroyers at over 30 knots, whatever his mission. Burke had done so again during these recent bombardment operations in support of the Bougainville invasion. Burke had always been ahead of the rest of TF 39 and Merrill had continously called Burke to slow down and stay close to the rest of the fleet. Still, Merrill could not really fault Burke, as the Desron 45 commander's habit of fast-stepping up and down The Slot with his destroyers had trained his sailors to escape tight situations against heavier Japanese naval units, or to reach a designated area in record time.

Burke was an aggressive commander who generally succeeded on a mission. He had honed his men to near perfection with continual maneuvers and gunnery practice. But Burke was also a fair and sympathetic man, and the sailors under him showed a great respect for their captain. They had learned that Burke's insistence on sharpness and accuracy had paid off during several naval engagements against Japanese ships in the Solomons.

Adm. Tip Merrill sipped more of his coffee while the sailors of Crudiv 12 and Desron 46 relaxed after their recent forays. When the TF 39 commander finished his coffee he turned again to Parker.

"What's the latest from Admiral Reifsnider?"

"Everything is going according to plan," the TF 39 chief of staff answered. "The marines have established a strong perimeter about six miles square, and so far they've only met light opposition. Those gyrenes have now hit the swamps and they intend to bivouack there for the night. It might be this time tomorrow before they reach that flat, dry area where they want to build an airfield."

"No more air attacks?" Merrill asked.

"No sir," Parker said.

"What about the transports?"

"Admiral Reifsnider has them moving southward," Captain Parker said. "He's going back to Guadalcanal to pick up more supplies and more troops."

"And our air units?"

"CAPs are still over the bay. They'll maintain a patrol until dark and then come back at dawn."

Merrill nodded, ducked inside the wheelhouse, and poured himself another cup of coffee. The TF 39 commander could not quite relax because he had heard about the Japanese fleet in Bougainville waters yesterday, a fleet that had sailed all the way down to the Shortlands and then returned north, apparently back to Rabaul. Merrill wondered why this enemy flotilla had come across the Solomon Sea from New Britain, sailed past the length of Bougainville, and then simply returned to the Gazelle Peninsula.

Merrill knew that Japanese recon planes had seen his own TF 39 fleet at least two or three times during the past 24 hours. Yet the enemy warship fleet had made no attempt to find and engage him. Even more curious, this enemy armada had made no attempt to attack the III Amphibious Force in Empress Augusta Bay, especially since the Japanese warships had passed within spitting distance of the American transport and supply ships.

Merrill had not guessed, of course, that Omori's fleet had returned to Rabaul to escort reinforcements to Bougainville.

Tip Merrill also wondered why the Japanese had thus far only sent two air formations over the American invasion site, one that had caused minor damage and another that had astonishingly aborted its mission. Yet, Merrill knew as well as anyone that the airfields at Rabaul were jammed with planes and the harbors were filled with ships. They had been spared from attacks by 5th Air Force for the past few days because of the poor weather. Why hadn't the Japanese sent these massive air and surface ship units into action?

By 1800 hours on this late afternoon of November 1, with the setting sun now silhouetting Merrill's ships on the expansive Sealark

Channel, the American fuel and supply ships steamed into sight. At almost the same moment, Capt. Arleigh Burke sailed into Vella Gulf with his Desron 45: Destroyers USS *Dyson, Ausburne, Stanley,* and *Claxton.*

By 1815 hours, the ammo ships were transferring tons of AP and GP 6″ and 5″ shells to Merrill's cruisers and destroyers, while tankers refueled the cruisers of Crudiv 12 and the destroyers of Desron 46. By the time the last aura of blue had faded into a night sky, the loading had been completed.

"All finished, sir," Parker told Merrill.

The TF 39 commander nodded. "Okay , tell those supply ships to get out of here and back to Barakoma Bay. We might get some night air attacks."

"Yes sir."

"Then put our destroyers on anti-submarine alert," Merrill continued. "We don't know how many Nip subs might be in these waters."

"I'll notify the destroyers at once," Parker said.

By 1900 hours, near total darkness hung over Vella Gulf. Thick clouds drifted across the sky and an occasional light rain squall fell over the American vessels. The sea had calmed and only the slightest breeze, no more than three knots, whispered over the gulf. Men on watch had never recalled a more peaceful evening in the Solomon Islands waters. They found their vigil so calm and monotonous, that they needed continuous coffee to stay awake.

Men in the radar room saw only black screens in front of them: no aircraft about, no submarines, and no surface ships. They too sat bored, breaking the monotony with idle talk and card playing.

Meanwhile, the officers and men of TF 39 had finally sat down to evening mess, late because of the busy afternoon and early evening in taking on fuel, ammo, and stores. Evening mess had ended for all hands at about 1945 hours and then Merrill and his staff retired to the flag room of cruiser *Montpelier*. Here, Merrill studied his maps before he looked at his officers.

"I think we'd best get under way by twenty-two hundred hours so we can be in Empress Augusta Bay by oh-one hundred hours. We'll maintain a slow shuttle patrol around Torokina Bay for the rest of the night. We'll keep our anti-aircraft destroyers to the west and north in case the Nips send out more air formations in the morning."

"Which they'll most likely do," Captain Parker grinned.

Merrill nodded and then continued. "Okay, signal all ships with blinker lights. We weigh anchor at twenty-two hundred and move north on a zero-zero-five course at twenty knots. That should get us into the bay at oh-one hundred with minimum fuel usage."

"Yes sir," Parker said.

Meanwhile, Admiral Omori was again heading for Bougainville from Rabaul with his

Torokina Interception Fleet, this time with ten marus. By 1930 hours, he had cleared St. George's Channel and was heading into the open waters of the Solomon Sea. Omori had grown impatient because the transports and freighters could not make more than 20 knots with their heavy loads. The Japanese admiral feared he could not reach Torokina and unload his troops, guns and supplies before daylight. He stood on the bridge of cruiser *Myoko* with his chief of staff in a mixture of impatience and frustration.

"What is the time?"

"Nineteen-thirty-five hours," Captain Yamada answered.

"Is there no way to increase the speed of the marus?"

"They are too heavily laden," the chief of staff answered.

Omori scowled and he then jumped from the sudden whine of whoop alarms about his cruisers. "What is that? What is that?"

Before Yamada answered an aide came into the bridge. "Honorable Omori, we have sighted enemy submarines and we must slow our speed until the picket destroyers deal with them."

"Bakyra!" Omori cursed. "We are delayed even more."

More than an hour passed before the screening destroyers had chased off the real or imagined American submarines in the area. As Omori reformed his fleet to proceed again, he got a new alert—enemy planes overhead. The vessels of the Torokina Interception Fleet broke formations and took up anti-aircraft patterns. As the destroyers spit streaking anti-aircraft fire into the heavens, whistling bombs came down from the darkness above and shuddered cruiser *Sendai* with near misses.

A half hour passed before calm returned to the Japanese fleet. The time was now 2130 hours and Omori saw no chance whatever of reaching Torokina before daylight with his plodding marus. The American planes that had dropped the bombs had no doubt reported Omori's position, and he might find himself facing both enemy surface ships and air formations by dawn. He called the Southeastern Fleet commander at Rabaul.

"Honorable Samejima, we have been disrupted and slowed by enemy submarines and aircraft, while the marus plod like turtles. We find impossible the task of discharging these troops, guns, and supplies before dawn. The enemy obviously knows our position now and their aircraft will no doubt attack us in the morning."

"What do you suggest?"

"I suggest we retire the marus to Rabaul and take them out again in a day or two during the early morning, so we can easily reach Torokina and discharge men and supplies at night. Meanwhile I will continue south with the cruisers and destroyers to attack the enemy's marus and their beachheads with naval guns."

"Very well," Admiral Samejima agreed.

So at 2145 hours, the heavily laden APDs and cargo laden AKDs about-faced and sailed back to Rabaul with two destroyer escorts. Omori reformed the rest of his fleet, four cruisers and six destroyers, and turned south. He quickly opened speed to 32 knots to reach the American invasion site by dawn.

Meanwhile, the recon planes, B-24s from COMAIRSOL's 5th Bomb Group, loitered overhead long enough to notice the marus turning back while the warships picked up speed and continued southeast. The Liberator pilots quickly radioed COMAIRSOL in Guadalcanal with the same message:

"Japanese cruiser-destroyer fleet heading south, southeast toward Empress Augusta Bay, at an estimated speed of 30 knots. They'll probably reach the bay by 0300 hours."

The dispatched at Guadalcanal quickly relayed the B-24 recon reports to flagship *Montpelier* of TF 39. Moments later, Captain Parker brought the message to Admiral Merrill. "Sir, that Japanese surface fleet is now heading toward Empress Augusta Bay. Recon reports say the fleet includes about a half dozen cruisers and a half dozen destroyers."

"Goddamn," Merrill hissed, "they *are* looking for a fight. Okay, notify all ships: increase speed to 32 knots. We want to catch that enemy fleet before they reach our landing site on Cape Torokina."

"Aye, sir."

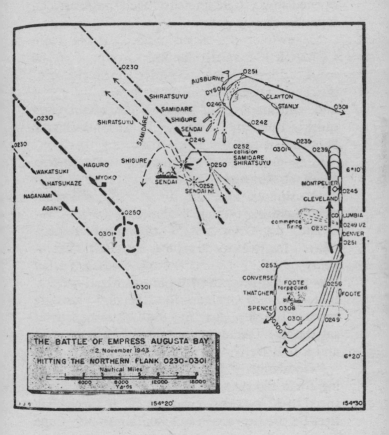

THE BATTLE OF EMPRESS AUGUSTA BAY
2 November 1943
HITTING THE NORTHERN FLANK 0230-0301
Nautical Miles
4000    8000    12000    16000
Yards

## Chapter Six

By the last hour of November 1, about midnight, everybody in the South and Southwest Pacific—on both sides—knew of the approaching confrontation between the Japanese Torokina Interception Force and the American TF 39 surface fleet. Shortly after the American B-24s reported Omori's cruiser-destroyer fleet heading for Empress Augusta Bay, long range Emily recon planes from the 11th Air Fleet at Rabaul had discovered the TF 39 fleet sailing swiftly northward. The Japanese planes quickly reported the information to Rabaul.

When the report of the American fleet reached his headquarters, General Imamura felt some relief. His troops and supply ships were heading back to the New Britain stronghold. Still, he urged the maru commanders to make top speed so they could reach Blanche Bay before American surface ships or air units caught up to them. Imamura then called Captain Goro Furugori of the 22nd Sentai.

"You will prepare every available fighter

plane to protect Rabaul against possible enemy air strikes in the morning. The marus returning to Blanche Bay are heavily loaded with troops, guns and supplies and they will be quite vulnerable."

"Yes, Honorable Imamura," Captain Furugori answered. "Starting at dawn, we will maintain two squadrons of fighter planes on combat air patrol over Rabaul at all times."

Imamura next called his antiaircraft commanders. "Make certain that all gunners remain alert throughout the night, and be certain they have plenty of ammunition in their gun pits. The Americans may be aware that our heavily laden marus are returning to Rabaul and they might make a special effort to attack these marus in the morning."

Adm. Tomushige Samejima issued a constant stream of orders to Admiral Omori. "Be sure your torpedo crews are ready. Make certain that gunners have stacked enough ammunition and shells in their gun turret pits. Be sure that lookouts remain alert so that your fleet does not suffer surprise by the enemy."

Adm. Junichi Kasaka was equally active. He roused both Capt. Takeo Shibata and Cmdr. Minoru Genda out of bed. "Your ground crews must work throughout the night to fuel, arm, and prepare aircraft. They will make morning strikes against this American surface fleet that now streams northward to engage Admiral Omori's fleet."

"We will act at once," Captain Shibata promised.

"We shall mount every available aircraft of the Twenty-sixth Wing to escort the Fourth Wing bombers," Commander Genda said.

In the Shortlands, Cmdr. Benji Shimada received a call from Rabaul to get as many planes as possible together for an attack on the American fleet in the morning. "You must also maintain float planes over the expected battle area to furnish star shell illumination for our battle fleet," Admiral Kusaka said.

"We will do our best, admiral," Shimada answered.

The Yokoyama Wing commander, of course, had seen the B-24s paste his airfield only this morning after the wing's near disastrous foray on the American invasion site. Shimada still had some 30 to 40 serviceable planes, along with a dozen float planes for nighttime reconnaisance. He urged every member of his ground crews to work hard in repairing the potted runways so that planes could take off. He also urged ground crews to ready as many planes as possible for sorties in the morning.

On south Bougainville, the troops of the Japanese 6th Division also learned of the apparent imminent sea fight in the Empress Augusta Bay area. Gen. Noburu Sasaki calmed his troops and asked them to maintain an alert vigil on their coastal guns, while they sought favors from heaven to aid Omori's fleet against the enemy.

"We must seek divine help," Sasaki told his officers and men. "With a great naval victory, the Americans will be forced to withdraw their invasion forces from Empress Augusta Bay, and we can then move a full regiment to Cape Torokina to thwart any further American invasion attempts."

The men of the Japanese 6th Division would indeed pray, for they understood a numbing fact: if the Americans solidfied their hold in the center of Bougainville as they had entrenched themselves in other recent sites, like the Treasuries or at Choiseul, the 6th Division would be trapped. They would either be annihilated or they would wither away from lack of food and supplies, as had so many other Japanese garrisons on other by-passed islands in the Solomons. They knew that Adm. Matsuji Ijuin had done well in evacuating trapped troops in these islands, but Ijuin would certainly find almost impossible a task of evacuating some 20,000 troops.

On the American side, bristling activity had similarly erupted at New Caledonia, Guadalcanal, and New Guinea. At Noumea's COMSOPAC headquarters, Adm. Bill Halsey had mustered his staff, getting men out of bed, from officers clubs, or from anywhere else he could find them.

"Make sure Tip Merrill knows where that enemy fleet is at all times. We don't want him surprised with long lance torpedoes." Halsey knew the devastating ability of Japanese surface fleets in nighttime engagements. Although the Americans had won some nighttime fights, they had lost most of them.

"Get COMAIRSOL on the line," Halsey told one of his staff members, "and make sure Twining is keeping recon planes continually over that enemy fleet so he can launch air attacks in the morning."

"Yes sir," the aide answered.

Adm. Len Reifsnider, the III Amphibious Force transport commander, had already pulled his troop and supply ships out of Empress Augusta Bay. However, when Reifsnider heard of the Japanese cruiser-destroyer fleet barrelling toward Cape Torokina, he increased speed. He wanted to get his ships as far south as possible before the Japanese and American fleets ran into each other.

On Bougainville itself, Gen. Al Turnage and his marines felt uneasy. These combat veterans had experienced previous Japanese surface ship bombardments after the Americans had landed on other islands in the Solomons. Turnage knew the accuracy of Japanese warship salvos and the power of 8″ cruiser shells.

"Get every man under cover," Turnage told his officers. "Have them dig foxholes, and dig them deep."

"Yes sir," one of the subordinates answered.

On Guadalcanal, Gen. Nathan Twining roused three of his COMAIRSOL group commanders out of bed: Col. Dick Mangrum of MAG 24, Col. Aaron Tyer of the 18th Fighter Group, and Col. Henry Wilson of the medium 42nd Bomb Group. Twining knew that Wilson had spent long hours in training his B-25 crews on minuimum altitude bombing techniques during the 42nd Group's stay in the Fijis before coming to the Solomons. The 42nd's Mitchell bombers had caught and sunk more than 20 Japanese ships with their low level tactics, including cargo vessels, barges, and two destroyers. The bombing at 75 to 100 feet above the surface of the sea had proven quite accurate against fast moving, zig zagging ships.

"Hank," Twining told Colonel Wilson, "this enemy fleet coming down from Rabaul is a real threat. You'll have to plan a low level strike against them in the morning."

"I thought they were running head on into our own warship fleet."

Twining nodded. "They'll probably have a nighttime action within a couple of hours. Our navy ships haven't been too successful in these witching hour engagements with the Japanese. That Nip fleet might drive off Merrill's fleet, and by daylight the enemy fleet could be heading for the invasion beaches at Cape Torokina to bombard the hell out of those marines."

"Okay," Colonel Wilson nodded. "We'll have our B-twenty-fives out there in the morning."

"Good," Twining said. The COMAIRSOL commander then turned to the MAG 24 and 18th Fighter Group commanders. "Colonel," the general told Mangrum, "can we get a squadron of your Avengers up there in the morning to help out Wilson's B-twenty five mediums?''

''Yes sir,'' the MAG 24 commander said, ''at least sixteen torpedo bombers.''

''Fine,'' Twining said. ''How about fighters? The Japanese will probably send planes after Merrill's ships. We need a couple of squadrons to protect those cruisers and destroyers.''

''I'll send out both the Two-fourteenth and Two-twenty-first Squadrons,'' Mangrum promised.

Twining now looked at Col. Aaron Tyer. ''I'd like a couple of your fighter squadrons out by dawn to escort the marine and army bombers.''

''We'll have two squadrons up,'' Tyer promised.

Far across the Solomon Sea, at Port Moresby, New Guinea, Gen. Ennis Whitehead also held a conference with his staff. By midnight, the last hour of November 1, Whitehead also knew that ten heavily loaded transports and freighters were on the way back to Rabaul, where the harbors were crammed with other ships and the airdromes were jammed with planes. Finally, Whitehead knew that his responsibility in Operation Cartwheel lay in neutralizing Rabaul and he was determined to act.

The 5th Air Force ADVON commander had thus far known only frustration because of the poor weather that still hung tenaciously over the Bismarck Archipelago. He had not been able to mount even a nuisance raid since the last air attack on Rabaul on October 26. Still, Whitehead wanted to remind his air group leaders to remain alert for an air strike on the Japanese stronghold on a moment's notice.

The 5th Air Force ADVON commander looked at his staff officers. "Are all air units still ready to go?"

"Yes sir," an aide answered. "The B-twenty-five groups at Dobo are still loaded and fueled and the fighter groups on Kiriwina and the Woodlarks can take off on a moment's notice."

"What about the heavies here in Moresby?" Whitehead asked.

"The Ninetieth and Forty-third Groups are set to go."

"Send a memo to all air group headquarters," Whitehead gestured. "Inform them of the latest around Bougainville: that impending naval battle, the return of those transports and freighters to Rabaul, and the countless ships and planes now up there in Rabaul. All group commanders must expect dawn take-offs for Rabaul."

"Yes sir."

Both the Japanese and the Americans, from Rabaul to Noumea, had made frantic preparations to support the expected nighttime sea battle between Adm. Sentaro Omori's Torokina Interception Force and Adm. Stanton Tip Merrill's TF 19 cruiser force.

During the wee hours of November 2, the

seas around Empress Augusta Bay were relatively calm. A slight breeze blew from the southwest, and occasional lightning flashed from the south. The four days' moon had set early, leaving the sky unusually dark, with stars twinkling through patches of clearing in the overcast. Rain squalls, often less than a minute in duration, intermittently drenched the crews of Merrill's ships. The night, uncannily quiet and with low humidity and pleasant temperatures, was good for sleeping in the usually stifling climate of the South Pacific. But no sailor aboard the four cruisers and eight destroyers of TF 39 slept, for they knew that a sea fight with the Japanese might be hours away.

Adm. Tip Merrill himself had been in his flag room with his staff since about 2045 hours to prepare for battle with the enemy fleet on its way to Cape Torokina. At 0115 hours, November 2, Merrill and his aides still discussed plans for the expected night action.

"We're not going to make the error we've made so often before in night actions," Merrill said. "I don't want our destroyers hanging back to protect our cruisers. While the DDs hung back, the Nips sent schools of long lance torpedoes that caused consternation before we got a shot at them."

Capt. Ralph Parker nodded. He knew that back in August of 1942, at the beginning of the Solomons campaign, American tactics in night actions had brought them tragedy. In the Battle of Savo Island, a disastrous naval defeat, the

U.S. and Australian destroyers had clung to the cruisers to protect them while long lance torpedoes tore the Allied fleet to shreds. The Americans had suffered similar defeats with these same stay-close-to-home tactics, the most recent at Vella Lavella, where Japanese Adm. Matsuji Ijuin had macerated an American fleet in night action, while Ijuin had successfully evacuated hundreds of Japanese troops from the island.

"Where do you think we'll fight, sir?" Captain Parker asked.

"I'd like to conduct this action well to the west of Empress Augusta Bay," Merrill said. "Set a course for two-eight-zero degrees to take us west by northwest. The further out we engage the enemy fleet, the further we'll keep them away from Cape Torokina."

"Aye, sir," Parker said.

"We'll deploy our ships on a north-south line, with our picket destroyer about three miles ahead of our flagship *Montpelier*. I want the cruisers on a thousand yard spread, with Desron Forty-six at three thousand yards off the port. We'll send Burke's Desron Forty-five ahead of us off starboard. The destroyers should be flexible and loose, free to act whenever they need to. As soon as we make contact, Burke can shoot ahead with his destroyers for torpedo launches and Austin can shoot west to make torpedo attacks on the flank."

"What about the minesweepers?" Parker

asked. "They've been laying mines off Cape Torokina all evening and they'll be right off our starboard just about the time we engage."

"Maybe we'll have to send them southward."

"Yes sir," Parker said.

Then, at 0130 hours, one of the recon B-24s of the 307th Bomb Group flew out of the overcast and spotted the Japanese fleet. The U.S. Liberator dropped two bombs, one of which hit cruiser *Hagura* and loosened some hull plates that forced Omori to slow his fleet to 30 knots. Much more important, however, was this up-to-the-minute sighting of the Japanese fleet. The recon pilot immediately radioed TF 39.

"Enemy fleet of six destroyers and four cruisers now at six degrees one minute north by one fifty-three degrees fifty minutes east. Now on a one-seven-zero degree course, at about thirty knots, and sailing in three columns."

When Merrill read the report, he scowled. This enemy fleet was in the same disposition as that enemy fleet that had done so well against the Allies in that horrible Battle of Savo Island in August of 1942.

"Our job is clear," Merrill told his staff. "We've got to be disposed in a position to drive the enemy fleet away. We'll need to maintain our cruiser column in a position to stop a single ship from entering Torokina Bay, while our destroyers plow off to make torpedo launches. If we can push the enemy to the westward, we'll have plenty of sea room to fight."

"That means we'll need to keep the fleet

about sixteen to twenty thousand yards away from us," Parker said.

Merrill nodded. "We can do this if our destroyers get out fast enough. Send a message to both Captain Burke and Commander Austin."

"Aye, sir," Parker said.

"Make certain they understand exactly what they must do," Merrill gestured emphatically.

"Aye sir," his chief of staff said again.

"And be sure we maintain our two-eight-zero degree bearing at twenty-eight knots."

Meanwhile, a Japanese sea plane from cruiser *Haguro* had also been searching the sea around Empress Augusta Bay and at 0200 hours, the sea plane spotted a U.S. destroyer column, Desron 45, that had taken up a position to the northwest of the main TF 39 cruiser force. The observers aboard the Japanese Emily assumed that these destroyers constituted the U.S. war fleet in the area, so they sadly underestimated the size of the American warship fleet.

"We have located the enemy fleet," the Emily observers radioed cruiser *Myoko*. "The fleet includes a mere cruiser and three destroyers, not the huge cruiser fleet that was erroneously reported earlier. This enemy fleet is now about fifty miles west of Cape Torokina and sailing west by northwest at thirty-two knots."

The report delighted Admiral Omori—a mere cruiser and a few destoyers. He could dispose of them quickly. He immediately altered course to

160 degrees to barrel ahead at flank speed to engage. He had barely made the course change when the Japanese snooper plane sent Omori a second radio report.

"Many transport marus are in Empress Augusta Bay," the airmen aboard the Emily recon plane reported.

The observers of the float plane had vaguely sighted ships in the bay after they had discovered Desron 45. The plane had then dropped flares over Empress Augusta Bay and the observers had seen a number of ships which they mistook for transports and freighters. Actually, the Japanese airmen had seen the three minesweepers that had been laying mines in the bay: USS *Breese, Gamble,* and *Sicard*. The fourth ship was destroyer USS *Renshaw* that had been escorting the minesweepers.

As soon as this small fleet of three minesweepers and one destroyer found themselves exposed by the Japanese reconnaisance plane, the ships sailed quickly out of Empress Augusta Bay. They suspected along with everyone else that a heavy surface warship battle was in the works on this dark night and they did not want to catch any stray torpedoes, especially Japanese long lances; nor did they want to catch any errant shells, particularly the 8″ shells from Japanese heavy cruisers.

But the four ships would not get completely away—they would have front row seats when the sea fight commenced.

As the second recon report reached Admiral

Omori, his delight intensified. Not only did he have a mere four American warships to contend with, but beyond these U.S. combat ships lay a small fleet of fat transport and freighter marus that he could pulverize with the big 8″ guns of his heavy cruisers.

"We will remain on our one-six-zero degree course and we will increase speed," he told his chief of staff. "We will position Admiral Ijuin's Desron Twenty-seven on the port of our heavy cruisers and Captain Osugi's Desron Sixty-one on the starboard of our heavy cruisers."

"Yes, admiral," Captain Yamada said.

Omori's naval force slid forward through the dark night and over the calm sea at 30 knots. In the center were flag *Myoko* and fellow heavy cruiser *Haguro*. On the starboard in column, 5,000 meters off, was Desron 61: flag light cruiser *Agano* and destroyers *Naganami, Hatsukaze* and *Wakatsuki*. In the port column, also some 5,000 meters off sailed Ijuin's Desron 27: flag light cruiser *Sendai* along with destroyers *Shigure, Samadare,* and *Shiratsuyu*. The Japanese fleet was sailing straight into the flank of the American TF 39 fleet.

Sailors aboard the Japanese warships psyched themselves eagerly for battle. They had won a nighttime engagement against the Americans many times and they hoped to come out ahead again this time. Gunners in the 8″, 5″, and 4″ gun pits waited excitedly by their guns, making certain they had plenty of shells. Torpedo crews stood by their launch racks, ready to send off fish against the American ships as soon as they got the word. Lookouts in crowsnests squinted intently into the darkness to the south, southeast, and east, waiting to pick up the first silhouette of an American ship.

Aboard American ships, a similar excitement prevailed. The U.S. bluejackets, although aware that American fleets had lost substantial night battles to the Japanese, expressed faith in Merrill's proposed tactics—send the destroyers out quickly and aggressively to attack the Japanese with torpedo spreads. American sailors also waited alertly at their gun pits, although their light cruisers did not carry anything bigger than a 6″ gun.

Torpedo crews also stood restlessly at their stations to launch fish as soon as the order came. Lookouts in the crowsnests of American ships, like their Japanese counterparts, also waited to see the first silhouette of an enemy ship.

As Task Force 39 and the Torokina Interception Force closed toward each other, both the Americans and the Japanese recognized the importance of the battle's outcome. If the Japanese won the battle, Omori's fleet could sail close to the marine beachheads and blast the invaders to pieces with 8″ naval shells. General Imamura could then send reinforcements to Bougainville to wrest the invasion site from the Americans.

At 0232 hours, Capt. Ralph Parker got another report from an American B-24 snooper.

"Enemy fleet still on its one-six-zero degree course, directly northwest, and sailing at about thirty knots; still in three columns, with heavy cruisers in the center and destroyer lines on the flanks." The TF 39 chief of staff brought the message immediately to Merrill.

The TF 39 commander read the recon report and then pursed his lips. "Okay, Ralph, steady as she goes."

"Aye, sir."

"Alert all men at their battle stations."

"All hands have been on alert for quite a while."

"As soon as we make contact," Merrill said, "send Burke off at once to get into position for torpedo launches from his destroyers. He's got to do this in a hurry, before the enemy can hit our columns with long lances."

"Aye, sir," Parker said again.

At 0235 hours, a Japanese snooper, another Emily float plane from the Shortlands, spotted the American fleet once more. The observers sent a new report to Omori. "American vessels steaming at twenty-eight knots on a three-four-five degree course. They are now twenty-five kilometers from Cape Torokina. Estimated position is six degrees thirty minutes south by one hundred fifty five degrees east."

Captain Yamada brought the report immediately to the admiral. "Honorable Omori, the latest report on the American fleet. The enemy is a mere twenty-five kilometers off, and they will soon come into visual sighting."

"Remind all ship lookouts to remain fully alert. You will inform Admiral Ijuin to increase the speed of his Desron Twenty-seven to flank so that he may launch torpedoes as soon as we have visual sightings."

"Yes, admiral."

"Make certain that gunners on our heavy cruisers are prepared to fire eight-inch salvos as soon as they get the order. We will release star shells as soon as we sight the enemy."

"Yes, Honorable Omori."

Adm. Sentaro Omori now walked out of the flag room to the open catwalk of the bridge and stared into the dark night, squinting at the silhouettes of his Desron 61 destroyers and then peering up at the low-hanging, broken clouds. He took a deep breath, inhaling the pleasant late evening air. Omori felt no fears and no regrets for the upcoming battle. First, he had the excellent Admiral Ijuin with him. Second, he believed the Japanese superior to the Americans in night action. Finally, he was under the erroneous impression that the American war fleet only included a light cruiser and a few destroyers. His own gunners, quite courageous and well trained, would quickly deal with this American fleet.

But the Americans had a tremendous advantage over the Japanese by the fall of 1943. Although both sides were about equal in strength, with the Japanese slightly ahead with eight-inch guns, the Americans had radar.

Two things were important for this night action. First, the side that found the other first could take the initiative and set the pattern for battle. Second, any battle action, especially at night, demanded accuracy. Radar would enable Merrill to find the Japanese long before any lookouts in crowsnests saw anything, and radar would enable the Americans to shoot straight regardless of how obscured the target.

At 0240 hours, in fact, radar blips showed up on the screen of the American picket destroyer USS *Ausburne* of Burke's Desron 45—and the Japanese still 22 miles away from the American fleet. The radar men quickly called the bridge of *Ausburne*.

"Enemy ships, south by west of Cape Torokina; bearing, one-six-zero degrees; speed, approximately thirty knots; distance, thirty-five thousand yards; sailing in three columns."

The report went immediately to flagship *Montpelier* where the communications officer brought the message to Merrill. "Radar has the enemy fleet, sir. They're on a one-six-zero degree course, only about thirty-five thousand yards off."

Merrill looked at the report and nodded. "Okay, the wait is over." He turned to Captain Parker. "Ralph, notify all ships. Prepare to fire."

"Yes sir," the TF 39 chief of staff said.

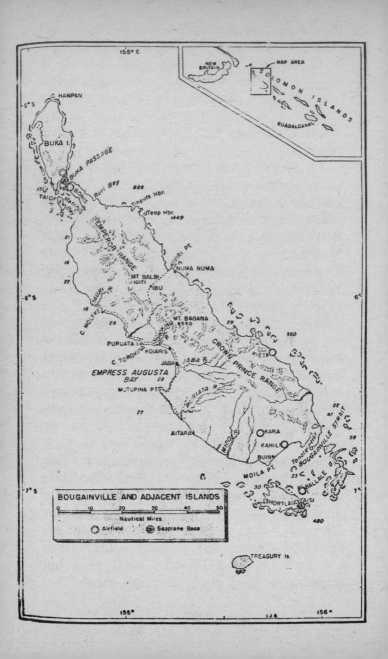

# Chapter Seven

The TF 39 fleet was now steering almost directly west at a speed of 28 knots, on a course of 345 degrees. "I want Desron Forty-five on the flank for torpedo launches," Adm. Tip Merrill said.

"Aye, sir," Parker answered.

Capt. Arleigh Burke responded elatedly to the order from flagship *Montpelier*. Burke quickly relayed the information to all Desron 45 commanders. "We're going west by northwest at full ahead for torpedo launch. Make sure all radar personnel have those enemy ships pinpointed. We'll send out torpedoes as soon as we come within ten thousand yards."

Admiral Merrill then ordered Cmdr. Bob Austin of Desron 46 to alter course so these other TF 39 destroyers could also get into a flank position for torpedo launches against the Japanese fleet. Austin quickly called his destroyer commanders. "Keep launch crews and radar crews on alert. We'll send out torpedoes as soon as we come into range."

Thus, while the destroyer squadrons plowed ahead, Admiral Merrill turned his four light cruisers 90 degrees to lay to for long range shell fire. The TF 39 commander had positioned his ships in what he considered proper battle order. No tin cans would hang back to shelter cruisers, while Japanese destroyers skimmed about the dark waters to launch torpedoes all over the sea. Merrill, certain he had found the Japanese without detection, hoped to get in the first blow before the enemy discovered his TF 39.

However, although the Japanese had none of the radar equipment of the Americans, Admiral Omori certainly suspected that the U.S. fleet was close by. He followed the usual Japanese technique—keep recon planes continually aloft. And, in a fortunate stroke of luck, one of the Japanese sea planes dropped star shells that blossomed right over the American cruisers. The glaring flares enabled a lookout aboard cruiser *Sendai* to see these heavier U.S. ships.

"Enemy cruiser fleet! Cruiser fleet! Forty thousand meters off!" the lookout called the bridge. "Enemy column at an estimated forty thousand meters."

Admiral Ijuin was aghast! The Americans had more than mere destroyers. The reconnaissance planes had apparently missed these cruisers. Ijuin recovered quickly from this shock and he ordered his Desron 27 column into a sharp 70 degree turn, southeast, at full ahead speed. His flag cruiser *Sendai* led the three destroyers. "We will launch torpedoes at once!'' Ijuin cried into a radio phone.

"Yes, admiral," somebody answered.

At 0250 hours, the crews on *Sendai* sent a spread of eight long lance torpedoes toward the American ships. Unfortunately for Ijuin, the American cruiser lookouts had seen the Japanese ships both visually and on radar. Further, they had seen the torpedoes coming. So the U.S. ships veered to avoid the hits. Still Merrill was irate because he had lost the element of surprise.

"Goddamn it," Merrill cursed, "they're already sending long lances at us." He turned to his communications officer. "Get a radar fix on those enemy ships and then give the order to open with cruiser guns."

"Aye, sir."

By 0252 hours, Merrill had the exact location of the enemy vessels, now sailing in three columns: Ijuin's Desron 27 on the right, Osugi's Desron 61 on the left, and heavy cruisers *Myoko* and *Haguro* in the center. Then, the gunners aboard light cruisers USS *Montpelier, Cleveland, Columbia,* and *Denver* opened with 6″ shell salvos. The shells from the American ships proved quite accurate on this dark night thanks to radar control range finding. Every one of the dozen 6″ shells came close to the Japanese cruiser column, with four of the six inchers slamming into cruiser *Sendai.*

One shell exploded on the aft, warped the steering, and jammed the cruiser's rudder. Another six incher struck the starboard and blew away the midship torpedo racks. A third shell hit a storage locker and disintegrated stacks of supplies. The fourth shell hit *Sendai*'s aft magazine, shuddering the cruiser with numbing explosions before fire and smoke enveloped the flagship of the Japanese Desron 27.

"Damage control, damage control!" the Desron 27 commander cried frantically over his radio phone. "You must repair damage and put out fires."

"Yes, Honorable Ijuin," the damage control officer answered.

The Desron 27 staff were utterly shocked by the accurate, heavy hits from the American ships. Admiral Ijuin could not recall when the Americans had done so well, especially during nighttime engagements. But, the Japanese did not know that the Americans were now aiming at targets with radar.

Although the next salvo from Merrill's cruisers missed the Desron 27 column, the shells came so close to the Japanese vessels that two ships collided in an effort to avoid hits. Destroyers *Samidare* and *Shiratsuyu* had zigzagged frantically about the dark sea at flank speed as exploding geysers from 6″ shells fell dangerously close to them. In their haste to escape the shells, the two destroyers collided, putting a huge hole on *Samidare*'s starboard and crumpling *Shiratsuyu*'s bow like cardboard. Crews then worked furiously to stem flooding aboard both destroyers. So temporarily at least, both ships were out of the fight. The destroyers veered to the westward in a 180 degree turn.

In the first few minutes of battle, the turret gunners aboard the American cruisers had put a Japanese cruiser and two destroyers out of business. Only destroyer *Shigure* had escaped damage in Ijuin's column and she became busy helping out the other ships.

When Omori got the report on the sudden maceration of Desron 27, the admiral paled. Captain Yamada tried to mitigate the admiral's shock. "They were simply fortunate, Honorable Omori. The Americans have never shown this kind of accuracy in night actions, and they are not likely to repeat this feat." Like Ijuin, Yamada and Omori were also ignorant of the fact that the Americans were finding the range with radar.

"We will turn right and open fire with our heavy guns," Omori said.

"Yes, admiral," Captain Yamada answered.

Omori had made a fortunate decision, for even as *Myoko* and *Haguro* made their turns, some 25 torpedoes were skimming in the direction of the heavy cruisers. Torpedo spreads from Burke's Desron 45 were heading straight for the Japanese warships. The U.S. torpedo crews had not anticipated the right turn by the Torokina Force vessels so all torpedoes missed.

In an added piece of luck for Omori, another Japanese float plane illuminated some of the TF 39 ships, once again Merrill's light cruiser column.

"They are no more than thirty thousand

meters off," Captain Yamada told the admiral.

"Commence fire at once," Omori said.

The gunners on heavy cruisers *Myoko* and *Haguro* then opened with salvos of big 8″ shells. While the shells came perilously close, none of the American cruisers caught hits. Admiral Merrill yelled into his JV.

"Make smoke! Make smoke! Alter course to two-zero-zero degrees and increase to flank speed."

The American ship commanders responded quickly and the American cruisers soon enveloped themselves in thick smoke. Merrill's cruisers had come within a mere 19,000 yards of the Japanese heavy cruisers and the TF 39 commander did not relish this close range to big 8″ guns. So he ordered a course change and the cruiser column steered south, southwest. Merrill had acted wisely, for Omori's gunners now lost sight of the American cruisers and the Japanese did not know where to send their next salvos.

At 0255 hours, Omori ordered his two big cruisers to the southward. However, after sailing through the darkness for several minutes, his lookouts still could not find the American ships that had slipped away in their smoke screen. The Torokina Fleet commander then sent out more float planes that dropped more star shells over the sea. But none of the flares burst over American ships.

Meanwhile, Capt. Morikzau Osugi had failed to shoot ahead with his Desron 27 column of destroyers to locate the American ships and launch torpedoes. Such launches were vital since the other Japanese Desron unit had been mauled during the first moments of battle. Instead of rushing forward, Osugi merely followed the two big Japanese cruisers with his Desron 27 column.

While Omori searched unsuccessfully for the Americans, Tip Merrill's radar men had again pinpointed the Japanese ships on radar screens. Merrill then ordered an immediate radar controlled resume fire.

A moment later, salvos of 6″ shells again whizzed through the darkness with good accuracy. Several near misses slightly damaged one of the Japanese destroyers, while two six inchers slammed squarely into the starboard quarter of flag cruiser *Myoko*. One shell blew away a storage locker and the other shell destroyed a 40mm gun pit. Fortunately *Myoko*'s helmsman deftly maneuvered the big cruiser away from further hits.

More radar controlled salvos caught destroyer *Hatsukaze*, the third ship in Captain Osugi's Desron 61 column. One shell shot away the forward turret, while another shell disintegrated a torpedo launch port. The explosions ignited several torpedoes that zoomed about like giant Roman candles and prompted the Japanese crew to scatter in panic. The *Hatsukaze* skipper ordered a sharp turn to right and full ahead speed.

The destroyer's helmsman, totally rapt in his effort to escape further American shell hits, did not see his own heavy cruisers ahead of him. While dodging TF 39 gunfire, the helmsman brought destroyer *Hatsukaze* between cruisers *Myoko* and *Haguro* and at 0307 hours, the destroyer ran into *Myoko*. In the collision, *Myoko* sheered off two of *Hatsukaze*'s torpedo tubes and a chunk of the destroyer's bow. The debris became imbedded in *Myoko*'s hull and the big cruiser would carry these souvenirs back to Rabaul.

Omori was rattled by the collision for he feared that *Hatsukaze* would go down. He called his chief of staff. "Captain, check damage on *Hatsukaze* at once. If she is sinking, we must take off survivors."

"Yes admiral," Captain Yamada answered.

Although damaged, with torpedo tubes gone and bow crumpled, the Japanese destroyer was in no danger of sinking, but the destroyer was out of the fight and Omori ordered *Hatsukaze* to retire.

Merrill's cruisers, meanwhile, continued to send 6" salvos against the Japanese ships. After steering his cruiser column on a south, southwest course for 20 minutes, Merrill ordered his cruisers into a figure eight maneuver to give Austin's Desron 26 plenty of room for torpedo launches. The TF 39 commander wanted his cruisers constantly in erratic movements to keep off balance the Japanese gunners and torpedo crews.

The deft maneuvers proved effective. Two spreads of torpedoes from Desron 61 failed to come anywhere near the American ships. By the time the Japanese torpedoes had skimmed toward their potential targets, the American ships were elsewhere. Further, the same erratic U.S. fleet movements had enabled the American cruisers to avoid several Japanese 8" shell salvos.

"The American cruisers are in constant movement, and quite haphazardly," Captain Yamada told the Torokina Interception Force commander. "We have been unable to score with shellfire or torpedoes."

"If they are in such constant, unstable maneuvers, how can they fire their own salvos with such accuracy?" Omori grumbled.

"I do not know, Honorable Omori," Captain Yamada said.

The answer, of course, was radar controlled gunfire. In truth, the new radar directional systems recently installed on many American combat ships had been the best innovation for sea battles since the war began. Radar had become especially useful at night, because even as the American light cruisers of TF 39 twisted and turned violently in speeds up to 30 knots, and even though the U.S. ships fired salvos without visual sighting of the enemy ships, the 6" shells hit home in many instances.

Light cruiser *Sendai* was already sinking, *Myoko* had taken serious hits, and four Japanese destroyers had either suffered hits or collisions because of the accurate American gunfire. In return, the American fleet was yet to suffer a scatch.

Now, cruiser *Haguro* caught some telling blows. A half dozen 6″ shells from the American light cruisers either struck or near-missed the big Japanese warship. One near-miss opened a hole on the port that started flooding. Another near-miss temporarily jammed a rudder. Two solid 6″ hits slammed into the superstructure, knocking out a signal house and an antiaircraft post. Two more near-misses opened a hole on the port side that temporarily flooded one of *Haguro*'s engine rooms and slowed the cruiser to 15 knots.

Then the Japanese got lucky. Another descending star shell from yet another Japanese float plane once more illuminated Merrill's light cruiser column. As soon as Japanese lookouts spotted the American ships and reported their location to flag cruiser *Myoko,* Admiral Omori ordered increased speed and a quick course change from 180 to 160 degrees. As the two heavy warships closed on Merrill's light cruiser, Onori cried into his radio phone.

"Launch torpedoes and resume shell fire!"

A spread of ten torpedoes soon splashed toward the American cruisers that were now only 13,000 yards off. Then 8″ Japanese gun salvos from *Myoko* and *Haguro* boomed toward the American ships. This time the Japanese showed better accuracy, with light cruiser USS *Denver* catching the bulk of the 8″ hits. One shell slammed into *Denver*'s stern and opened holes that started flooding. Another shell knocked out the rear gun turrets before erupting fires and smoke. Fortunately, the other two 8″ hits were duds, but even these opened holes in the American cruiser's hull to cause more flooding.

*Denver* was soon ablaze and slowed to 20 knots. However, repair crews worked swiftly to seal flooding and snuff out fires.

At the time that *Denver* was catching the 8″ hits, Merrill's cruiser column was still sailing south, southwest. Merrill ordered another 180 degree turn and he increased speed to open range. 13,000 yards was too close against the heavy cruiser shells and he needed to avoid the Japanese torpedoes.

Meanwhile, the U.S. destroyers columns had failed miserably thus far. Arleigh Burke's Little Beavers of Desron 45 had accomplished nothing since launching the torpedoes early in the battle. Burke had lost both visual and radar contact with the Japanese because he had scooted too far to the northwest and his ships had become separated in the darkness. Now the Desron 45 destroyers had come full circle to seek out the battle area. At 0335, the lookout aboard Desron 45's flag, destroyer USS *Dyson,* spotted the burning *Sendai.*

"Enemy ship about seven thousand yards off," the lookout called the bridge. "Looks like a Japanese cruiser in trouble."

"Okay, we'll finish her off," Burke answered.

Gunners on USS *Dyson* opened with 5″ guns

and sent a half dozen shells into *Sendai,* even as *Dyson* plowed past the cruiser at 32 knots. More fire and smoke erupted from the battered Japanese warship and the U.S. bluejackets cheered. As *Dyson* moved past the floundering, burning *Sendai, Dyson*'s radar crew picked up destroyers *Samidare* and *Shiratsuyu* on their screens.

"We've got more bogies," an EM called the bridge. "They're about eight thousand yards off the port bow."

"Increase speed," Capt. Arleigh Burke said.

A moment later, Burke's lookouts spotted the silhouetted ships ahead. The vessels, turning north, were apparently in a bad way. "Prepare to fire!" Captain Burke cried into a JV.

But, the Desron 45 commander suddenly got a call from Cmdr. Bob Austin aboard flag destroyers USS *Spence* of Desron 46. "Hold off, Arleigh. Don't shoot! It's us out here!"

"Goddamn, Bob," Burke hissed. "It's a good thing you called."

Ironically, the call from Austin had given grace to the Japanese destroyers *Samidare* and *Shiratsuyu.* Burke's lookouts had indeed seen these two Nippon ships, but after the call from Austin, Burke assumed the Japanese ships were destroyers from the U.S. Desron 46. Crews on the two Japanese vessels had been busy making repairs from their collision when the Americans spotted them. The Nippon sailors now sighed in relief when at 0417 hours USS *Dyson* turned 180 degrees and headed east, with the rest of the

Desron 45 column following the flag destroyer.

But, destroyer *Hatsukaze* was not as fortunate as *Samidare* and *Shiratsuyu*. As Cmdr. Bob Austin led his four destroyers of Desron 46 northward, he ran into the Japanese ship that was barely moving, while repair crews tried to mend damage from the collision with cruiser *Myoko*. In fact, Austin's flag *Spence* had come within 2,000 yards of *Hatsukaze* when one of the destroyer's searchlight beams clearly lit up the Japanese ship.

"Open fire!" Commander Austin cried.

The U.S. destroyers laced the Japanese destroyer with endless salvos of five-inch shells a moment later, at close range. An array of hits opened the hull to start uncontrolled flooding. More hits blew away compartments, gun pits, storage lockers, and magazines. Within minutes, *Hatsukaze* was aflame from bow to stern and listing badly. But still the Americans gunners pumped five-inch shells into the hapless Japanese destroyer. The blazing ship soon split in half from the heavy, ceaseless, point blank gunfire. Finally, at 0439, the bluejackets aboard USS *Spence* watched the ship go down. The American sailors saw no survivors.

But, as Commander Austin's Desron 46 turned 90 degrees to join the rest of TF 39, destroyer *Foote*, at the rear of the column, made a wrong turn and lost the rest of the destroyer column. Lt. Cmdr. Alston Ramsey, *Foote*'s skipper, was peeved by the error and he called the engine room.

"Full ahead! Full ahead to join column!"

"Aye sir."

USS *Foote* then plowed forward at a full 35 knots. But she had only sailed for several minutes when a sudden, numbing explosion rocked the ship and shuddered the American tin can to a stop. A torpedo from one of the Japanese destroyers had slammed into the aft of the American vessel and blown off her stern. With his destroyer dead in the water, Lieutenant Commander Ramsay became frantic.

"Repair crews, check damage and stop flooding. Stop flooding!"

Meanwhile, as the remainder of Desron 46 continued on its altered course, salvos of Japanese 5″ shells erupted geysers of water around them. Commander Austin ordered flag *Spence* into a quick starboard turn to avoid the Japanese gunfire. But in making the sudden turn, *Spence* sideswiped destroyer USS *Thatcher* that had made its own quick turn to escape Japanese shells. Luckily, the scraping hulls did not cause serious damage and neither destroyer was even slowed down.

At 0440 hours, a 5″ Japanese shell hit USS *Spence* at the waterline and shrapnel punched a hole in the fuel line that allowed salt water to leak into the oil tanks and contaminate fuel; *Spence* stopped dead in the water, until repair crews made improvisions. The ship then moved on, but intermittently stopped when salt water again seeped into the fuel lines and forced crews to clear the lines again.

Cmdr. Bob Austin's Desron 46 was in disarray: flagship *Spence* with fuel problems, *Foote* dragging her stern, *Thatcher* damaged, and able destroyer *Converse* trying to help the other three. Austin could not even answer Admiral Merrill when, at 0445 hours, the TF 39 commander ordered all destroyers to rejoin the cruiser columns so that Merrill could reform for further attacks on the Japanese fleet. The Desron 46 sailors had a tough time rejoining, but they had one consolation: as they struggled back to the U.S. cruisers, they saw cruiser *Sendai* rolling over in her final death throes before going down.

The Japanese had not yet given up. Their float planes still hovered overhead as they had since the battle started over two hours ago. At the request of Admiral Omori, Capt. Benji Shimada had been continually sending out recon planes from his base at Ballale in the Shortlands. The starshell-loaded aircraft left the Shortlands harbor as fast as Shimada could get them off. This time, two seaplanes came over Merrill's ships to drop a confetti of new star shells. A thin cloud cover hung over the American warships, and when the star shells blossomed in bright illumination directly over the cruisers, the clouds acted as a silver reflector to brilliantly light up the four graceful U.S. warships.

With an excellent view of the American cruisers, Omori's gunners fired new salvos of 8″ shells at the TF 39 column. The shells erupted colored geysers of water like fountains in a palatial garden—red, green, and golden, depending on which Japanese ship had fired the shells. American bluejackets might have enjoyed the colorful nighttime exhibition, but they knew that the next eruption could blow them to oblivion.

Fortunately for the Americans, in their anxiety to score hits, the Japanese gunners performed shoddily during the waning hour of this dark night. Some of the shells fizzled, others fell short, and only a few luckily near-missed. The Japanese scored only minor damage on the American cruisers. But worst of all, when Admiral Omori saw the huge geysers erupting near the American cruisers, he astonishingly assumed that torpedoes had struck the American ships. Further, he believed the smoke screens from the U.S. vessels were the residue of solid, fiery hits on the American cruisers. So, at 0448 hours, certain he had put the American cruisers out of action and on their way to the bottom, Omori ordered retirement to reform his fleet.

"Honorable Omori," Captain Yamada said, "perhaps we should make certain we have destroyed these enemy cruisers."

"No," Omori answered, "it is obvious our shells and torpedoes have taken care of these Yankee vessels. We must now concern ourselves with our own damage. Cruiser *Sendai* is sinking and four of our destroyers have been severely damaged. We must attend to these vessels and their sailors. Then we will sail into Empress

Augusta Bay to destroy the enemy transport marus and their beachheads."

"Yes, Honorable Omori."

While the Japanese fleet veered away to the westward, Adm. Tip Merrill and his chief aide, Capt. Ralph Parker, were standing on the bridge of flagship *Montpelier*. Merrill had been squinting into empty seas to the west and he then turned to watch the first huge patch of daylight rise over Empress Augusta Bay. Then he looked at Parker.

"Ralph, have you ordered all ships to rejoin?"

"Yes sir."

"What's our damage?"

"Destroyer *Foote* is quite bad and she'll need a tow," Parker said. "We've had hits on some other ships, too, but nothing serious. They're all under their own power and none is in danger of sinking."

"Good," Merrill nodded. He then peered again into the still dark horizon to the west. "I don't see anything."

"We have nothing on our radar screens, either," Captain Parker said. "I think that whatever's left of that enemy fleet has retired. We have definite proof we sank at least one destroyer and one cruiser, and maybe we hurt two or three of their destroyers."

"That's a good score," Merrill nodded.

"Will we pursue?" Parker asked.

"No," Merrill said. "If they're scurrying back to Rabaul that's good enough for us." He looked to the east again and now squinted into the still brightening sky. "Looks like a beautiful day on shore. Our gyrenes should make some good progress from their beachheads today."

"Yes sir."

"As soon as all ships are back in column, we'll close toward the bay. I want you to call COMAIRSOL for CAP's. Those Nips may launch an air strike on us this morning."

"After the beating their air units took during the Bougainville landings, do you think they'll send out more air formations?"

"I'm not taking any chances," Merrill said. "You call COMAIRSOL for those combat air patrols. I want them here by sun up."

"Aye sir," Parker answered.

## Chapter Eight

In the Battle of Empress Augusta Bay, American casualties had been relatively light. TF 39 losses included 19 killed and 17 wounded on destroyer USS *Foote,* with another 20 killed and 23 wounded from hits on other American vessels. But most important, Merrill had stopped the Japanese fleet from sailing into the bay to bombard the American beachheads with their heavy 8″ guns.

In the Pacific war, the Japanese almost invariably exaggerated the results of any battle action. Adm. Sentaro Omori, although losing two ships and suffering damage to others, had radioed Rabaul at 0500 hours that he had destroyed most of the American ships, and left several U.S. cripples floundering around the entrance of Empress Augusta Bay. Japanese air units, Omori said, could finish off these damaged American ships with little difficulty. So, the brass in Rabaul acted at once.

At 0505 hours, immediately after receiving reports from Omori, both Admiral Kusaka and

General Imamura ordered air strikes. Kusaka instructed Capt. Tokeo Shibata to send out bombers at once, while he asked Commander Genda to furnish Zero escorts for this attack on the supposed damaged American ships now wallowing off the coast of central Bougainville. The 11th Air Fleet commander also called on Capt. Benji Shimada at Ballale.

"Captain, I have asked Captain Shibata to launch air strikes from Rabaul and he will be over Empress Augusta Bay by oh-nine-hundred hours. Meanwhile, you will attack the American warships as soon as possible with all available aircraft from your own Yokoyama Wing."

"Yes, Honorable Kusaka."

"If you complete the destruction of these American warships, Captain Shibata can attack the enemy's transport marus and his beachhead."

"We will act at once," Shimada assured Admiral Kusaka.

General Imamura gave Capt. Goro Furugori essentially the same order. "Mount your Mitsubishi bombers (Bettys) with an escort of Kawasaki fighters (Tonys) for an immediate air strike at Bougainville."

"Yes, Honorable Imamura," Furugori answered.

At the same early morning hour, at Guadalcanal, COMAIRSOL headquarters received the request from TF 39 for CAP's over Merrill's fleet. General Twining immediately called both Col. Dick Mangrum of MAG 24 and Col.

Aaron Tyer of the 18th Fighter Group to get their fighter planes off for the CAP over Empress Augusta Bay. "We can expect the Japanese to launch air strikes from Rabaul this morning."

Both air group commanders acted at once. Maj. Greg Boyington would take out his VMF 214 squadron of Corsairs and Maj. Bob Westbrook would again take out his 44th Squadron of Lightnings.

Meanwhile, after the surface ship night action, both Merrill and Omori began rescue operations. Neither fleet commander knew the whereabouts of the other, but each assumed that the other still loitered in the area. Both admirals expected morning air attacks, so the two fleet commanders carried out rescue work cautiously to save as many men and ships as possible.

Destroyer *Foote,* though still afloat, could not move under her own power and destroyer *Claxton* took her in tow, with destroyers *Converse* and *Thatcher* acting as escort. And as soon as 31 Knot Burke returned with the rest of his destroyers, Merrill ordered fleet retirement southward.

Merrill's task of reforming his fleet and caring for survivors was quite easy, for he had lost no ships and he had no sailors overboard. The Japanese ships were scattered all over the Solomon Sea beyond Empress Augusta Bay, and perhaps 60 to 100 miles away from TF 39. Omori, upon learning that cruiser *Sendai* and destroyer *Hatsukaze* had been sunk, sent out destroyers to search for survivors. Omori got a fearful report at about 0530 hours.

"American aircraft are flying up the Sealark Channel," Yamada told the admiral, "perhaps fifty to sixty aircraft."

Omori squeezed his face, irritated. Even though he expected the Americans to begin air strikes at daylight, he now grew squeamish. Like so many other Japanese admirals, Omori too feared American air power. He cravenly abandoned all plans to conduct rescue operations or to sail toward the American beachheads for warship bombardments. He decided to retire.

"We cannot be certain that our fighter planes will arrive to protect us from enemy air attacks," he told his staff. "We must withdraw to Rabaul. We have accomplished a good night's work in destroying the bulk of the enemy's cruisers and leaving their other ships badly damaged."

"But what of the survivors from *Sendai* and *Hatsukaze?*"

"We know their positions and we will send submarines to rescue them." He looked at Captain Yamada. "You will order a starboard turn to a three-four-zero degree course."

"Yes, Admiral Omori."

Fortunately for Omori, submarines would pick up over 400 survivors from *Sendai,* including the cruiser's captain and Adm. Matsuji Ijuin. 100 others from the sunken cruiser would make their way to Bougainville. But, *Sendai* lost 320 of her crew. The Japanese did not find a single survivor from *Hatsukaze*. Apparently, all 250 officers and men from this destroyer had been killed or drowned in the vicious pounding by American naval guns. Omori had also lost about 50 sailors from hits on other ships, especially the hits on heavy cruiser *Haguro*. By 0700 hours, Omori was well on his way back to Rabaul with his surviving ships and men. They had left the area before the arrival of the American CAP's.

The Americans were not so lucky. At 0740 hours, November 2, hordes of blips appeared on the radar screens of U.S. picket destroyer *Ausburne*. "Bogies approaching from the south, southeast; maybe fifty planes," the radio man aboard *Ausburne* reported.

As soon as he got the report, Tip Merrill rushed to the bridge of *Montpelier* with Captain Parker. Both men scanned the southern horizon and they squinted up at the sky. "Where the hell are the CAP's?" Merrill growled.

"On the way," Parker said.

"They should have been here by now," the TF commander barked. "Order anti-aircraft formation at once."

"Aye, sir."

Moments later, the warships of TF 39 spread out and assumed a circular, zigzag formation to battle the approaching Japanese planes. Anti-aircraft gunners hurried to gun pits, while other sailors cleared the decks of anything that might get damaged from bomb hits. By 0750 hours, lookouts aboard the American ships got visual sightings of the Japanese planes.

The aircraft, 18 Val dive bombers with 20 Zero escorts, had come from Ballale. Capt. Benji Shimada had done an excellent job in mounting this many planes, considering the pounding Ballale had taken from American bombers. Shimada himself led the dive bombers while Lt. Cmdr. Toyotara Iwami led the Zero escorts.

At almost the same time, Maj. Bob Westbrook arrived in the vicinity with 16 P-38 fighter planes. Blips of the Japanese planes soon emerged on Westbrook's radar scope and the major picked up his JV to call Capt. Bill Harris.

"Bob, about a dozen or more enemy dive bombers are heading for those TF thirty-nine surface ships. They've got about a squadron of Zero escorts with them."

"I've got them on my own scope," Harris said.

"I'll take the bombers; you take the fighters."

"Roger," Harris answered.

Before the Japanese dive bombers reached the American surface ships, Captain Shimada saw the American fighter planes approaching from the south, southeast and he licked his lips nervously. He and other Japanese pilots dreaded the P-38. The American Lightning had proven itself quite superior to the Japanese

Zeros and the American pilots often took a heavy toll against Nippon air formations. Still, the Yokoyama Wing commander was determined to attack the American ships. He called Lieutenant Commander Iwami.

"You must deal with these American interceptors. They must not stop us from our attack on the enemy vessels."

"We will attack them at once, captain," Iwami answered.

Iwami had 20 Zeros, slightly more than the 16 P-38s. If he could not dispose of the superior Lightnings, perhaps he could engage them long enough to keep them away from Shimada's Vals until the dive bombers attacked the American warships. But as Iwami peeled off his Zeros to meet the American P-38s, he got another call from Shimada.

"More enemy fighter planes coming from the southeast. You will need to send some of the Mitsubishi escorts to engage."

"Yes, captain," Iwami said. But he scowled irritably. He would need to split his squadron into ten plane units to engage the American P-38s and these new American planes approaching the Japanese air formation.

The second squadron that now arrived was the 16 Corsairs under Maj. Greg Boyington from VMF 214. Boyington had also taken off promptly from Guadalcanal after getting the call from Colonel Mangrum to maintain a CAP over Empress Augusta Bay. The Black Sheep commander had arrived in the area only moments after Westbrook's arrival. He now called Westbrook over his TBS.

"This is Baa Baa leader. You were here first, major, so it's your choice. Do you want the escorts or the bombers?"

"Glad you're here, Baa Baa. Those Zeros are coming after us, so we may as well tangle with them. Take your Corsairs after those Vals."

"Will do, major," Boyington answered.

As soon as Corsairs droned off, Westbrook veered his 16 P-38s into the oncoming Japanese fighter planes from the Yokoyama Wing. Lieutenant Iwami did not even have time to split his squadron and send half of his 20 planes after the Corsairs.

"Okay, in pairs, and don't get fancy with those Zeros," Westbrook cried into his radio.

As the Lightning pilots peeled off, they followed the cautious system of avoiding loops and turns and spins against the more maneuverable Zeros. The 18th Fighter Group airmen had learned long ago that the P-38 was superior to the Zero in speed, climb, and dive, but not in versatility. So the American Army Air Force pilots followed the pattern of diving down on the Zeros to hit them with their tremendous fire from six .50 caliber wing guns and from 37mm cannon. When a Zero banked or looped away, the P-38 pilot simply zoomed high and came down again on the Japanese plane.

In a matter of minutes, the 44th Squadron pilots shot down eight of the Zeros. Westbrook got a kill when he tailed a Japanese plane and chopped off the tail with a stream of .50 caliber hits. The Zero simply tumbled like a jagged rock and plopped into the sea. Capt. Bill Harris also got a Zero when he caught the engine of the Japanese plane with a 37mm cannon hit. The subsequent explosion enveloped the Zero in fire and smoke before the plane plunged into the sea.

Some of the Zeros dropped low and skimmed along the top of the sea to avoid destruction. But Westbrook's pilots zoomed down after them and opened with thumping 37mm cannon shells and blistering .50 caliber strafing fire. Zeros exploded, or fell apart, or simply splashed into the sea.

Among the eight victims of the aggressive P-38 pilots was Lt. Cmdr. Toyotara Iwami. He had deftly maneuvered his Zero to catch a P-38 with 20mm cannon fire and a stream of .30 caliber machine gun fire. The hits knocked out both Lightning engines and the American plane tumbled into the sea, with its pilot already dead from .30 caliber fire. However, before Iwami banked away, a pair of P-38s tailed his Zero and opened with twin barrages of .50 caliber fire. The Zero literally fell apart from the heavy assault, but Iwami successfully ditched the battered plane and then scrambled out of the cockpit.

Iwami was luckily rescued by the same Japanese submarine that rescued survivors from cruiser *Sendai*.

The 12 surviving Zero pilots simply zoomed their planes into cloud banks to avoid further suffering from the aggressive Lightning pilots.

Capt. Benji Shimada, now without escorts, also sustained serious losses. Pappy Boyington and his Black Sheep pilots waded into the Japanese Vals with withering machine gun fire. The Japanese rear gunners on the dive bombers fired back, but their twin .30 caliber guns were no match for the six .50's and 37mm shells of the American Corsairs.

Boyington himself got his 14th kill in the Pacific war when he caught a Val in the gas tank. The explosion tore the plane apart, killing pilot and gunner. Capt. Bob McClurg got a dive bomber with withering .50 caliber fire that killed both the rear gunner and pilot. Black Sheep Lt. Bob See also got a Val when he came down on the bomber and unleashed three 37mm shells. One shell smashed through the cockpit, exploded, and killed the pilot. The Val simply tumbled tail over nose and into the sea.

Although losing six bombers en route, Shimada miraculously brought his other 12 Vals over the spread out, zigzagging American vessels. Shimada led a trio of Vals over the disabled USS *Foote* and released his bombs. However, the bombs from two of the planes missed the U.S. destroyer and heavy anti-aircraft fire from *Foote*'s gunners knocked down a Val before the dive bomber came close enough to release bombs. The Val exploded in midair and its fragments plopped into the sea.

As other Vals roared toward the TF 39 ships, Merrill ordered a quick 90 degree turn to bring more anti-aircraft batteries to bear. The move proved effective. At about 0805 hours, five-inch batteries from the U.S. cruisers and destroyers began firing like oversized machine guns. 40mm and 20mm anti-aircraft guns soon joined. Incredibly, the Vals broke formation and came after the ships in delayed intervals, allowing American ack ack gunners to concentrate on one Val before they needed to switch attention to the next dive bomber.

The American bluejackets knocked down three more of the attacking Vals while the other Japanese planes failed utterly. Some Vals broke off before their attack and simply zoomed away. Others released bombs too soon or too late, wildly missing targets by wide margins. One Val roared in at masthead height toward an American destroyer but crashed before reaching target.

The Yokoyama Wing pilots only scored two hits on the entire American TF 39 fleet, both on cruiser *Montpelier*. One 500 pounder struck the catapult and blew away the ramp and its plane. Miraculously, only one American sailor suffered injury. The other bomb knocked out *Montpelier*'s rear turret and wounded eight sailors.

By 0817 hours, the attack on the American ships had ended. Captain Shimada had lost over half of his Val dive bombers and eight of his Zero fighters—a terrible toll for two hits on a

U.S. cruiser. The Yokoyama Wing commander had no choice but to break off the action and take his survivors into cloud banks to avoid further assaults by the American pilots.

Soon, only the P-38s and Corsairs were circling over the American ships. The bluejackets of TF 39 gave the U.S. army and marine pilots a rousing cheer.

Maj. Bob Westbrook called the bridge of *Montpelier*. "No more bogies; no more bogies; we'll maintain CAP over your ships until relieved.'

"Very good," Capt. Ralph Parker answered.

As TF 39 continued its retirement inside Empress Augusta Bay, the sailors on the American ships did not yet relax. Although the bluejackets had welcomed the American air victory, they feared that more Japanese air units might come from the stronghold of Rabaul. And, in fact, the American sailors had reason to worry.

At 0800 hours, 2 November 1943, dozens of aircraft were warming up on the Rabaul airfields. After Capt. Tokeo Shibata had briefed 24 Val air crews and 20 Zero pilots of his 4th Kokutai Wing, he led these airmen toward their waiting planes at Rapopo and Tobera Dromes at Rabaul. Shibata himself would lead the dive bombers and Lt. Tetsuzo Iwamoto would lead the Zero escorts.

At Lakunai Field, Capt. Goro Furugori had briefed his Betty bomber crews and Tony fighter pilots. The army's 22nd Sentai, with about 50 aircraft, would follow on the heels of the navy's 4th Kokutai. Furugori would make a second strike on the American fleet, on the transports in Empress Augusta Bay, and on the American beachheads.

Meanwhile, Admiral Kusaka kept Cmdr. Minoru Genda on alert to make perhaps a third attack in the Empress Augusta Bay area. "You will prepare fifty aircraft of the Twenty-sixth Kokutai Wing to attack the Americans," Kusaka told Genda. "You will load half of your Mitsubishi (Zero) aircraft with bombs to be used as fighter-bombers, while the other Mitsubishi fighter aircraft will furnish escort."

"Yes, admiral," Genda answered the 11th Air Fleet commander.

Some 150 Japanese planes prepared to leave Rabaul for further attacks on the Americans in and around Bougainville. The two American CAP squadrons, 16 P-38s and 16 Corsairs, could hardly handle this many planes. COM-AIRSOL would certainly need to send more planes up to central Bougainville.

But the Americans got an unexpected respite from an air attack out of Rabaul. Shortly after 0800 hours, following the unsuccessful attack by the Yokoyama Wing on the American TF 39 fleet, bad news reached Rabaul. The weather had suddenly worsened over the Solomon Sea. Dense, low hanging rain clouds had now moved over Bougainville waters, unleashing intermittent rain squalls and frequent thunderstorms. The foul weather that had kept 5th Air Force planes grounded in New Guinea, the

149

Woodlarks, and at Kiriwina, had now spread over the northern Solomons to close the air routes between Rabaul and Bougainville.

"Severe atmospheric conditions now deepening throughout the northern Solomons as well as the Bismarck Archipelago," the Rabaul weather station reported to the 8th Area Forces headquarters.

When Gen. Hitoshi Imamura got the report, he scowled. He had enjoyed his respite from 5th Air Force raids on Rabaul because of the same weather disturbances, but now his own interests had been jeopardized since he could not send out swarms of planes from Rabaul to finish off the "crippled" American fleet in Empress Augusta Bay and then destroy the American invasion site. Imamura had no word yet on the results of the air sorties by the Yokoyama Wing out of the Shortlands. However, his disappointment would have certainly worsened had he known the minimal damage of these air strikes and the heavy losses suffered by Capt. Benji Shimada.

Imamura called the weather station at Rabaul. "Are you certain that we cannot mount air strikes?"

"None, Honorable Imamura," the weather station chief answered. "In fact, the two navy reconnaisance aircraft (four engine Emily sea plans) that patrol over the Solomon Sea cannot return to Rabaul. The flying boats will go south to the Shortlands and land at Ballale."

"I see," Imamura said in disappointment. The

8th Area Forces commander then called Junichi Kusaka. "Admiral, we have received reports of very unstable weather conditions between Rabaul and Bougainville. I fear we must delay these air sorties scheduled to go off within the hour."

"That is unfortunate," Kusaka said.

"I will so inform Captain Furugori. I will ask him to remain on full alert to fly off as soon as the weather permits."

"I will instruct my own air commanders of this delay," Kusaka said, "and I too will ask them to remain on full alert to take off as soon as we have word of improved weather conditions."

General Imamura then called the weather station to issue new instructions. "You are to keep reconnaisance planes out continually and they are to report any weather improvements immediately. Our air units are on full alert and they will mount their sorties as soon as they can leave."

"Yes, Honorable Imamura," the chief at the weather station answered.

When the order came to scrub air missions, the Japanese airmen from the Rabaul air units expressed disappointment. Captain Shibata, Commander Genda, Captain Furugori, and other flyers had been anxious to attack both the American fleet and the American beachheads at Bougainville.

The cancelled air strikes would be a fortunate blessing. Within a few hours, the Japanese would need every fighter plane at Rabaul to defend their New Britain stronghold against a massive air attack by 5th Air Force.

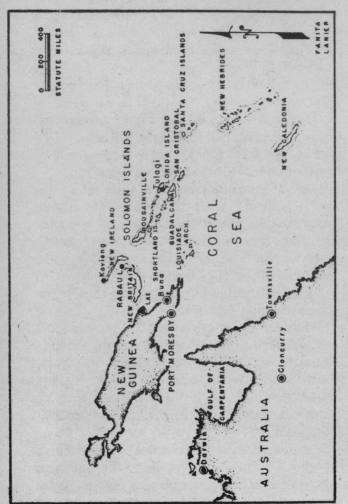

NEW GUINEA AND THE SOLOMONS

Admiral William Halsey, CinC of COMSOPAC directed the U.S. Operation Cartwheel.

General Nathan Twining, commanded COMAIRSOL, the mixed bag of air units operating out of the Solomons.

General Ennis Whitehead commanded ADVON, U.S. 5th Air Force out of New Guinea.

Admiral Stanton "Tip" Merrill commanded the TF 39 U.S. cruiser fleet that engaged the Japanese in the night time surface ship battle off Empress Augusta Bay.

Colonel Dick Mangrum commanded the marine air unit, MAG 24 out of Guadalcanal.

(L) Admiral Len Reifsnider and (R) General Al Turnage conducted the Bougainville invasion.

Major Bob Westbrook of the U.S. Army Air Force's 18th Fighter Group led the fighter planes in protecting U.S. carrier strike on Rabaul.

Capt. Tom Lamphier of the 18th Fighter Group downed 3 enemy planes during the campaign.

Major Greg Pappy Boyington, squatting left, with members of his outcast Black Sheep Squadron. The Black Sheep performed brilliantly during the Bougainville campaign.

Captain Murray Shubin of the 347th Fighter Group led army squadron that macerated Japanese bomber unit trying to hit the U.S. marine invaders at Bougainville.

Colonel John Henebry of the 3rd Bomb Group led his Grim Reapers on a devasting air attack against Rabaul on November 2, 1943. The Reapers sunk 7 ships; damaged 6.

Major Ray Wilkins of 3rd Group won the CMH for efforts on the November 2 raid.

Lt. Col. Charles MacDonald of the Satan's Angels 47th Fighter Group did good job of protecting bombers during the November 2 attack on Rabaul.

Cmdr. Henry Caldwell of carrier USS *Saratoga*, led naval air strikes on Rabaul on November 5. The strikes were first by carrier planes against the Japanese stronghold.

Major Tom Lynch led the fighter sweeps into Rabaul on November 2.

Lt. Cmdr. Robert Farrington, also of USS *Saratoga*, damaged 2 ships on November 5 raid.

Lt. Cmdr. Harold Funk of carrier USS *Princeton,* led carrier's fighter bombers against ships in Blanche Bay on the November 5, 1943, raid on Rabaul.

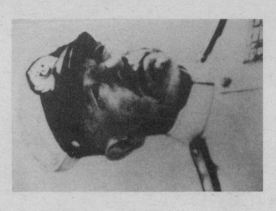

General Hitoshi Imamura, CinC of Japan's 8th Area Forces, devised the I-110 Operation designed to destroy U.S. air bases with air and surface ship strikes.

Admiral Mineichi Koga, CinC of Japanese Combined Fleet, promised Imamura full naval support for the I-110 operation.

Admiral Takeo Kurita had planned to destroy U.S. invasion site on Bougainville with his heavy cruiser fleet.

Admiral Junichi Kusaka promised full air support with units of his 11th Air Fleet.

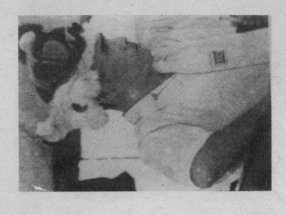

Cmdr. Minoru Genda of the 26th Kokutai Wing brought his unit to Rabaul from Truk to help stop the American invasion at Bougainville.

Captain Goro Furugori (r) with one of his airmen of the 22nd Sentai Air Division.

Admiral Sentaro Omori commanded the Torokina Interception Fleet. He performed so badly in Battle of Empress Augusta Bay that he was sent home in disgrace.

Admiral Matsuji Ijuin of Desron 27 lost his flag cruiser *Sendai* in the sea battle and was rescued by submarine.

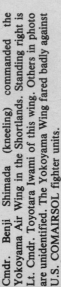

Lt. Takeo Tanimizu of the carrier 26th Kokutai Wing did well against American air units, but his efforts were not enough.

Cmdr. Benji Shimada (kneeling) commanded the Yokoyama Air Wing in the Shortlands. Standing right is Lt. Cmdr. Toyotara Iwami of this wing. Others in photo are unidentified. The Yokoyama Wing fared badly against U.S. COMAIRSOL fighter units.

Lt. Hiroshi Nishizawa, The Devil, downed a half dozen American planes during the U.S. air strikes on Rabaul.

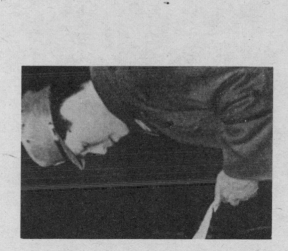

Captain Tokeo Shibata commanded the Japanese 4th Kokutai Wing at Rabaul. His fighter pilot, however, could not stop American air attacks against Rabaul.

Lt. Tetsuzo Iwamoto, also of the 4th Wing, was Japan's biggest air ace of WW II, with a total of 212 kills. He died in 1958 of septicemia.

Wrecked Japanese planes at airfield at Buin, Bougainville. U.S.
COMAIRSOL aircraft destroyed Japanese airfields before
Bougainville invasion.

U.S. marines from 3rd Marine Division land on Bougainville on
November 1, 1943.

American destroyers fire at Japanese ships during the night surface ship battle.

Cruiser USS *Montpelier* fires at Japanese ships during Battle of Augusta Bay night action of Nov. 2, 1943.

Booming naval guns light up the sea during Battle of Empress Augusta Bay.

American gunners down a Japanese scout plane during the night action.

B-25 medium bomber from the 3rd Bomb Group wings its way towards Rabaul for the heavy November 2, 1943, raid.

Phosphorous bombs from the U.S. 345th Bomb Group fall on Japanese planes at the Vunakanau Airfield on Rabaul. The group destroyed hordes of planes on the ground.

A B-25 skims over Simpson Harbor after skip bomb hits on Japanese ship.

B-25 of the 3rd Bomb Group skip bombs a freighter in Simpson Harbor. In background, Rabaul shoreline lies in flames from other B-25 attacks.

Direct bomb hit on a Japanese freighter by a U.S. 38th Bomb Group Mitchell during the November 2, 1943 air attack.

Rabaul shore line burns furiously after U.S. 5th Air Force attack.

Debacle lingers at Rabaul after air attack, with sunken freighter in foreground.

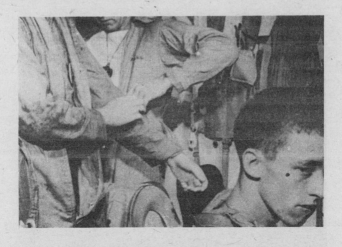

U.S. carrier pilots from carrier *Saratoga* prepare glumly for attack on Rabaul. The carrier airmen dreaded the idea of attacking the Japanese stronghold.

U.S. Navy fighter planes leave deck of USS *Princeton* for the November 5, 1943, raid.

Japanese ships in Rabaul harbors try desperately to escape in open waters as U.S. carrier planes roar into Rabaul on November 5 air attack.

Direct torpedo hit by U.S. Avengers on a destroyer during the
November 5 raid.

A 500 pound bomb from a U.S. Dauntless dive bomber scores a
direct hit on Japanese ship in Simpson Harbor on November 5.

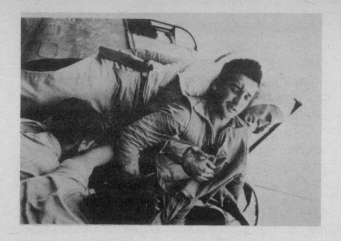

Gunner AOM Kenneth Bratton is helped from Cmdr. Caldwell's damaged Dauntless after the November 5 raid. Caldwell's plane got jumped by eight Zeros but he and crew shot down three of the attackers and damaged two more.

American supplies burn furiously after Yokoyama Wing raid on invasion site on Bougainville. This Japanese air attack was only bright spot in the Operation Cartwheel battle.

# Chapter Nine

For three days the bomber crews of the 3rd, 38th, and 345th Bomb Groups, 5th Air Force, had sat idly in Dobodura, New Guinea, because of poor weather over the Bismarck Archipelago. The combat flyers had felt a mixture of relief and apprehension. None of these Americans were anxious to hit Rabaul again, for they remembered vividly the swarms of interceptors and heavy ack ack fire during the mid to late October raids when they came into the Rabaul Bowl. Still, with the landings at Bougainville, the recent sea fight in Empress Augusta Bay, and the Japanese attempts to hit the U.S. invaders, these 5th Air Force airmen recognized the necessity of knocking out the Japanese fortress on New Britain.

The morning of November 2 had dawned as dreary as had the previous three mornings. The rain laden, unsettled weather front still lingered over the Bismarck Archipelago and had even spread over the Solomons. Dark clouds still hung low in the sky and the Dobodura airmen expected another day of inactivity. Recon reports at 0930 hours from PBY planes over northern New Britain sent a report to 5th Air Force headquarters at the rickety Port Moresby Hotel.

"Weather clearing over Rabaul and expected to remain clear throughout the day. Clearing conditions will spread south and east of Rabaul by nightfall. Latest observation over Gazelle Peninsula shows Rabaul harbors jammed with ships."

An aide quickly brought the report to General Whitehead, the ADVON commander of 5th Air Force. When he read the report, the general licked his lips and walked to the window of his office where he peered at the gray, low hanging overcast. If the weather front was clearing over Rabaul, maybe they could still hit the target today. And, as the recon planes reported, this same clearing front would probably cleanse the rest of the Bismarck Archipelago by nightfall. If planes left New Guinea by late morning, they would return from their strikes at late afternoon. By then, favorable weather would prevail and they could land at the New Guinea bases in relative safety. Whitehead turned to an aide.

"Okay, notify all group commanders at Dobo, the Woodlarks, and Kiriwina—the mission to Rabaul is on. They've already been briefed on FO two-six-three, so each group knows its part of this mission. Time of take off for all units will be eleven hundred hours," he gestured. "That should put them over Rabaul at about thirteen hundred hours. All units will follow the same arrangements. The fighters will come in first to sweep the harbor. Then, the Three-forty-fifth Group will hit the ground batteries before the Third and the Thirty-eighth come in to hit shipping in the harbor."

"Yes sir," the aide said.

Within moments, word had reached the 3rd, 38th, and 345th Bomb Groups at Dobodura on New Guinea's north coast. Word also reached the 8th, 35th, and 49th Fighter Groups on the Woodlarks and the 475th Fighter Group at Kiriwina Island. All total, 108 B-25 medium bombers and 102 P-38 fighters would make the sortie to Rabaul.

Less than ten minutes after the all go order from Port Moresby's 5th Air Force headquarters, an aide to Col. John Henebry posted an order on the bulletin boards of the 3rd Bomb Group's squadrons: the 13th, 8th, and 90th. "Briefing at once for FO two-six-three." Then, 3rd Group aides sent ground crews to revetment areas to ready the group's B-25s that would carry 500 pound bombs, phosphorous incendiary bombs, and fragmentation bomb clusters, along with loaded machine gun belts in the ten front firing guns of the Mitchells.

By 0955 hours, airmen had seated themselves in the 3rd Group operations tent, where Colonel Henebry mounted his dais and pulled down a wall map of Rabaul.

"Okay," the colonel began, "take off time is

at eleven hundred hours. Our mission is still the shipping in Simpson Harbor. Recon aircraft reports this morning indicate that at least one hundred ships of all types are anchored in Simpson Harbor and Blanche Bay. The ships include freighters, transports, destroyers, and maybe some cruisers. There isn't much doubt that the Japanese are massing a convoy for a counter invasion at Empress Augusta Bay. If these ships get off, the marines at Bougainville could be in for a rough time." He paused and then placed a finger on the map. "We hit the targets in Simpson Harbor as I said, and the Thirty-eighth Group hits the ships in Blanche Bay."

"What about planes at Rabaul?" Maj. Ray Wilkins asked.

"That's another thing we're worried about," Henebry said. "They may have as many as three hundred planes in Rabaul right now, with at least half of them fighters. Besides using those ships in the harbors to send reinforcements, they could mount huge formations of aircraft to pound the marine invasion sites. Some of the fighter units and our heavies, who come after us, will hit those planes and airfields at Rabaul."

"What about antiaircraft guns? Who hits those?"

"The Three-forty-fifth Group has the land battery assignment," Henebry said. "We follow them in to hit the shipping in Simpson Harbor and the Thirty-eighth Group follows us to hit the shipping in Blanche Bay. The Four-seventy-fifth fighter Group will provide escort."

"My God," Capt. Joe Walker of the 90th Squadron gasped. "We're only going to have one group of fighter planes as escorts?"

"We'll also have a squadron from the Forty-ninth Fighter Group," Henebry said, "and the two squadrons of fighter planes that sweep the harbor will also double as escorts. That would be the Thirty-ninth Squadron from the Thirty-fifth Group and the Eightieth Squadron from the Eighth Fighter Group."

"We got jumped real bad the last time, Colonel," somebody said. "And with all those planes reported at Rabaul, can we expect the same thing this time?"

"Probably," Henebry said. "But, our fighter pilots are damn good. They'll keep most of those interceptors away from us."

The man did not answer.

"Okay, one more time," Colonel Henebry continued. "I'll come in first with the Thirteenth Squadron to take the ships at the south end of Simpson Harbor. The Ninetieth Squadron will attack ships in the central part of the harbor, and the Eighth will hit the ships at the north end of the harbor near Lakunai. The Thirty-eighth will follow with their two squadrons to hit Blanche Bay." Henebry then looked at an aide. "The photo, sergeant."

"Yes sir."

The non-com flashed a light on a huge blow-up of a photograph before Henebry continued.

"This is Simpson Harbor, in case you don't remember. You can see from this latest photograph that at least a couple dozen transports and freighters, and maybe three or four destroyers, are anchored here. That'll be the Third Group's target. This photo was only taken yesterday so we can assume that most of these ships are still there and probably still anchored in the same position. Only a few warships sailed south to engage our naval fleet in the Solomons, so we're sure most of these ships in this photo are still there." He paused and scanned his 3rd Group airmen. "Any questions?"

"Will we rendezvous in the same place today as we did on the twenty-sixth?" Maj. Ray Wilkins asked.

"Yes," Henebry nodded, "Longitude one-five-one, latitude five. You navigators please make notes." He then turned to the map and tapped the tip of the Gazelle Peninsula. "We'll come straight in through St. George's Channel between Cape Gazelle and the Duke of York Island. We'll fly straight over Blanche Bay and then veer right into Simpson Harbor. After we make our runs, we'll continue on over Rabaul township and shoot out of the bowl north of Mount Tovanurdarie. We then head toward Watom Island before we turn west and head for the Bismarck Sea for the flight back to Dobo. Any questions?"

None.

"Okay, let's go."

The 3rd Group airmen left the briefing tent with somber faces and near silence. None of them relished the flight to Rabaul, this deadly dragon in the Southwest Pacific. "The best way to hit Rabaul," a grizzly veteran bomber pilot once said, "is to hit the place from outer space."

The pilot may have been correct. Nonetheless, the 3rd Group airmen, like airmen throughout the 5th Air Force, had come to New Guinea to do battle against the Japanese and they would not falter in that responsibility, regardless of their fears. They clambered into waiting jeeps and personnel carriers outside of the 3rd Group briefing tent for the ride to their waiting B-25s in the revetment areas of the Dobodura airdrome.

In other 5th Air Force groups assigned to FO 263, the same apprehensions prevailed among the bomber crews. Col. Larry Tanberg of the 38th Bomb Group briefed his crews on the ships in Blanche Bay, while Col. Clinton True of the 345th Bomb Group briefed his Mitchell crews on their mission to attack the Rabaul ground batteries and perhaps grounded planes. Then, the crews of these medium bombers also boarded jeeps and personnel carriers for the silent, somber ride to their waiting B-25s on the Dobobura airdrome.

On this dreary morning of November 2, fighter group commanders also briefed their airmen. Lt. Col. Charles McDonald briefed the pilots of his 475th Fighter Group at Kiriwina

Island. Maj. Tom Lynch of the 35th Fighter Group's 39th Squadron, Maj. Jay Robbins of the 8th Fighter Group's 8th Squadron, and Maj. John Landers of the 49th Fighter Group's 9th Squadron all briefed their pilots at the 5th Air Force fighter base on Woodlark Island. The pilots heard the same thing from the air commanders: the 9th Squadron of the 49th Fighter Group and the three squadrons of the 475th Fighter Group would act as escort. The 39th and 80th Fighter Squadrons would be the first into the Rabaul Bowl to make strafing sweeps on the ships in the harbors. Then the two squadrons would join the other 5th Air Force fighter units to protect the Mitchell bombers.

These American fighter pilots did not share the fears of the bomber crews, for the P-38 pilots had already proven that the Lightning fighter plane was a superior plane to the Zero in straight runs, climbs and dives. The P-38 pilot needed only to remember not to engage in aerobatics with the more maneuverable Zero.

By 1100 hours, the 108 B-25s and the 102 P-38s had left their bases at Dobodura, Woodlark, and Kiriwina to rendezvous at the 131, 5 degree position, just south of Gasmata on New Britain's south coast.

As soon as the 5th Air Force bombers and fighters were gone, Gen. Ennis Whitehead called the commanders of the 90th and 43rd Bomb Groups. These heavy B-24 units would leave Port Moresby at 1200 hours to arrive over

Rabaul at about 1500 hours. The Liberators would make runs over the harbors to complete the attack on shipping and runs over the airfields to knock the runways out of commission. The other two fighter squadrons of the 8th Group and squadrons from the 35th and 49th Fighter Groups would escort the B-24s on the afternoon mission.

Whitehead would clear his airfields of aircraft in the hope of taking out Rabaul today. Only the RAF air units would be around to intercept any attempted Japanese air strikes today on Allied bases.

In the cabin of his B-25, Col. John Henebry looked grimly ahead at the Mitchell formations of the 345th Bomb Group. He then looked downward at the expanse of Solomon Sea under him, and finally he looked at the dense clouds above him. He hoped the meteorologists were correct—the weather was clearing over Rabaul. Henebry would need to remain alert, for Zeros sometimes came after American air formations long before they crossed the New Britain coast.

Henebry droned on for about a half hour when the Mitchells of the 38th Bomb Group came in behind him. The colonel looked at his watch: 1140 hours. The 38th Group was right on time. The 108 medium bombers continued on and soon the coast of New Britain loomed ahead of them. Colonel True, who was leading the mission, called the other B-25 group commanders.

"As soon as we cross the coast, we'll drop to

treetop level for the flight across the island," the 345th Group commander said. "We'll fly within fifty miles of the Rabaul Range and then veer east to come in through St. George's Channel."

The B-25s then crossed the coast, dropped to almost treetop level and continued on. About 15 minutes later, the escorting P-38s arrived and soon jelled around the bombers. Henebry heard Colonel True call Lieutenant Colonel MacDonald of the 475th Group who was leading his own three fighter squadrons and the 9th Fighter Squadron of the 49th Group.

"This is Dobo leader," True said. "Please maintain escorts at the laterals and above us at a thousand feet."

"Will do," MacDonald answered. "We'll also keep scouts up ahead to keep an eye out for bandits. If they spot anything, Dobo leader, you'll be the first to know."

"Okay," Col. Clinton True answered.

Henebry then watched a half dozen P-38s zoom ahead in the van scout position where they soared, darted, banked, and arched about the sky like restless fledglings. And above the B-25 formations hung a high cover of Lightnings, while more P-38s jelled around the bombers in a symmetrical ring. Soon, the more than 200 U.S. planes droned northward over the New Britain jungles.

Over the desolate tropical wilderness, Henebry felt a shudder race through his tall muscular body. If he went down in this remote, inland area of New Britain he knew he would probably be lost forever, a victim of the elements or of starvation, no matter how thoroughly he had been trained in jungle survival.

The dense rain forests of New Britain, unfriendly and uncompromising, as were the jungles in most of the Bismarck Archipelago, looked ominous to the 3rd Group leader. Few men who had bailed out of a disabled aircraft or who had survived a crash landing in these dense forests had ever found their way out of the wilderness. Only those lucky few whom natives found and brought to their villages had lived to talk about their experiences. But in this sparsely populated, isolated terrain, the chances of discovery by natives was remote.

Henebry looked again at the P-38s far ahead that soared and darted about the sky. Then he stared at the B-25s about him that hung in the air like suspended centipedes. He looked at his watch again: 1210 hours. They had passed the halfway point to target. The 3rd Group colonel picked up his radio phone and called Capt. Lee Walker.

"This is Reaper leader to Reaper Two; Reaper Two."

"I read you," Captain Walker of the 90th Squadron answered.

"When we reach target area, keep your squadron at least three minutes behind us. We don't want to catch any of the explosive fire from our bomb drops."

"Okay, colonel," Walker said.

Then, when Colonel Henebry gave the same instructions to Maj. Ray Wilkins of the group's 8th Squadron, he got a call from Col. Clinton True. "This is Dobo leader to all units. We're thirty-five minutes from IP; thirty-five minutes. Each unit know its job, so please follow through. After the strikes we rendezvous at latitude four-point-six degrees by longitude one-thirty-two-point-four degrees over the Bismarck Sea at thirteen-forty hours. Anybody not at rendezvous point will be left behind. Please note again: rendezvous point at four-point-six degrees by one-thirty-two-point-four degrees at thirteen-forty hours." True paused. "Okay, from here on we maintain radio silence. Good luck to all of you."

Almost as though following a subconscious instinct, the fighter and bomber pilots on the FO 263 mission tightened their formations, as if seeking protection from each other against the powerful, seething, fiery dragon ahead—Rabaul Bowl.

The U.S. airmen had reason for fear on this 2nd day of November, 1943. Despite the series of air raids in October, and despite Japanese military commitments elsewhere in the Pacific, Rabaul remained strong in its number of men, ships, and planes. Col. John Henebry's apprehensions might have been even worse had he known of the increased air strength at the Japanese stronghold. Some of Japan's finest pilots were also now at Rabaul.

Among the pilots from the 3rd Mobile Carrier Fleet who had come to Rabaul to bolster the 11th Air Fleet were Cmdr. Minoru Genda and Lt. Takeo Tanimizu. Genda had been a fighter pilot for many years and had served in the Pacific since the attack on Pearl Harbor. The veteran had been among the few successful pilots during the Battle of Midway. Lt. Tanimizu had also been a veteran pilot, who already had more than 50 kills to his credit.

In the 4th Kokutai Wing itself was "The Devil," Lt. Hiroshi Nishizawa, a gaunt, sober faced fighter pilot who had caused consternation among American pilots in the Pacific. Also with the 4th Wing was Lt. Tetsuzo Iwamoto, Japan's highest scoring fighter ace.

At midday on November 2, Capt. Tokeo Shibata, commander of the 4th Wing, and Cmdr. Minoru Genda, commander of the 26th Wing, sat at the officers mess table of the 11th Air Fleet. Shibata turned to Genda while they waited for stewards to serve them the noon meal.

"I am grateful for the improving weather. Perhaps we can yet launch an air strike against the American invaders at Bougainville."

"My pilots are anxious to fight," Commander Genda said. "They have seen little action for many weeks because we have been on alert at Truk to meet the threat of an American invasion in the Marshalls. But since the Yankee invasion has not materialized in these islands, we are now quite sure that the Americans are not planning any assaults in the Central Pacific at this time."

"They cannot attempt further incursions through the Pacific as long as we maintain our strength at Rabaul and Truk," Captain Shibata said. "I was quite surprised by the Bougainville landings, only two hundred miles from here. I did not believe the Americans would attempt an invasion so close to Rabaul."

"Surely, they must have guessed that we would react with heavy air assaults."

"Unfortunately, we have not done well so far," Shibata said, "but with the aid of your pilots from the Third Carrier Fleet, we will have adequate fighter planes with many experienced pilots to escort our Mitsubishi and Aichi bombers against the invaders at Bougainville. No doubt you have seen the many transport and supply marus in the harbors. The Honorable Omori has destroyed the American fleet at Empress Augusta Bay and as soon as he returns to Rabaul with his Torokina Interception Fleet he will escort the marus to Bougainville."

"And are there enough troops at Rabaul to dislodge the Americans from Bougainville?" Genda asked.

"We have three combat divisions here who are ready to fight," Shibata said, "not counting numerous engineer, service, and construction battalions, both army and navy. Yes, we have plenty of troops. As soon as the cruiser fleet arrives, we will make a concerted attack against the

Americans at Bougainville with air, sea, and ground forces."

"I look forward to that," Commander Genda said.

For the next half hour, Captain Shibata, Commander Genda, and other officers at Rabaul's 11th Air Fleet officers mess enjoyed their noon meal, a repast that included fish cakes, rice, cooked vegetable shoots, tea, and rice cakes for dessert. The officers had finished their meal at about 1230 hours and then stiffened when sirens suddenly whined from a dozen different places around the Gazelle Peninsula. The siren blasts echoed from ships in the harbor, from Rabaul township, from the five Rabaul airfields, from the supply and maintenance areas, and from this 11th Air Fleet mess hall.

Most of the soldiers and sailors at Rabaul ran for shelters where they could watch the American aerial assault from relative safely. Ships in the harbors immediately weighed anchor to speed out of Simpson and Blanche into the expansive St. George's Channel where they had plenty of room to maneuver against aerial bombs. Others at Rabaul took offensive measures. Both army and navy fighter pilots hurried to their aircraft at the first sound of sirens, even before the voices of various executive officers in air unit orderly rooms blared over PA systems: "All fighter pilots will man their aircraft! All fighter pilots, man your aircraft to intercept enemy bombers!"

Orders also went out to antiaircraft gunners, who quickly donned helmets and hurried to the dozens of anti-aircraft guns in and around Rabaul.

Commander Genda himself hurried to the nearest radio phone to call his temporary headquarters for the 26th Wing at Vunakanau Drome. He spoke quickly to his executive officer. "How many aircraft are we mounting?"

"Two squadrons, commander; forty-eight aircraft."

"You will inform Lieutenant Tanimizu that he will lead one squadron, while I will come at once to lead the second squadron."

"Yes, Honorable Genda," the executive officer said.

Other air leaders at other units had also called pilots to man aircraft. At Tobera Drome, Lt. Hiroshi Nishizawa hurried to his aircraft along with 39 more fighter pilots of the 4th Kokutai Wing. At Lakunai Field, Army Air Force Captain Goro Furugori quickly mustered 60 Tony fighter planes, two squadrons from his 22nd Sentai Air Division. These army aircraft would also fly out to meet the American air formations.

The air raid sirens continued wailing around the Gazelle Peninsula as screaming aircraft engines echoed from the fields at Vunakanau, Tobera, and Lakunai. As the U.S. 5th Air Force planes entered St. George's Channel, still 15 minutes from target, the Zeros and Tonys of the 26th Kokutai, 4th Kokutai, and 22nd Sentai began roaring down runways before rising high into the sky to meet the oncoming American planes.

Lieutenant Nishizawa of the 4th Wing took his Zero fighters high above the Rabaul Bowl, to 20,000 feet, where he waited for the American interlopers. To the east, the Zeros from the 26th Wing were already over St. George's Channel to meet the Americans, now less than ten minutes away. And finally, Captain Furugori himself led the 60 Tony fighter planes of his 22nd Sentai high over the volcanic hills surrounding Rabaul.

By 1300 hours, most of the thousands of men at Rabaul had sheltered themselves in foxholes, bunkers, and pillboxes to wait out the air raid. Meanwhile, ships in the harbor worked up steam to hurry out of the harbors into open water. And finally, the small harbor crafts, barges, tugs, and motor launches were scooting like water bugs to the beaches and coves at the edge of the bays to hide themselves under the overhanging trees until the air attack was over.

Now the Japanese waited for the 208 American planes.

Maj. Tom Lynch, who would come in first with his 39th Fighter Squadron, soon saw the volcanic hills in the distance, including the highest peak, that of Mother Volcano. Then Lynch heard the first echo of antiaircraft fire in the distance. As Lynch led his P-38s into the Bowl, the Lightnings of the 8th Group's 80th

Squadron, also assigned to harbor sweeps, followed on Lynch's heels. Lynch hoped that the efforts of the two American fighter squadrons would reduce to a minimum the expected ack ack fire from the ships in the harbor against the oncoming B-25s.

But even as the P-38s of the 39th and 80th Squadrons roared toward Blanche Bay, ships in the harbor sent up plenty of ack ack fire. And worst of all, almost 150 Japanese fighter planes now waited in the skies over Rabaul for the 5th Air Force P-38s and B-25s. Could the Mitchell gunners and the Lightning pilots successfuly contain such a horde of Japanese Zeros and Tonys?

In a few minutes the Americans would find out.

# Chapter Ten

Lt. Hitoshi Nishizawa and Lt. Tetsuzo Iwamoto of the 4th Kokutai Wing loitered high above the Rabaul Bowl. Nishizawa, a tall, lean pilot, with the perpetually sober face, rarely smiled, never engaged in social activities with fellow pilots, and usually wandered about the campsite areas alone. His gaunt face and frail, thin body gave the appearance of a man with some terminal illness rather than a crack fighter pilot. But once in the air, Nishizawa became a demon, a man who feared nothing, and a pilot who showed uncanny fighting ability. Fellow pilots called him "The Devil."

On one particular day during the Guadalcanal campaign, Nishizawa had fought alone against a dozen American pilots. Incredibly, he had downed six of the enemy planes before he escaped unscathed. By November of 1943, Nishizawa had scored more than 150 kills. He would raise this score today.

Lieutenant Tetsuzo, also of the 4th Wing, had already spent more than six years in combat and he had built an enviable record. By November of 1943, he had already downed 176 planes: 22 planes while fighting in China, another 60 while fighting off carrier *Zuikaku* in the Indian Ocean, and 88 more while operating out of Rabaul during the past year. Iwamoto's total kills would reach 212 before the war ended. He too would raise his kill total today.

Like Nishizawa, Iwamoto was also a loner, but a fine combat leader. He would not tolerate mental lapses in combat, but the pilots of his squadron almost worshipped him because of his courage and fairness. Captain Shibata, CO of the 4th Wing, considered Iwamoto the most reliable, trustworthy, honest, and dedicated pilot in his unit.

"If I had fifty men like Iwamoto," Shibata told an interpreter after the war, "we might have won every air battle in the Pacific."

Lt. Takeo Tanimizu, the fighter ace of the 26th Kokutai Wing, had enjoyed considerable success in the Pacific war. He had scored two kills during the Battle of the Coral Sea, along with 30 kills in the Indian Ocean battles, and several more during the Guadalcanal campaign. Tanimizu offered a sharp contrast to the air aces of the 4th Wing. The *Junyo* pilot was an outgoing airman who always smiled, enjoyed social relationships, and showed a confident optimism. No matter what the Americans threw against him, Tanimizu was always sure he could win. He too would add to his kill score today.

Tanimizu had scored all of his victories while

flying off carrier *Junyo*. He had been among the irritated pilots of the 3rd Carrier Fleet who had tired of waiting for more combat. So when Genda took the 26th Wing to Rabaul with the warning that they would probably see plenty of combat, Lieutenant Tanimizu had been elated. He now waited eagerly in the skies over Rabaul for American planes.

But if a wealth of Japanese aces hovered over the Gazelle Peninsula to meet the American interlopers, the 5th Air Force had brought some remarkable fighter pilots of its own to Rabaul on this November day. The P-38 team of Capt. Dick Bong and Maj. Tom Lynch had probably been the most dreaded combination in the Southwest Pacific. Lynch was a superlative leader who would finish his tour in the Pacific with 20 confirmed kills. The 39th Squadron leader from the 35th Fighter Group had an uncanny knack for anticipating the moves of opponents and Lynch usually got into an advantageous position to shoot down his aerial adversary.

Lynch was a friendly man, a dedicated pilot, and an airman who loved combat. He had scored his first kill in May of 1942 when the Japanese still controlled the skies in the Southwest Pacific. During the ensuing months, as the 5th Air Force gained air superiority, Lynch gained more confidence. The 39th Squadron major fully expected to meet opposition over Rabaul today, but he was sure he would get a couple of kills without harm to himself.

In the 8th Squadron was the highly successful Jay Robbins, a man who would finish his tour in the Pacific with 22 kills. Robbins, too, had scored his first kill during the early months of the Papuan campaign in New Guinea. On June 30th, 1942, against a swarm of Japanese planes, Robbins had downed three enemy aircraft from the highly touted Tianan Wing in Lae. The 80th Squadron major would rise to the rank of lieutenant general before retiring from the U.S. Air Force in 1962 to settle down in San Antonio, Texas.

Robbins, like Lynch, hoped to get his harbor strafing chores down quickly so he could tangle with Japanese interceptors.

And, of course, Lt. Col. Charles MacDonald, heading the P-38 escorts from the 475th Fighter Group, had already compiled a remarkable record in the Southwest Pacific. The Pennsylvania born air leader had won his wings in 1940 and in 1941 he had come to Wheeler Field, Hawaii, to join a pursuit squadron. He had been asleep in his barracks on that infamous December 7, 1941 when the din of screaming bombs and the chatter of machine guns abruptly awoke him. MacDonald had been among the few pilots to reach planes and take off. But by the time he got airborne, the enemy attack had ended and the Japanese planes were gone.

The attack on Pearl had left on the young pilot a deep hatred for the Japanese. MacDonald had then worked with determination to make himself a thoroughly professional fighter pilot. The effort had paid off, for by the time he assumed command of 432nd Squadron of the 475th Fighter Group, the Satan's Angels, he had scored 19 victories. He would finish combat with 27 kills, a score second only to Bong and McGuire among U.S. Army Air Force pilots in the Pacific.

Capt. Dan Roberts of the 475th's 433rd Squadron had scored his first kill during the Papuan campaign while a pilot in the 8th Fighter Group. On August 26, 1942, as part of a ten plane P-40 formation, his squadron ran into 10 Zeros over the Owen Stanley Mountains. The 8th Group pilots had knocked down eight of the enemy planes, with Roberts getting two of them with his inferior P-40—an amazing feat for a new pilot. He would get 12 more enemy planes, including one this afternoon, before he ended his tour in the Southwest Pacific.

Maj. John Landers of the 49th Fighter Group's 9th Squadron had also scored his first kill during the Papuan campaign. He had downed two Zeros on the day after Christmas, December 26, 1942, before he got shot up himself and bailed out of his aircraft. Fortunately, he landed on the Dobodura plain south of Buna, where Australian led natives found him and brought him to Allied headquarters. Landers later scored three more victories in the Southwest Pacific. He would get his 6th kill today before returning to the States. Landers would then command a fighter group in England where the aggressive U.S. pilot would score 15 more victories against the Luftwaffe.

Among the B-25 leaders, Col. John Henebry had been flying bombing missions for over a year as had Maj. Ray Wilkins of the 3rd Group's 8th Squadron. Lee Walker of the Group's 90th Squadron had come to Australia in February of 1942 with the original complement of 3rd Group personnel. He had been in combat for more than a year and a half and he had personally destroyed more than 50 grounded Japanese planes and sunk three enemy ships.

In the 345th Bomb Group, Col. Clinton True had been a bomber pilot with the old 19th Bomb Group that had been so badly macerated during the opening months of the Pacific war. He had returned to the U.S. a beaten and demoralized man. But in early 1943, he had returned to the Pacific with the new 345th Bomb Group, the Air Apaches. For the past few months the 345th Group had been pasting Japanese bases, much to True's delight. The Air Apaches commander hoped to knock out Rabaul today, the principal source of all his distress during those early months of the war.

Col. Larry Tanberg of the 38th Bomb Group had been in combat since the fall of 1942 when his group finally got its B-25s. His Sunsetters' had come into battle during the latter stages of the Papuan campaign and the 38th Group had played a major role in finishing off the enemy at Buna. Since the Papuan campaign, Tanberg's

38th Group bomber crews had taken a heavy toll against Japanese bases, enemy shipping, and Nippon airfields. He hoped to succeed today.

The stage was set for a vicious donnybrook over the Japanese stronghold on the Gazelle Peninsula of New Britain. The American bomber crews hoped to sink ships, knock out parked planes, and destroy the defenses at Rabaul, while the U.S. fighter pilots longed to raise their kill scores. Conversely, the Japanese fighter pilots hoped to raise their own scores while defending the Japanese base. The Americans expected resistance, but they would be shocked by the aggressiveness of the enemy pilots. In turn, Japanese pilots, even renowned airmen like Nishizawa, Iwamoto, or Tanimizu, would be surprised by the tenacity of the Americans.

The battle opened at 1315 hours when Maj. Tom Lynch led his 18 P-38s of the 39th Squadron over Blanche Bay, despite heavy anti-aircraft fire. The major and his pilots skimmed over the water and unleashed withering .50 caliber strafing fire at very low level. The harbor sweeps were designed to rattle, disorganize, and kill Japanese antiaircraft gunners aboard the ships so that the B-25s of the 3rd and 38th Bomb Groups could make their runs with minimum ack ack.

Lynch found in Blanche Bay eight transports, two freighters, and three destroyers. He and his wing man braved the intense flak to rake one of the destroyers with spitting streams of tracers. Other 39th Squadron pilots followed, in pairs, to spray the decks of other vessels with telling .50 caliber fire from the wing machine guns of their P-38s. If Lynch and his fellow pilots did not seriously damage the array of ships, the heavy fire killed, wounded, or scattered dozens of Japanese sailors, while the ships themselves tried to weigh anchor and plow out of the bay.

As soon as Lynch made his sweep over Blanche Bay, however, 20 Zeros dove from above to attack the P-38s. The 4th Wing fighter planes, led by Lt. Hiroshi Nishizawa, opened viciously on the American Lightnings. Nishizawa scored against one P-38 with chattering machine gun fire and thumping 20mm cannon fire. The U.S. Lightning burst into flames and smashed into the jungles beyond Rabaul township.

"Zeros! Zeros!" an American pilot cried into his radio.

Maj. Tom Lynch looked up, gasped at the diving Zeros, and then frantically called his pilots. "Increase speed and climb! Climb!"

Fortunately for the Americans, most of the Japanese pilots released machine gun fire and 20mm shells too soon and most of the fire did little damage. By the time Nishizawa's P-38 victim had crashed into the trees, the Americans had fully alerted themselves. So, before the 4th Wing pilots came close enough to hit the Americans with a second fusilade of tracers, the P-38s were zooming swiftly skyward and away from the Japanese planes. Some of the Zero pilots started after the P-38s, but Lieutenant Nishizawa severely scolded them over his radio.

"Idiots! You cannot overtake them! Reform into Vs and we will remain at this low altitude to meet the next formation of Yankee aircraft."

"Yes, Honorable Nishizawa," somebody answered The Devil.

The next swarm of American planes, the 18 P-38s of the 80th Squadron under Maj. Jay Robbins, soon skimmed over Simpson Harbor. The 80th Squadron pilots quickly attacked the ships here: six transports, four freighters, four destroyers, and one tender. Robbins concentrated on the destroyers that were sending out heavy antiaircraft fire.

"Get the tin cans, the goddamn tin cans!" the major yelled into his radio. "Their flak will pulverize those Mitchells coming in after us."

"Yes sir," one of Robbins' pilots answered.

But then, the major saw ahead and above him the swarms of Zeros, like a huge flock of angry hawks. He squeezed his face and then called his pilots once more. "Don't use up too much ammo. Looks like we'll be taking on a horde of bandits."

Despite the Zeros, the 18 planes of the 80th Squadron peppered the ships in Simpson Harbor with heavy .50 caliber fires that caused panic among the Japanese sailors. The intense fusillade again killed, wounded, and scattered Japanese gunners, and so alleviate as much of the ack ack oppositions the B-25s of the 3rd and

38th Groups might find in the harbors.

Even as Major Robbins and his pilots worked over the ships with their wing guns, Zero pilots jumped the Americans. Not only was Lt. Nishizawa waiting for this new squadron of Lightnings with his 20 Zeros, but now Lt. Tetsuzo Iwamoto with his 20 Zeros and Capt. Minoru Genda with 24 Zeros came into the fray. The swarms of Japanese planes pounced on the first two flights of P-38s like angry bees from a disturbed hive.

"Zeros! Dozens of them!" Robbins yelled to his fellow pilots over his radio. "Let's get the hell out of here and climb high! High!"

However, before the pilots of these American figher planes cleared Vulcan Crater to the west of Rabaul township, the Japanese raked the Americans with .30 caliber machine gun fire.

Commander Genda sent withering fire into the cockpit of one P-38, shattering the canopy and killing the pilot. The P-38 flopped over and plopped into Simpson Harbor—pilot dead and plane lost. A second 26th Wing pilot caught a P-38 in the right engine, setting the plane afire. The pilot tried desperately to maneuver his Lightning and escape further damage. But, with the engine gone, the aircraft could not clear the Vulcan Crater. The plane smashed into the mountainside before the fragments cascaded downward in a waterfall of flames. Four other P-38s of the 80th's lead flights also caught hits, but the pilots managed to clear Rabaul Bowl.

Now Lt. Takeo Tanimizu scored against the

80th Squadron. The *Junyo* pilot caught a P-38 with two 20mm cannon shells that struck the Lightning's twin tails and blew away the aft. The American plane splashed into the bay. Other 26th Wing pilots jumped on the 3rd and 4th Flights of the 80th Squadron to down still another Lightning. The aircraft fell like a huge boulder and smashed into the trees south of Rabaul township.

Three more planes from the tail flights of the 80th Squadron suffered damage. One Lightning got its fuselage riddled, but the skillful U.S. pilot cleared Vulcan Crater and escaped. Another P-38 got its left wing shot up, but this pilot deftly controlled the plane and zoomed upward and away. A third U.S. fighter plane caught a hit in one engine, but even on the remaining engine, the American pilot successfully roared the powerful P-38 out of the harbor to escape further damage from the Zeros.

By the time Maj. Jay Robbins had taken his 80th Squadron high and away, he had lost three planes and suffered damage to four more. Robbins called his pilots. "You guys with damage; get your planes to Kiriwina. Keep in constant contact with the Dumbos at Woodlark and stay on the emergency flight path back to base. If you have to ditch, the Dumbos will find you."

"Yes sir," one of the pilots answered Robbins.

Soon, the 80th Squadron commander joined

Maj. Tom Lynch who had only lost one of his 39th Squadron planes on the run over Blanche Bay.

Maj. Jay Robbins had issued wise orders to the pilots of damaged planes, for if the pilot crash landed or ditched, he would need to radio his position at once. If the plane went down on the established emergency flight path, a 4th Recon Squadron PBY from Woodlark Island could find the downed pilot with minimum difficulty. The Dumbos, those PBY rescue sea planes, had done a remarkable job in the Southwest Pacific, fishing out of the water more than two-thirds of the 5th Air Force airmen who had been forced to ditch in the sea. So, the four pilots of the 80th Squadron with damaged planes had at least a 75 percent chance of rescue if they followed instructions on their retirement from Rabaul.

Meanwhile, after macerating the 80th Squadron, the hordes of Zeros now dipped and arced about the low skies over the Gazelle Peninsula, waiting to hit the next formation of American planes. Capt. Goro Furugori, since he was the ranking officer aloft, took command of the nearly 150 Japanese fighter planes in the air over Rabaul. He had been loitering in the sky with the 60 Tony fighter planes of his 22nd Sentai, when he saw the B-25s now heading for the land areas south of Blanche Bay and Simpson Harbor. The air commander knew well enough that the Mitchell pilots intended to knock out AA batteries, perhaps some of the grounded Japanese bombers, and most likely the wharves and stacks of beachside supplies. He called the other air leaders over his radio phone.

"Enemy bombers now approaching Gazelle Peninsula, no doubt to attack the shoreline installations on Blanche Bay, Keravia Bay, Marupi Point, and perhaps the township itself. We must intercept."

Commander Genda was the first to answer. "Are there any escorts?"

"I believe they are above the Yankee bombers," Furugori said. "I will take my pilots to deal with the escort aircraft. I ask that the pilots of the Twenty-sixth and Fourth Wing intercept the enemy bombers before they cause serious damage. Commander Genda, your squadrons may attack the first wave of American aircraft and the Fourth Wing pilots may attack the second wave of enemy bombers."

"We will do so," Commander Genda answered.

"We understand, captain," The Devil Nishizawa answered Furugori.

So Col. Clinton True and the air crews of his 345th Bomb Group faced a serious challenge. Nonetheless, True came in low over St. George's Channel with his Mitchell bombers. He called his squadron leaders.

"I'll hit the Cape Gazelle batteries with A (498th) Squadron; B (499th) Squadron will hit Rapopo Drome, C (500th) Squadron will hit the

Keravia Bay and Vunakanau batteries, and D (501st) Squadron will hit the Matupi Point and Lakunai areas. Those Mitchells coming in after us will need as little ack ack resistance as possible if they're going to hurt those ships in the harbor."

"Yes sir," answered Maj. Ralph Wallace of the 501st Squadron.

Wallace was quite tense as were the crew members of *Betty's Dream*. The major had already suffered one trauma during the October 18 raid on Rabaul only two weeks ago. His aircraft had been among the mere six planes from his group that had reached target to make sweeps over Blanche Bay. The 501st Squadron leader had hit a freighter with a bomb that had literally torn the maru apart. But, as his Mitchell droned on, he got jumped by a dozen Zeros whose pilots had knocked off one of the B-25 engines. Miraculously, the B-25s gunners had held off further Zero attacks and Wallace had managed to sputter his plane to Kiriwina Island where he made an emergency landing.

Major Wallace feared the Japanese would jump him again and he had feared correctly. His 501st Squadron would be the last unit in to make the strikes on the Matupi and Lakunai batteries at the extreme end of the twin Rabaul harbors.

As Col. Clinton True roared in with the 498th Squadron of the 345th Group, he met intense antiaircraft fire. True himself luckily escaped hits and he and his two wingmen quickly silenced the AA guns on Cape Gazelle with spitting .50 caliber fire from nose guns and with dozens of parafrag demolition bombs that floated out of the bomb bays from tree top level. The frag bomb clusters squarely hit three gun pits, disintegrating both guns and crews.

"Scratch three guns," True's co-pilot grinned.

Then came the rest of the 498th Squadron to lace other batteries on Cape Gazelle with spitting strafing fire and descending parafrag bombs. The low level Mitchell assault wrecked a half dozen antiaircraft positions, along with three wharves and a half dozen harbor boats tied up on the cape.

But the 498th Squadron paid a price.

Lt. Takeo Tanimizu pounced on the Mitchells with his 20 Zeros. The carrier pilots sent withering .30 caliber fire and thumping 20mm cannon shells into the attacking American bombers. Tanimizu himself got one Mitchell, his second kill within a few minutes, when his 20mm cannon fire hit the fuselage of a B-25 and almost cut the bomber in half. The American aircraft, suddenly enveloped in fire and smoke, wobbled precariously for several hundred yards and then smashed into the ground south of Rapopo Drome before exploding. The crew perished.

More Zeros pounced on the 2nd Flight of the 498th Squadron, again slamming the Mitchells with strafing and cannon fire. The gunners aboard one B-25 got one of the Zeros with their own twin .50 caliber guns and the Japanese plane exploded before falling to earth in a ball of fire. But the Zeros pressed their attack tenaciously and soon tore apart a second 498th Squadron plane, killing the U.S. bomber crew before the plane crashed into the jungles south of the township.

Still the Zeros came on, spitting more .30 caliber fire and 20mm cannon shells into the American B-25 formations. One 20mm shell blasted the fuselage of a Mitchell, but the B-25 remained airborne and luckily cleared Rabaul Bowl without further damage. A second Mitchell caught two hits that knocked out one engine, but again, the sturdy B-25 continued on with one engine until the aircraft escaped the Japanese pursuers.

Ack ack fire greeted the next squadron of B-25s from the 345th Bomb Group. The 499th Squadron Mitchells raced in low towards Rapopo Drome. Two of the B-25s caught ack hits and .30 caliber strafing fire. But neither bomber went down and both strafed and bombed as did other planes of the 499th Squadron.

In fact, the attack by the second squadron from the Air Apaches group not only knocked out antiaircraft guns around Rapopo Drome but also destroyed some grounded planes. A half dozen Mitchells dropped a string of phosphorous and fragmentation parachute bomb clusters on the airfield and destroyed 14 of the Japanese Aichi (Val) bombers and damaged four more.

From a shelter in Rapopo Drome, Capt. Tokeo Shibata of the 4th Wing cursed in anger. He had forty Zeros topside under the well experienced Nishizawa and Iwamoto. The Japanese also had over 100 more fighters topside. How could they allow these B-25s to cause such destruction? But Shibata had underestimated the determination of the Mitchell crews and the destructive power of the B-25 payloads—eight .50 caliber guns in the nose and the bomb bays full of frag and phosphorous bombs that the B-25s dropped via small parachutes from tree top level with great accuracy.

More Air Apaches bombers now roared along the southern shore of the Rabaul harbors. The 500th Squadron hit the Keravia Bay-Vunakanau areas, despite the Zero fighters that jumped the squadron of bombers. Miraculously, the Japanese fighter pilots failed to down a single 500th Squadron Mitchell, although they damaged two of the bombers. In turn, the 500th Squadron left the Keravia Bay area in flames: wharves, supplies, and AA gunpits went up in thundering explosions from the heavy descent of parafrag and phosphorous bombs. The bomber pilots had also ignited several tons of supplies. By the time this third Air Apache squadron veered away from target, they had left behind a length of fire and smoke along the semi-circle of shoreline.

Lieutenant Nishizawa, Lieutenant Iwamoto, and 38 more pilots from the 4th Kokutai Wing waited for the last squadron of planes from the 345th Bomb Group, the 12 Mitchells under Maj. Ralph Wallace. The 501st Squadron aircraft had just reached Matupi Point when Nishizawa and Iwamoto swooped down on the Mitchells with their 40 odd Zero fighter planes.

"Holy Christ!" Lt. Harlon Peterson of the 501st's 2nd Flight cried, staring at the swarm of interceptors. "We don't have a prayer." He called his gunners. "Shoot! Shoot! You've got to hold them off." Peterson then searched the skies for American fighter planes, but saw none. "Where the hell are the goddamn escorts?"

Despite his horror, Peterson joined Major Wallace and the other B-25 crews of the 501st to successfully hit both Matupi Point and Lakunai Field with bombs and strafing fire. The B-25s knocked out four large antiaircraft gun positions and a row of Betty bombers of the 22nd Sentai that were parked on Lakunai Drome. The 501st destroyed or damaged ten of the Japanese bombers before the Air Apaches paid for their efforts.

As Maj. Ralph Wallace raced away from target, he saw the right engine of his medium bomber catch a 20mm cannon hit that severed the fuel line. The 501st Squadron leader veered his damaged plane away from target, however, and sputtered back to Kiriwina Island for an emergency landing.

Lt. Harlan Peterson of the same 501st Squadron was not so lucky. Zeros chopped up his plane with strafing fire and Peterson flew his damaged aircraft towards St. George's Channel to escape. But his B-25 caught two more 20mm cannon shells and more .30 caliber strafing fire. The plane crashed and exploded in the channel, killing Peterson and his crew.

Next, Capt. Lyle Anacker of the 501st's 3rd Flight had just laid his parafrags atop a pair of Betty bombers on Lakunai Field when his Mitchell got hit with a half dozen 20mm shells from a swarm of Zeros. A series of explosions wracked the U.S bomber, tearing the plane and crew to shreds before the aircraft smashed into Mount Tarvurvur northeast of the Lakunai Drome.

The rest of the 501st Squadron escaped the gauntlet of enemy fighter planes and cleared Vulcan Crater to escape Rabaul Bowl before heading out to sea. The 345th Bomb Group gunners had shot down four planes, two Zeros from the 26th Kokutai and two Zeros from the 4th Kokutai. The Air Apaches had knocked out two dozen antiaircraft positions and destroyed or damaged 26 planes on the ground, while also smashing harbor facilities.

Overall, the 5th Air Force had thus far suffered quite badly. The 39th Squadron had lost a P-38 and the 80th Squadron had lost three P-38s, with damage to four more Lightnings. Meanwhile, the 345th Bomb Group Air Apaches had lost four B-25s with damage to five other Mitchells. Lieutenant Peterson had certainly seemed justified in cursing the absence of American fighter plane escorts. The interceptors over Rabaul had thus far done quite well and they had seemingly pounced on American planes with impunity.

Now the Japanese fighter pilots waited for the B-25s of the 3rd Bomb Group Grim Reapers and the 38th Bomb Group Sunsetters, Mitchells slated to hit shipping in the harbors. However, while the Japanese had done well with Round I of this melee over Rabaul, Round II would be a different story.

# Chapter Eleven

The first goal of this 5th Air Force strike on Rabaul had been accomplished. The initial attacks by the 345th Bomb Group had paved the way for the 3rd and 38th Bomb Groups. The Air Apaches had silenced most of the antiaircraft guns as had been their mission, while they had also destroyed wharves, supply dumps, and planes on the ground.

By the time the 345th Group had completed its run over target areas, the American fighter units had organized themselves for their principal duty—protecting the B-25s as they attacked shipping in the harbor. Lt. Col. Charles MacDonald of the 475th Fighter Group called his pilots.

"The Third Group Reapers are coming in over St. George's Channel now and they'll need plenty of protection. We'll need to use all three squadrons to hold off Zeros. I'll take them high, Four-thirty-first and Four-thirty-second Squadron will take them low."

"We read you, Colonel," Capt. Marion Kirby answered.

MacDonald then called the squadron leaders of the 39th, 80th, and 9th Fighter Squadrons. "You guys did well on those harbor sweeps, but we've got a skyful of Japanese planes that are coming after the third and thirty-eighth Bomb Groups in the harbors. My squadrons will protect the Reapers over Simpson Harbor. Major," he said to Tom Lynch, "I'd like your Thirty-ninth Squadron, Major Robbins' Eightieth Squadron, and Major Landers' Ninth Squadron to protect the aircraft of the Thirty-eighth Group over Blanche Bay. Can you do it?"

"Yes sir, Colonel," Lynch answered.

"We're on our way," Maj. John Landers of the 9th Squadron said.

"We'll give the Thirty-eighth all the help we can," Maj. Jay Robbins of the 80th Squadron said.

The Japanese, in turn, had prepared their own plan to meet the B-25 bombers heading towards the Rabaul shipping. Captain Furugori radioed quick orders to the various unit commanders, beginning with Minoru Genda. "Commander, the Second Sentai will attack the first formation of bombers (3rd Group) now coming into Rabaul to attack our vessels. You will take the fighter aircraft of the Twenty-sixth Wing to attack the second formation of bombers (38th Group) that also comes toward the harbors."

"Yes, captain," Genda answered.

Furugori then called Hiroshi Nishizawa of the

4th Kokutai Wing. "Lieutenant," he said, "you will keep your squadron with my own Twenty-second Sentai against the first group of Yankee bombers coming into the harbor."

"Very well, captain," Nishizawa answered.

Furugori then called Tetsuzo Iwamoto. "Lieutenant, you will take your squadron from the Fourth Wing to join the fighter aircraft of the Twenty-sixth Wing in attacking the second group of Yankee bombers."

"I understand," Lieutenant Iwamoto said.

Moments later, Col. John Henebry successfully passed the North Daughter Volcano crater where he met only minimal antiaircraft fire thanks to the 345th Group airmen who had effectively disposed of many of the gun pits in and around Matupi Point and Lakunai Drome. Then the colonel led his three squadrons of B-25s from the 3rd Group into Simpson Harbor, the inner haven. By the time Henebry was skimming over the harbor at near sea level altitude, the six transports, four freighters, four destroyers, and one tender were frantically weighing anchor to sail into the open waters of St. George's Channel. The ships offered little antiaircraft fire resistance since the American pilots of the 39th and 80th Fighter Squadrons had done an effective job in silencing many of the ships' gunners.

"Okay, pick your targets," Henebry cried into his radio, "but attack in pairs and keep your eyes peeled for bandits. I'll hit the transports with the Thirteenth Squadron.

Ninetieth Squadron will hit the freighters and tenders, and Eighth Squadron will hit the destroyers."

"I read you, colonel," Maj. Ray Wilkins answered Henebry.

"Let's get on them," Capt. Lee Walker said.

Henebry then roared over Simpson Harbor with his wingman at his side. The two pilots unleashed vicious .50 caliber strafing fire from the eight forward guns on each B-25. The tracers sprayed the deck of a transport with devastating fire. Japanese sailors aboard the ship scurried for cover, but dozens did not make it. Meanwhile, the ship's helmsman tried to veer the ship away. But, Henebry's two delayed fuse 1,000 pound skip bombs slammed into the ship at the water line. The colonel then arched safely away from target before two numbing explosions tore the transport apart. The ship quickly sank.

However, before Henebry got out of Simpson Harbor, a flight of Zeros led by Lieutenant Nishizawa jumped on the three lead B-25s of the 3rd Bomb Group. The Devil poured spitting .30 caliber fire into one B-25 and the fusillade of tracers tore off one engine and a wing. The Mitchell flipped over and plopped into the sea. Then, another Zero pilot unleashed a second stream of .30 caliber fire into Henebry's Mitchell. The hits killed one of the engines and riddled the fuselage and wing. However, the Grim Reaper commander worked his damaged bomber away from target on one engine.

"We can't make it, sir," Henebry's co-pilot cried.

"We'll make it," the 3rd Group colonel answered grimly.

Henebry did make it. Between his own extraordinary airmanship and the tough hide of the Mitchell, the Grim Reaper colonel skimmed and yawed away from the battle area until he got free of Rabaul Bowl. However, he would need to ditch in the Solomon Sea. But he brought his plane down only a dozen miles from the emergency landing strip at Kiriwina Island. Within an hour, a PBY Dumbo out of Woodlark Island would rescue Henebry and his crew from their rubber life rafts.

Meanwhile, other Grim Reaper B-25s also skimmed into Simpson Harbor to unleash more blistering .50 caliber strafing fire and thousand pound skip bombs. Two bombs hit a second transport and the explosion tore the ship apart, killing dozens of soldiers and sailors. Another pair of 3rd Group Mitchells from the 13th Squadron struck still another transport to set the ship afire before the next duet of Mitchells finished off the ship with more skip bombs. The final sextet of 13th Squadron bombers damaged more transports.

Now came Capt. Lee Walker and the B-25s of the Reapers' 90th Squadron. The Mitchells skimmed into the zigzagging freighters that tried to escape the attack. But the plodding marus could not elude the blistering low level assault by Walker and his bomber pilots.

Machine guns raked the decks of the Japanese ships, killing sailors and starting fires. The Mitchells then sent thousand pound skip bombs into the Freighters, erupting fires, destroying superstructures and opening holes in the hull.

Walker himself put two bombs into a freighter before the ship shuddered from concussioning blasts. The ship then literally fell apart from more internal explosions and sank rapidly. The vessel had apparently carried ammunition in its holds. More 90th Squadron planes damaged other freighters and blew the stern off the tender before the Mitchells roared away.

But the 90th Squadron did not get away clean. A half dozen Japanese Zeros broke through the American fighter screen and attacked the low flying Mitchells. A pair of Zeros caught a Grim Reaper just as the B-25 banked away from target. The Japanese pilots ripped the B-25 to pieces with thumping 20mm shellfire and withering .30 caliber machine gun fire. The American bomber simply flipped over and splashed into the bay in a ball of flame.

A second 90th Squadron Mitchell caught an array of .30 caliber strafing hits from a second trio of 4th Kokutai Zeros. The tracers shattered the B-25's cabin and killed both the pilot and co-pilot. Then a 20mm shell hit and exploded in the mangled cabin before the B-25 glided on and smashed into a grove of trees beyond Simpson Harbor. The crash killed the remainder of the B-25 crew.

And now, the Grim Reapers' last squadron came on to hit the harbor shipping. Palls of smoke from burning ships and the dense flak from antiaircraft guns now obscured almost everything in Simpson Harbor. Still, Maj. Ray Wilkins skimmed over the water through the smoke toward the four destroyers. Through intermittent clear spots, the 8th Squadron pilots saw the zigzagging destroyers. Wilkins came in first, strafing a destroyer and chasing its gunners to cover. Then the 8th Squadron major caught the destroyer squarely amidship with two skip bombs. The vessel exploded before going into a quick 30 degree list.

Wilkins' plane then caught an exploding anti-aircraft shell that wrecked his vertical stabilizer.

"We better get out of here, sir," the co-pilot cried.

"No," Wilkins answered. "There's too much ack ack coming from those other destroyers. We'll need to draw their attention so the other planes can score."

Despite the badly damaged plane, Wilkins continued on. He unleashed a new stream of strafing fire on a second destroyer, forcing the gunners to scurry for cover. But Wilkins drew more ack ack fire from the other destroyers than he expected. The three warships in Simpson Harbor almost chopped Wilkins' B-25 apart with antiaircraft. The major tried to arc his plane upwards to avoid more fire, but the Mitchell caught a five-inch shell hit that blew a gaping hole in the bottom of the aircraft. The same explosion knocked apart the fuselage, and the bomber then veered crazily over the harbor before crashing into the sea in a numbing explosion. All aboard were killed.

Maj. Ray Wilkins would win the Congressional Medal of Honor posthumously for his efforts that had enabled other planes of the 8th Squadron to strafe and bomb the other destroyers in Simpson Harbor against minimum ack ack fire. Before the other pilots of the 8th Squadron left the target area, they had put down a second destroyer and damaged the other two so badly that these Japanese warships would be useless for escort duty.

But the 8th Squadron suffered three more damaged Mitchells. Japanese fighter pilots knocked off part of the tail on one plane with strafing fire. They blew away the top turret and its gunner on another B-25, and they hit a third 8th Squadron Grim Reaper with 20mm cannon shells that left gaping holes in the fuselage. All of these damaged Mitchells limped successfully back to the emergency landing strip on Kiriwina Island.

Col. John Henebry and the Grim Reapers of the 3rd Bomb Group, though losing three planes and suffering damage to several others, had scored heavily in Simpson Harbor: three transports sunk and three damaged, two freighters down and one damaged, and two destroyers sunk with two more damaged. Only a single freighter in the harbor escaped unscathed. The Japanese fighter pilots had failed to stop the 3rd Group's devastating assault in Simpson Harbor.

Now came the two squadrons of the 38th Bomb Group Sunsetters. The 24 Mitchells, in eight V's, headed for the ships in Blanche Bay: eight transports, two freighters, and three destroyers. Lt. Col. Larry Tanberg peered at the palls of fire and smoke far ahead in Simpson Harbor, but he then stared at the swarms of planes far above him where American P-38s were tangling with Japanese Tonys and Zeros. The Sunsetter commander called his pilots.

"I'll take the 71st Squadron into the transports; 405th Squadron will hit the freighters and destroyers."

"We read you, colonel," Maj. Carl Lausman of the 405th Squadron answered.

As Tanberg came in low with the first trio of Mitchell bombers, the B-25s unleashed heavy .50 caliber fire from their nose and side guns that raked the decks of the Japanese marus. Then the trio of planes sent a half dozen skip bombs at the zigzagging transports. Two of the bombs found their mark. One hit opened a hole on the starboard side of the transport and the other bomb chippped away the aft deck of the ship. The maru listed quickly to the right and then sank in the bay. Another trio of planes blasted a second transport that burst into flames until the entire superstructure became enveloped in fire and smoke.

The first six B-25s of the 38th Group had

successfully put down one transport and badly damaged another without loss or damage to any of the half dozen planes.

The next trio of Sunsetter Mitchells caught a third transport with heavy .50 caliber fire and whistling thousand pound skip bombs. Heavy explosions chopped the maru apart, and the 4,000 ton ship settled quickly to the bottom of Blanche Bay. The last V of medium bombers from the 71st Squadron scored hits on other transports in the harbor, erupting fires and causing flooding that kept Japanese repair crews desperately busy.

In these quick first few minutes over Blanche Bay, the 38th Group's 71st Squadron had sent two ships to the bottom and damaged four others, leaving only two transports unscathed. And remarkably, the 12 Mitchells had all escaped with nothing more than minor damage from Zero interceptors and ack ack fire. In turn, the American B-25 gunners had knocked two of the pouncing Tonys out of the air.

Now the 38th's 405th Squadron skimmed across the water and into the three destroyers and two freighters that were zigzagging about Blanche Bay. Maj. Carl Lausman quickly sent a thousand pounder into the hull of a destroyer, blasting away the bow of the ship. Another destroyer also caught a thousand pounder, this one amidship, and the explosion knocked down one of the vessel's stacks. The third destroyer in Blanche Bay caught three bomb hits. One thousand pounder blew away the stern, the next opened the hull on the starboard, and the third struck a magazine that exploded with a deafening concussion. By the time the first sextet of 405th Squadron bombers left the bay, the destroyer was already halfway to the bottom. The ship sank within ten minutes.

Finally, the last sextet of 405th Squadron Mitchells laced the two freighters in Blanche Bay with strafing fire and skipping thousand pound bombs. A bomb hit sheared off the boom of one of the freighters, although the ship remained afloat. However, the second freighter took two hits in the hull that opened a huge gap before tons of uncontrolled salt water poured into the holds. The ship fell into a quick, heavy list before the vessel capsized, taking most of her crew to the bottom with her.

The 405th Squadron did not share the good fortune of the 71st Squadron. A pair of Zeros downed one Mitchell with heavy tracer fire that lopped off both B-25 engines. The U.S. bomber simply plopped into the bay and quickly sank, taking her crew with her. A second B-25 caught a 20mm shell hit in the cabin, exploded, killed the co-pilot, and wounded the pilot. Still the pilot managed to get the ship away. And, despite his shrapnel wounds, he would bring the plane safely back to base. A third Sunsetter Mitchell saw its fuselage opened by a pair of 20mm hits from an aggressive Tony pilot. Fires erupted inside the plane, but gunners quickly put out the flames and the pilot brought the plane back to Dobodura.

Although losing one Mitchell and suffering damage to others, the 38th Bomb Group had done extremely well. The Sunsetters had sunk or damaged every ship in Blanche Bay, sinking two transports, a freighter, and a destroyer.

While rattling explosions and fires prevailed in Simpson Harbor and Blanche Bay, a vicious dogfight had been going on high above Rabaul Bowl. American and Japanese fighter pilots mixed with each other, with the Americans keeping most of the Japanese pilots away from the 3rd and 38th Group bombers.

Before the Grim Reaper and Sunsetter bombers had made their runs over targets, Lt. Col. Charles MacDonald had taken the 16 P-38s of his 432nd Squadron, 475th Fighter Group, high in the sky, while Capt. Marion Kirby of the 431st Squadron and Maj. Dan Roberts of the group's 433rd Squadron had kept their 32 Lightning fighters at a low altitude. The Satan's Angels soon clashed with the Zeros under Lt. Hiroshi Nishizawa of the 4th Kokutai Wing. The thunder of thumping Japanese 20mm and American 37mm cannon shells, along with the rattle of .30 caliber and .50 caliber machine gun fire echoed above Simpson Harbor.

MacDonald and his Satan's Angels successfully held off most of the Japanese pilots. The 475th Group lieutenant colonel and his wingman waded into the first V of Zeros with heavy machine gun fire. The lieutenant colonel caught one Zero before the Japanese plane could veer away and he chopped the aircraft apart before the Zero plopped into the harbor. MacDonald's wingman also hit a Zero, knocking off its engine with 37mm cannon shells before the 4th Wing fighter plane dropped like a hideous bird into the sea.

"Stay in pairs! Stay in pairs!" MacDonald warned his pilots.

The other pilots from the 432nd Squadron also dove viciously into the Zeros from the 4th Wing. As usual, the American pilots followed the prescribed technique of avoiding loops and turns with the more maneuverable Zeros. Instead, the American airmen used the superior speed, climb, and dive of the Lightnings to catch Zero after Zero, knocking them out of the sky like hunters shooting down flocks of ducks. The Satan's Angels bagged 12 kills and damaged at least four other planes. Lieutenant Nishizawa's squadron had been totally macerated.

Lieutenant Nishizawa himself had personally downed one of the P-38s before striking the Mitchells of the 3rd Group that were sweeping over Simpson Harbor. The Devil had caught the Lightning as the American pilot veered away after shooting up a Zero. Two well aimed 20mm shells from Nishizawa's plane caught the P-38. The shells exploded and knocked off the left engine and wing before the P-38 cartwheeled into the bay. The Devil had his third kill of the afternoon.

But Nishizawa's kills were small consolation.

Very few of the 4th Wing interceptors in The Devil's squadron got through the P-38 fighter screen to strike the 3rd Bomb Group Mitchells.

The hordes of fighter planes from the 22nd Sentai that hung low had fared no better than the Japanese planes that had stayed high. The Tonys could not cope with the 21 P-38s of the 475th Group's 431st and 433rd Squadrons under Capt. Marion Kirby and Maj. Dan Roberts. These Satan's Angels at low level running interference for the Grim Reaper bombers, knifed into the waiting Tonys with deadly streams of machine gun fire from their six .50 caliber wing guns. The Lightning pilots also sent thumping 37mm cannon shells into the Tony formations. The heavy fire quickly knocked four of the Tonys out of the air and the other pilots of the 22nd Sentai simply broke ranks, zooming off in a dozen different directions.

"Maintain formation! Maintain formation!" Captain Furugori cried angrily into his radio. But few of his 22nd Sentai airmen listened. Most of them were inexperienced pilots and they panicked easily. The numbing fire from the American P-38s had simply stampeded them.

"Don't get cute," Maj. Dan Roberts warned his pilots after the Tonys scattered. "Take after them in pairs; in pairs. Protect your wingmen."

"Okay, major," one of the 433rd Squadron pilots answered.

The P-38 airmen then chased after the zooming Tony fighter pilots. Major Roberts himself flew under a low, thin cloud and caught a Tony just before the Japanese aircraft could duck into the overcast. Roberts' withering fire knocked the tail off the Japanese plane before the Tony tumbled nose first into the sea. Five more pilots from the major's squadron also downed enemy Tonys.

Meanwhile, Capt. Marion Kirby and the pilots of the 432nd Squadron had also chased the zooming, arcing Tony fighter planes. Kirby himself saw three Japanese planes working over a crippled Mitchell of the 3rd Bomb Group and he raced into the trio of enemy planes with withering machine gun fire and thumping 37mm cannon shells. He quickly downed one of the planes with machine gun fire and sent down a second with cannon fire. The third Tony maneuvered away from Kirby. However, before the Tony pilot could open range on the 431st Squadron commander, a fellow American pilot blew the Tony out of the sky.

Other 431st Squadron pilots also attacked Tonys that tried to reach the B-25s of the Grim Reapers. A half dozen P-38s simply loitered above the Mitchells, weaving back and forth and zooming off in pairs against any Tonys or Zeros that tried to hit the 3rd Group bombers. The Satan's Angels knocked down five more Tonys of the 22nd Sentai and two Zeros of the 4th Wing that had escaped MacDonald's squadron upstairs.

Since the 475th Fighter Group had administered serious losses to Fururogi's air units, the

3rd Bomb Group had met only minimal disruptions in the run over Simpson Harbor. The 475th itself had only lost two Lightnings to the Japanese interceptors.

To the east, American pilots of the 39th, 80th, and 9th Squadrons tangled with the more aggressive Zero carrier fighter pilots of the 26th Wing and with the other Zero squadron of the 4th Wing. Here, the stalwart pilots under Commander Genda and the willing pilots under Lieutenant Iwamoto fought back aggressively.

Lieutenant Iwamoto himself got two P-38s and Genda one, his second of the afternoon. Lieutenant Tanimizu damaged a Lightning. Other Japanese pilots, especially the carrier pilots, also scored against the Americans. The 39th Squadron lost two Lightnings, the 8th Squadron two, and the 9th Squadron three. Further, some of the Zeros broke through the American escort screens to hurt the 38th Group as the Sunsetters made their runs over Blanche Bay shipping.

However, the American pilots hardly came out on the short end. The Japanese paid heavily for their attempt to stop the Sunsetters from strafing and bombing the Japanese vessels. Maj. Tom Lynch and his 39th Squadron pilots downed seven Zeros. Maj. John Landers of the 9th Squadron got a Zero and damaged two more, while other 9th Squadron pilots downed an additional dozen Japanese planes. The U.S. pilots of the 80th Squadron scored highest, knocking down 14 enemy Zeros from the 4th and 26th Kokutai Wings. Maj. Jay Robbins of this squadron made the best score of the day among the American pilots—three Zeros downed and three more damaged.

Robbins caught one Zero with a burst of strafing fire that knocked off a wing before the enemy plane flipped over and fell into the bay. Then the 80th Squadron commander hit a second Zero with two 37mm cannon shells that ripped the fuselage apart. He got his third kill when he zoomed away from two attacking Zeros that had damaged his plane. Robbins suddenly found himself on the tail of a Japanese fighter plane and he opened with .50 caliber fire that set the plane afire. The Zero arced in flames and fell into the sea with a steaming hiss. Then as Robbins continued to ward off Zeros trying to reach the 38th Bomb Group bombers, the major damaged three more Zeros and chased off a half dozen other Japanese fighter planes.

Finally, at about 1330 hours, the attack on Rabaul ended. The township, airfields, gun batteries, wharves, and ships in the harbor were enveloped in fire and smoke. No doubt the 5th Air Force planes had caused serious destruction on this November 2 afternoon. Even as the U.S. air formations droned away from Rabaul Bowl and over the Bismarck Sea, the American airmen still saw and heard explosions inside Rabaul Bowl.

This November 2 strike on Rabaul had been the toughest thus far for the 5th Air Force. The

Americans had lost nine bombers and suffered damage to a dozen more. The 5th Air Force had also lost 13 fighter planes with damage to another dozen. The losses had been one of the highest tolls ever encountered in the Southwest Pacific on a single mission. Forty-five U.S. pilots and crew members were finally listed as killed or missing. Luckily, Dumbos from the 4th Recon Squadron plucked another 40 to 50 American airmen from the sea.

The 5th Air Force strike gave a welcome respite to the U.S. marine invaders at Bougainville. The Japanese had lost five transports sunk and seven transports damaged; three freighters sunk and two damaged, and all destroyers in both harbors either sunk or damaged. Further, the Americans had destroyed 26 Japanese planes on the ground and damaged some 50 more at the Rapopo and Lakunai Airdromes. B-25 gunners had shot down 13 planes, while the American fighter pilots had downed 42 planes. American airmen had also claimed damage to at least 50 more Japanese fighter planes. And finally, 8,000 tons of supplies had been destroyed at Keravia Bay and at Matupi Point.

By the late afternoon of November 2, 1943, one truth was evident. If Gen. Hitoshi Imamura intended to send reinforcements to Bougainville as soon as Admiral Omori returned to the Japanese stronghold with his Torokina Interception Force, the 8th Area Forces commander would not be able to do so from Rabaul.

# Chapter Twelve

When Adm. Sentaro Omori reached Rabaul's Blanche Bay late in the evening of November 2, palls of smoke from the afternoon air raid still hung over the Japanese stronghold.

Admiral Omori and his sailors had heard of the enemy air raid while sailing homeward from Bougainville waters. They did not yet realize the extent of destruction. Omori and his chief of staff, Capt. Usho Yamada, stood on the bridge of their damaged cruiser *Myoko* and gaped at the holocaust: the wrecked and burning wharves along the shoreline, the array of sunken ships, and the occasional sight of a sailor still floundering in Simpson Harbor or Blanche Bay.

About midnight, Omori heard sudden air raid sirens. Next, searchlights pierced the darkness as the drone of planes echoed over the dark sky of Rabaul Bowl. A squadron of New Zealand Beaufort light bombers had arrived over the Japanese stronghold. Suddenly, the thunder of antiaircraft fire and the flashes of exploding flak deafened Omori and his sailors before the

RNZAF light bombers sent whistling bombs into Rabaul. Erupting balls of fire came from the shoreline again as the New Zealand 18 Squadron unleashed 500 pound GP bombs. Soon more supply dumps went up in flames along the length of the Keravia Bay coastline.

When the nighttime air raid ended, launch boats came to Omori's cruiser to carry the fleet commander and his staff to shore. Cmdr. Yosuni Doi, the Southeastern Fleet harbor craft commander, met the Torokina Fleet officers.

"You must excuse our delay, Honorable Omori," Doi said, "but the most unpleasant enemy air assault this afternoon has kept our harbor boats busy in rescue operations. We lost nine vessels sunk and more than a half dozen ships quite badly damaged. Despite our heavy antiaircraft fire and interceptor planes, the enemy bombers showed extremely good accuracy, especially against our vessels in the harbor."

"I understand," Omori said.

"I was told to inform you, Admiral, that you and your desron commanders are to meet with General Imamura in the morning," Doi continued. "He has asked that you join him for breakfast at his bungalow at o-seven-thirty hours."

"We will be there," Omori said before he entered the launch boat that would take him to shore.

The Torokina Interceptor Fleet commander felt quite frustrated. First, he had failed to bombard the enemy beachheads at Empress Augusta Bay and now Rabaul had suffered a disaster from the American air attacks. The admiral pondered these misfortunes as a staff car picked him up on the shore and drove him to his quarters. His near exhaustion had dominated his distress and by 0100 hours, November 3, he was fast asleep in his bungalow.

Far to the south, in New Guinea, the air crews of the 3rd, 38th, and 345th Bomb Groups were still celebrating. Aerial gunners had joined other EMs in NCO clubs, while officers talked with each other in the officers' clubs. At the 3rd Bomb Group club, Col. John Henebry, Capt. Lee Walker, and other Grim Reaper pilots drank jungle juice cocktails (a mixture of ethyl alcohol and fruit juice), while they discussed this afternoon's raid. Although tired from the long, dangerous mission to Rabaul, they were too excited to sleep. Besides, they had no mission scheduled for tomorrow, so they could sack out as late as they wanted the next morning.

Maj. Scott Denniston, the group operations officer, sat with the two men. "You guys sure did well."

"What was the score?" Captain Walker asked.

"All kinds of damage," Denniston answered. "Recon photos late this afternoon definitely showed a half dozen ships sunk in Simpson Harbor and at least six more aflame. The Third

211

cleaned out that harbor."

"Our gunners knocked some of those Zeros out of the air, too," Lee Walker said. "I personally saw a couple of guys from my squadron get at least two of those Japanese interceptors."

"We don't know for sure how many planes your gunners shot down," Denniston said. "But the score on enemy ships is accurate."

Col. John Henebry grinned. "This was the best job yet on Rabaul."

Suddenly, two young lieutenants came up to the table, "Sorry to interrupt, Colonel, sir, but we were arguing about the results in Simpson Harbor today. I say we downed two destroyers; Joe here says one."

"We got a lot of ships," the second young officer said, "but only one of the destroyers."

"No, you got two," Major Denniston grinned. He then handed the lieutenants a photo. "A recon pilot took these photos just before dusk. See here," he pointed to a spot on the picture, "two destroyers down."

"I'll be damned," the second officer grinned.

"Wilkins got one of them himself," Henebry said.

"Yeh," Walker said. Then he squeezed his face. "Too bad about Ray."

"We saw what happened," one of the lieutenants suddenly sobered. "He went straight into that ack ack, while he led us right over target to make sure we'd reach those destroyers." The young officer shook his head.

"We couldn't have scored on those warships if it weren't for the major. I never saw a plane get shot up so badly and still keep on course."

"If Major Wilkins didn't keep going," the second young co-pilot said, "we'd have never found those destroyers because of the thick smoke and ack ack."

"Some of the other pilots told me that Wilkins drew enough ack ack to himelf to allow you guys to hit those ships with minimum damage to your aircraft," Colonel Henebry said.

"Here's to Ray," Capt. Lee Walker said, raising his glass of jungle juice.

"To Ray, and the others who didn't come back," Henebry said.

Then, the colonel, Walker, Denniston, and the two young lieutenants downed their glasses of jungle juice. Besides Maj. Ray Wilkins, three other officers and four enlisted men gunners of the 3rd Bomb Group had also lost their lives that day. Maj. Ray Wilkins would win the CMH, while the other lost airmen would win Silver Stars and DFCs posthumously. Gen. Ennis Whitehead would personally award DFCs to Col. John Henebry for his leadership with the 3rd Group and to Lee Walker for the captain's efforts. In fact, more than half of the Grim Reaper airmen would win awards, medals ranging from the CMH to Air Medals. Such had been the success of their efforts on the November 2 mission to Rabaul.

Near the #2 bomber strip at Dobodura, the officers of the 345th Bomb Group began breaking up their celebrations by midnight. Col. Clinton True had congratulated his men on a job well done. The Air Apaches had gone in first to catch the brunt of the Japanese ack ack fire and intercepting Zeros. Still they had destroyed a large number of gun pits and grounded planes, while wrecking wharves and burning supplies. The 345th had lost two B-25s and eight men, but the Apaches had taken a heavy toll against the Japanese. Colonel True would win a DFC for his leadership today, while other pilots and gunners of his group would also win medals for their courage, daring, and success in the face of heavy enemy opposition.

Across the #2 bomber strip at Dobodura, the men of the 38th Bomb Group had also celebrated. Col. Larry Tanberg and Maj. Carl Lausman would each win a DFC while a dozen more airmen would be awarded Silver Stars, DFCs or Air Medals for their efforts in Blanche Bay. But the Sunsetters mourned the loss of four men.

While the B-25 bomber groups of the 5th Air Force had lost men and planes, the 5th's fighter units had suffered the worst casualties. Ironically, the fighter pilots had been much less fearful of this mission to Rabaul than the bomber crews. The worst losses had befallen the 80th Squadron: five P-38s down and five Lightnings damaged. The 80th Squadron pilots had themselves downed about 20 Japanese planes. So, despite the losses, Maj. Jay Robbins and his pilots had reason to celebrate.

Meanwhile, the fighter pilots of the 39th Squadron under Maj. Tom Lynch and the pilots of the 475th Fighter Group under Lt. Col. Charles MacDonald also had reason to indulge themselves in jungle juice for their fine efforts on the November 2 raid. These two fighter units had also downed more than a dozen planes each, while the 475th Group Satan's Angels had effectively cleared the way for the bomber groups that came after them.

When the sun rose over the Gazelle Peninsula on the morning of November 3, 1943, the daylight exposed clearly the wreckage inside Rabaul Bowl: sunk and damaged ships in the harbors, smashed and burned planes on the runways, collapsed wharves, smoldering ruins, burned supply dumps on the shoreline, and scores of downed Tony and Zero fighter planes in the brakes, clearings, and waters of the Gazelle Peninsula.

At 0730 hours, Adm. Sentaro Omori studied the destruction in Rabaul as he rode towards General Imamura's bungalow where other officers had already gone.

Imamura himself stood on the porch of his headquarters house to meet an array of visitors on this clear morning. The 8th Area Forces commander first greeted Adm. Tomushige Samejima who arrived with his aides from the Southeastern Fleet. Imamura next met Capt. Goro Furugori of the 22nd Sentai and Adm. Junich Kusaka who arrived with Capt. Tokeo

Shibata and Cmdr. Minoru Genda. Finally, the general met Admiral Omori and his desron commanders, Adm. Matsuji Ijuin and Morokazu Osugi, along with Omori's chief of staff, Capt. Usho Yamada.

"We will enjoy breakfast," Imamura said soberly, "and we will then retire to the conference room."

The Japanese brass in the general's bungalow ate a good meal of fish cakes, rice cereal, tea and juice. Despite the heavy raids on Rabaul during the past month, the New Britain stronghold got plenty of food and other supplies for the thousands of sailors, soldiers, and airmen who were stationed here. The Japanese officers ate their breakfast in near silence at the meal table, where Omori thought the others were throwing disparaging glances at him, including Samejima. Omori suspected that the Southeastern Fleet commander was upset with him.

When the officers retired to the conference room, Imamura took up first the subject of the Torokina Interception Force and the U.S. 5th Air Force raid on Rabaul yesterday. He rose from the table where Admiral Samejima had been sitting at his side.

"Gentlemen," the general began, "we have suffered a double tragedy in the past two days. First, our interception fleet failed in its mission and then our fighter pilots at Rabaul failed to stop the Yankee bombers from causing considerable damage to the Southeastern Fleet."

He now looked specifically at Omori. "I must tell you in all frankness, Admiral, that I cannot understand why you sailed back to Rabaul after you had caused so much damage to the enemy fleet. Surely, you could have sailed into Empress Augusta Bay to destroy both the American transports and their invasion forces on the beaches."

"As I explained," Omori said, "we had learned that a large enemy air formation was on the way to Bougainville."

"That was a poor excuse," Imamura said, "since it was my understanding that Admiral Kusaka had planned to send out fighter units from the Yokoyama Wing to protect you."

Omori did not answer.

"And now," Imamura gestured, "we must consider the unfortunate consequences of the enemy air attacks yesterday. Because of the extensive damage and losses to the transport and freighter marus, we cannot send reinforcements to Bougainville as planned. We will need to await the arrival of new marus from Truk." The 8th Area Forces commander now glared at the 11th Air Fleet commander. "I must tell you, Admiral, that both Admiral Samejima and myself are quite disappointed in the performance of your airmen against the Americans yesterday."

Adm. Junichi Kusaka pursed his lips before he answered. "The Americans were unusually aggressive yesterday. They showed a determination that we have seldom seen in them before."

"Still," Admiral Samejima suddenly spoke, "you had many more fighter aircraft in the air than did the Americans, three fighter planes to each two American fighter planes."

"Surely," Imamura said, "you should have dealt with them, especially since you had the airmen of the Third Mobile Carrier Fleet, whom I was told were among the best in the Imperial Japanese Navy."

"I must remind the Honorable Imamura," Kusaka said, "that the Twenty-second Sentai Air Division is considered one of the best units in the Japanese Imperial Army. Yet they too failed to stop the Yankee fighter pilots."

The comments by the 11th Air Fleet commander silenced Imamura, at least temporarily.

Meanwhile, Captain Furugori, Captain Shibata, and Commander Genda squirmed uneasily. They knew that the criticism of the Japanese airmen was a direct reflection on their own leadership. None of the three air commanders attempted to defend himself as had Admiral Omori. The air leaders simply sat at the conference table in silence.

Samejima now looked at Shibata. "Captain, what were the losses of the Fourth Wing?"

"I regret to say, Honorable Samejima, that we suffered the loss of twenty-three Aichi dive bombers destroyed or damaged on the ground. We lost an additional eighteen Mitsubishi fighter planes in the air."

"And what of the Twenty-sixth Wing?"

Samejima now looked at Genda.

"We lost twelve aircraft destroyed during the aerial engagements with the Americans," Genda answered, "but our own pilots claimed twenty Yankee planes shot down."

Samejima ignored Genda's weak attempt to justify his wing's poor effort yesterday. He now looked at Captain Furugori. "And what of the Twenty-second Sentai?"

"We lost twelve Mitsubishi G-four-M bombers on the ground and another ten fighter planes in the air."

"Then what is the complement of available aircraft at this time?" Imamura asked.

"The Fourth Wing still has some forty Aichi dive bombers and seventy-five Mitsubishi fighters available," Captain Shibata said.

"The Twenty-sixth Wing can mount some sixty fighter aircraft," Commander Genda said.

"We can still send out at least a squadron of G-four-M heavy bombers and at least two squadrons of Kawasaki fighter planes," Furugori said.

"One hundred fifty fighter aircraft and seventy bombers," Imamura nodded. "That is a consolation after the near disaster yesterday."

"I can also tell you, General," Kusaka said, "that our crews have been working diligently to mend our runways and to repair damaged aircraft where they can. Our fighters and bombers will be able to again operate from these fields by noon today. If it is your desire that we launch an air strike against the Americans at

Bougainville, we can do so this afternoon."

"We will launch no air strikes yet," Imamura said. He shuffled through some papers on his desk and then pulled out a sheet. "Gentlemen, Admiral Samejima and myself have received news from General Umezu and Admiral Koga at Truk. They gave us encouraging words. First, new maru transport and supply ships will arrive in Rabaul within two days to carry reinforcements to Bougainville. We will also get two new squadrons of bombers, one for the Fourth Wing and one for the Twenty-second Sentai. We are also getting another squadron of fighter planes from the Third Mobile Carrier Fleet. But most important," Imamura gestured, "we have been informed that the Honorable Takeo Kurita will bring his Second Fleet immediately to Rabaul."

"The heavy cruiser fleet?" Kuska asked.

"Yes, this powerful support fleet that includes seven heavy cruisers, the light cruiser *Noshiro* and four destroyers," Admiral Samejima suddenly spoke. "As soon as this fleet arrives, the Torokina fleet will join Admiral Kurita for a massive surface ship attack on the enemy invaders at Bougainville. We expect the Second Fleet to arrive in Rabaul by the morning of November 5, and Admiral Kurita will personally brief commanders for this new sortie to Bougainville."

"What of the aircraft?" Admiral Kusaka asked.

"The three new squadrons of fighters and

bombers are expected to reach Rabaul sometime today. These aircraft will attack Bougainville in conjunction with Kurita's fleet. Such a striking force can utterly destroy the Americans at Empress Augusta Bay."

"The Torokina Interception Fleet will be ready to join the Honorable Kurita when he gets here," Admiral Omori said.

"I regret to say, Admiral, that you will not join this new effort," Samejima told Omori. "Admiral Kurita insists that his own flag officers command the cruiser and destroyer divisions. Admiral Koga, General Imamura, and myself agreed that Admiral Kurita should have the right to select his own commanders since he will be responsible for this new effort against the Americans. However, Admiral Kurita has requested that Admiral Ijuin join his fleet."

Omori did not answer; nor did anyone else at the conference table speak. Samejima's comments were obvious: he had told Omori and Captain Osugi as tactfully as he could that they had been relieved of command. Apparently the VIPs of the Japanese Combined Fleet were disappointed because Omori had withdrawn from battle with his Torokina Interception Force. Apparently, the Japanese naval brass had also been irked by Captain Osugi's tactics during this battle against the American TF 39 cruiser fleet.

In truth, Admiral Ijuin had also performed poorly. But Ijuin's reputation had won him a respite and he would retain a desron command. Further, his experience of losing his ship and almost his life before being plucked from the sea had apparently won him sympathy from the staff of the Japanese Combined Fleet.

Within a day, both Adm. Sentaro Omori and Capt Morikazu Osugi would be on the way back to Japan in disgrace.

"Gentlemen," General Imamura again addressed the officers at the table, "both Admiral Samejima and myself expect the air commanders to prepare their units for battle. We will make air strikes on our enemy in conjunction with the Second Fleet's surface ship bombardment, as I have said. Our bombers will strike from the sky, while Kurita strikes from the sea. We will surely destroy the American invaders at Bougainville once and for all."

"Admiral," Samejima looked at Ijuin, "you will prepare the destroyers and cruisers of the Torokina Fleet that has just returned to Rabaul. The ships and sailors must be ready for combat by the time of Admiral Kurita's arrival."

"Yes, Honorable Samejima," the Desron 27 commander said.

The instructions to Ijuin, while ignoring Omori, represented another slap at the deposed Torokina Interception Force commander.

"Are there any questions?" Imamura asked.

No one answered.

"Good," the 8th Area Forces commander nodded. "Please return to your units and prepare your men for battle."

Despite the debacle in the Empress Augusta Bay sea battle and despite the destruction at Rabaul by 5th Air Force yesterday, the Japanese again prepared for a military effort against the Americans at Bougainville.

On the morning of November 4, 1943, two U.S. PBY recon planes from COMAIRSOL were patrolling the waters northeast of Bougainville. At 0730 hours, they sighted an enemy fleet steaming swiftly southward. The American airmen aboard the PBYs were flabbergasted when they counted seven heavy cruisers in the force along with one light cruiser, several destroyers, and more than a half dozen transports.

The U.S. airmen had sighted Adm. Takeo Kurita's powerful 2nd Fleet that included seven heavy cruisers: flag *Maya*, along with *Takao*, *Atago*, *Suzuya*, *Mogami*, *Chikuma*, and *Chokai*. Also with the fleet were light cruiser *Noshiro* and destroyers *Fujinami*, *Umikaze*, *Urakaze*, and *Suzunami*. Also accompanying these warships were four troop laden transports and three tankers.

"Jesus Christ, look at that!" one of the PBY pilots told his co-pilot.

"Goddamn," the co-pilot answered, "there's enough eight-inch guns in that force to blow the Bougainville landing site right off the map."

The airmen quickly radioed the sightings to COMAIRSOL headquarters on Guadalcanal.

Moments later, General Twining read the report in horror. "We've got to stop them," he told an aide. "Launch air strikes at once with the heavies."

"Yes, sir," the aide answered.

By noon of November 4, a squadron of B-24s from the 307th Bomb Group arrived over the Japanese convoy. However, the deft Japanese helmsmen avoided most of the 1,000 pound bombs dropped by the American Liberators. The B-24s only damaged two tankers. An hour later, another squadron of heavy bombers from Guadalcanal attacked the 2nd Fleet, but only damaged two of the transports with near misses. The marus were taken in tow by a pair of the heavy Japanese cruisers, while sailors made repairs. The fleet then continued on towards Rabaul.

At mid afternoon, B-24 recon planes again sighted Kurita's fleet, 19 ships in all. The flotilla was now entering the western entrance of St. George's Channel. By shortly after dark, the armada would anchor in Simpson Harbor and Blanche Bay and by sometime tomorrow this powerful Japanese surface fleet would probably leave for Bougainville, taking with it a counter invasion force.

The Americans had sunk or disabled eight transports on the November 2 air raid. However, another half dozen marus of the Southeastern Fleet, including those slightly damaged, were still available for use. So the Japanese could sail eight to ten transports to Bougainville—enough to carry a division or more of combat troops.

By late afternoon of November 4, Adm. Bill Halsey of COMSOPAC had decided that 5th Air Force must help out again. He sent an urgent message to Gen. Ennis Whitehead at Port Moresby, New Guinea. Could the 5th mount another heavy air assault against Rabaul as they had done on November 2?

"Yes, admiral," the 5th Air Force ADVON commander answered Halsey.

Whitehead then called the air commanders of his three B-25 groups and four P-38 groups. "Prepare for an oh-nine hundred air strike tomorrow, with take off time at oh-seven hundred." He also called his heavy bomb groups at Moresby, the 43rd and 90th. "B-twenty-four groups will make an early morning strike on Rabaul warships at oh-seven hundred hours. Take off time for the heavies will be at oh-four hundred."

However, by dark, Whitehead got a shocking report from his weather station at Dobodura: "A new low pressure front moving into the Bismarck Archipelago. Dense rain clouds, accompanied by severe thunderstorms, expected to cover the New Guinea and New Britain areas for the next twenty-four to fourty-eight hours. Recommend that all fifth Air Force air missions be cancelled."

Whitehead anxiously called the weather station. "It's imperative that we attack Rabaul in the morning. Are you sure we can't go out?"

"No sir," the weather officer said. "You won't even get your planes out of New Guinea, much less across the Solomon Sea and over New Britain. Tomorrow is definitely out, sir; maybe in a day or two."

"What about the Solomons? Can COMAIRSOL do anything? They're not really equipped for heavy strikes on Rabaul, but they're better than nothing."

"I'm sorry, sir, the Solomons is closed in, too. I don't think anything can fly out of Guadalcanal any more than they can fly out of New Guinea."

"Goddamn," Whitehead cursed.

"Sorry, sir, that's how it is."

The disappointed Whitehead now called Halsey with the bad news: poor weather had ruled out any air strikes against Rabaul from New Guinea or Guadalcanal. The COMSOPAC commander was shocked by the news and Halsey looked anxiously at his aides. "We've got to hit that Japanese fleet at Rabaul the first thing in the morning; we've got to. By this time tomorrow afternoon that fleet could be well on the way to Bougainville and by tomorrow night their eight-inch guns will blow our invasion site apart."

Halsey's aides did not answer. What could they say?

Halsey then called his own weather stations whose meteorologists confirmed the weather reports from New Guinea: An extremely poor weather front had moved over the Bismarck

Archipelago and the Central Solomons, cancelling any chance for air strikes from New Guinea, the Woodlarks, or Guadalcanal.

Admiral Halsey mulled over his problem for more than an hour. Then at 1800 hours, November 4, the COMSOPAC commander remembered that his carrier fleet was in The Slot south of Bougainville. Yes! he would send his carrier planes to make the strike on Rabaul. After all, navy Dauntless dive bombers and Avenger torpedo bombers had been making low level strikes against enemy ships for months. And Halsey knew that Adm. Fred Sherman, commander of the U.S. TF 38 carrier fleet, had kept his airmen constantly practicing such strikes. TF 38 included carriers USS *Saratoga* and *Princeton,* with a total complement of about 100 planes. Halsey called Sherman at once.

"Fred, we've got a problem. A severe weather front has ruled out any air strikes on Rabaul by the Fifth Air Force or COMAIRSOL. We're got to get those Japanese heavy cruisers before they can load up and head for Bougainville. I want air strikes from your carriers. Can you launch strikes by dawn?"

"But we've only got about one hundred available planes and thirty-three of these are fighters."

"Load the fighter planes with bombs, too."

"We've never hit land based targets and harbors with carrier planes."

"There's a first time for everything," Halsey

said. "It's got to be done. If that fleet reaches Empress Augusta Bay, nothing will stop them."

"If we load our Corsairs and Hellcats with bombs, what do we do for escorts?"

"I'll have COMAIRSOL furnish escort."

"But you said COMAIRSOL couldn't get off because of the weather."

"Fighter planes can. Without bomb encumberments, they can fly through anything."

"Admiral, sir," Sherman still protested, "if we get our two carriers that close to Rabaul, we'd be taking an awful chance. We might get macerated by Japanese land based planes. We could lose both *Sara* and Princeton."

"Those are the chances," Halsey said. "Turn to and head for Rabaul. Make arrangements with General Twining to rendezvous with COMAIRSOL fighter escorts."

"Okay, admiral," the TF 38 commander said.

Adm. Fred Sherman did not like this idea at all. He did not want his two carriers so close to a Japanese land base, especially Rabaul. And, he was not certain his carrier pilots could successfully hit anchored ships, especially against swarms of enemy interceptors and heavy anti-aircraft fire. While his pilots had trained to hit ships, they had not practiced hitting them in the confines of a harbor.

Sherman notified his fleet commanders to veer northwest. He then called his air group leaders, Cmdr. Henry Caldwell of *Saratoga*'s AG 12 and Lt. Cmdr. Harold Funk of

*Princeton*'s AG 23. Both men expressed astonishment at the order to attack Rabaul with carrier planes, something they had never done before. Caldwell and Funk quickly called their air crews to ready room briefings.

The carrier planes would leave their ships at dawn, November 5, to attack the Japanese stronghold on the Gazelle Peninsula.

## Chapter Thirteen

At 2100 hours, November 4, 1943, the 2nd Fleet arrived in Rabaul. Sailors and soldiers along the shoreline of Blanche and Keravia Bays looked in awe as the heavy cruisers moved into Simpson Harbor, for they had rarely seen so many big warships at one time at the New Britain stronghold. The appearance of this powerful surface fleet was a welcome sight.

A launch boat immediately carried ashore Adm. Takeo Kurita and his 2nd Fleet officers, despite the late evening hour. Then VIP staff cars took the naval officers to Admiral Samejima's headquarters. Both Samejima and General Imamura warmly greeted the 2nd Fleet commander, but Kurita only nodded and gestured with an air of confident authority.

"Let's get on with it."

"Yes, admiral," Samejima bowed.

At the conference table in Samejima's bungalow, Kurita dominated the meeting. Adm. Mineichi Koga and Gen. Yoshihiro Umezu had agreed to dispatch Kurita to Rabaul with special orders to take care of the problem of the Bougainville invaders. With the blessings of the ranking navy and army commanders in the Pacific, Kurita took control.

"My own warships and marus of the Second Fleet are fully prepared to leave for Bougainville," Kurita said. "We need only take on fuel and supplies. How many vessels can you furnish from the Southeastern Fleet?"

"Six transport marus, a supply ship, six destroyers, and two heavy cruisers," Samejima said.

"Good, good," Kurita nodded. "You will load these vessels at once with supplies, ammunition, and troops. By noon tomorrow, I will sail for Bougainville, so the fleet can reach Empress Augusta Bay by dawn of November 6. We have brought fresh combat troops on our marus and we expect more from Rabaul." He looked at Imamura. "General, how many troops can you board on the transport marus here at Rabaul?"

"Perhaps two regiments," the 8th Area Forces commander said.

"Good," Kurita said again. "That will give us well over a division of troops for the counter invasion. As soon as our cruisers smash the American beachhead, we will land troops to destroy whatever is left of the enemy forces at Empress Augusta Bay."

"Yes, admiral," Imamura said.

"Obviously," Kurita continued, "our fleet must have air cover. Can we expect at least two

231

squadrons of fighter planes to cover us during the sail eastward and during our bombardment at Bougainville?"

"We can easily keep two squadrons airborne from Rabaul," Samejima said, "but I am not certain that Captain Shimada can furnish fifty planes from the Shortlands."

"Then send two or three squadrons to the Shortlands at once," Kurita gestured brusquely. "Air cover will be most critical in Bougainville waters. I expect Captain Shimada to furnish us ample air cover on the morning of November six when we expect to be in Empress Augusta Bay with the cruiser fleet."

"Yes, admiral," Samejima said.

"If necessary, both army and navy service crews will work throughout the night and into the morning to make certain we can leave Rabaul by noon."

"I have already asked our Eighth Area Service Command to do just that," General Imamura said. "They will work without rest until these duties are completed."

"Navy service crews have received similar orders," Samejima said.

Kurita nodded. "I would now ask that Adm. Matsuji Ijuin join myself and my staff in a briefing for tomorrow's sail. We must be certain we have our cruisers, destroyers, and maru groups in proper formation to protect us against enemy submarine and air attacks. I would also ask that you send Captain Shibata and the army air commander to this briefing so that we may coordinate air operations with our mission to Bougainville."

"As you wish, admiral," Samejima said.

Throughout the night of November 4-5, the sailors, soldiers, and airmen at Rabaul worked continuously. Despite damage to wharves and the loss of so many supplies, the Japanese still had plenty of provisions and the harbor boats to carry these supplies to anchored marus. Barking sergeants and petty officers kept service crews working, while the harbor boat helmsmen deftly putted their laden craft around the sunken ships in the harbors to deliver provisions to the vessels still afloat.

Kurita was satisfied with the progress, and by midnight he was certain his ships would be under weigh by midday tomorrow. He could then arrive at Empress Augusta Bay as planned to carry out the job that these commanders at Rabaul had thus far botched up.

Also by midnight of November 4, the TF 38 carrier fleet was on a northwest course at a speedy 30 knots and heading towards Rabaul. U.S. deck crews readied planes aboard the American carriers for a morning strike: 32 Dauntless dive bombers, 16 Avenger torpedo bombers, and 33 Hellcat fighter bombers on USS *Saratoga;* and 19 Corsair fighter bombers and seven Avenger torpedo bombers on the smaller carrier USS *Princeton*.

At 0500 hours, Cmdr. Henry Caldwell, the AG 12 commander aboard *Saratoga,* held a briefing with his U.S. Navy airmen. "We take off at oh-six hundred hours. Night recon pilots report both Simpson Harbor and Blanche Bay packed with ships." He threw a light on a huge aerial photo of Rabaul Bowl. "Here's Simpson Harbor," he tapped the photo with a pointer. "Our group will hit the ships there. I'll come in first with the dive bombers, Lieutenant Commander Farrington will come in next with the torpedo bombers, and Lieutenant Commander Newell will come in last with the fighter bombers to hit anything we miss. Remember, every plane goes into Simpson Harbor. We want those ships and nothing else. And don't worry about sinking any of them," Caldwell gestured. "COMSOPAC would rather have us leave twenty cripples behind rather than a half dozen sunken ships. Our job is to stop that fleet from sailing to Bougainville."

"What about cover?" Lt. Cmdr. Bob Harrington asked.

"COMAIRSOL will furnish escorts. They'll rendezvous with us at about oh-seven hundred hours at one-five-three degrees east by four degrees south, due west of Bougainville. They'll cover us coming and going over Simpson Harbor." He paused. "Any questions?"

None.

"Okay, get some breakfast and then report back to the ready room for final instructions," Caldwall said. "We're in for a long day."

Aboard *Princeton* at the same 0500 hours, Lt. Cmdr. Harold Funk also held a briefing in

234

the carrier's ready room. He too threw a spotlight on a large photo of Rabaul Bowl. "Here's our target—Blanche Bay," Funk said. "*Saratoga*'s AG Twelve will hit the inner Simpson Harbor and our own AG Twenty-three will hit the ships in the outer Blanche Bay. I'll go in first with the Corsair fighter bombers. We'll hit as many ships as we can. Miller will come after us with Avengers to attack any ships we miss."

"Do we attack in two plane waves?" Lieutenant Henry Miller asked.

"Yes," Funk nodded. "And remember, we don't go after anything except those ships in Blanche Bay—nothing else. And don't worry about sinking any ships; we just want to cripple them and put them out of business."

"How about air cover?"

"COMAIRSOL will furnish about one hundred marine and army fighter planes," Lieutenant Commander Funk said. "They'll rendezvous with us at oh-seven hundred at a longitude of one-five-three degrees east and a latitude of four degrees south. They'll cover us all the way in and all the way out."

The AG 23 airmen felt uneasy. Although these navy fliers had practiced low level attacks against ships, they were not sure they could do so without running into each other, especially against land based interceptors and anti-aircraft guns.

Lieutenant Miller leaned forward and looked at Harold Funk. "Commander, are you sure we can do this?"

"I understand that one of the army air groups will go in first to knock out ack ack batteries," Funk said. "And I also understand that those COMAIRSOL fighter pilots are good. They'll protect us."

The *Princeton* airmen did not answer. They only knew they did not like the idea of hitting the Japanese stronghold on New Britain's Gazelle Peninsula.

Also at 0500 hours, fighter pilots from COMAIRSOL were sitting in briefing tents at their Guadalcanal fields. At fighter strip #3 on the Tenaru River, Maj. Bob Westbrook briefed his 31 fellow pilots from the U.S. Army's 18th Fighter Group. "We cover the planes from *Saratoga*," Westbrook told the Lightning pilots. "They'll be coming in first to hit the ships in Simpson Harbor. I'll keep the Forty-fourth Squadron high and Capt. Tom Lamphier will keep the Seventieth Squadron low. Is that all right?" he asked the 70th Squadron commander.

"Okay, major," Lamphier said, but he then shook his head. "I don't know how the hell we can get off in this weather."

"We've got to," Westbrook said. He paused and then continued. "We can expect to run into plenty of interceptors, so you'll need to keep a sharp watch. Don't go running off. The purpose of this mission is to knock out enemy ships. Our business is to protect those navy bombers—nothing more."

"We understand," Captain Lamphier said.

"Okay," Westbrook nodded, "let's get some breakfast and then we'll get to our planes. We rendezvous with the navy bombers at about oh-seven hundred hours."

On Guadalcanal's fighter strip #12, Maj. Gregory Boyington briefed the pilots of his VMF 214 Black Sheep squadron and the pilots of VMF 221 under Capt. James Swett.

"This will be our first flight to Rabaul," Boyington told the 31 assembled marine pilots. "We're supposed to cover the bombers from carrier *Princeton* who are assigned to hit the ships in Blanche Bay. Right here," he tapped a huge photo on the wall. "Two-fourteen Squadron will stay upstairs and Two-twenty-one Squadron will hang low around the bombers. Is that all right, captain?" he asked Jim Swett.

"Fine, major," the 221 Squadron commander answered.

"We're scheduled to rendezvous with the AG Twenty-three planes at oh-seven hundred at latitude 4 degrees south and longitude one-five-three degrees east. Any questions?"

"How about interceptors?" Captain McClurg asked. "Can we expect any?"

"Rabaul is jammed with planes," Boyington answered. "So we'll need to stay alert." He paused. "Okay, get off to breakfast and then man your planes. We'll be taking off at oh-six hundred. We've got a long way to go and we have to do it in this lousy weather."

And finally, at fighter strip #3 on the Tenaru

River, Lt. Col. John Mitchell briefed the pilots of his 347th Fighter Group. Mitchell would use all three squadrons, 48 Lightnings, of his Army Air Force group. Further, Mitchell would lead the air strike. He too threw a spotlight on a large photo of Rabaul.

"We go in first," Mitchell told his pilots. "Our job is to make harbor and shoreline sweeps. We need to eliminate as many ack ack guns as possible to make it easier for those navy bombers. I'll take Simpson Harbor with the Three-fortieth Squadron, Captain Shubin will attack the land batteries with Three-forty-first Squadron, and the Three-forty-second Squadron will come in last to attack the ships in Blanche Bay. As soon as we make our sweeps, we'll climb high and take on any Japanese interceptors that try to hit those carrier planes."

"Will we meet a lot of opposition, sir?" Captain Shubin asked.

"The Nips may have as many as two hundred fighter planes at Rabaul," Mitchell answered. "The Fifth Air Force attack on Rabaul a couple of days ago cost the Japanese plenty of aircraft, but we understand they've brought in more planes." He paused. "Any questions on target?"

"Are we supposed to protect those navy bombers, too?"

"We may take on interceptors after we make our sweeps," Mitchell said. He sighed. "Okay enjoy breakfast. We've got a long day and we need to be off by oh-fifty-five hundred hours to meet those navy bombers at the rendezvous position. As I said, we go in first, while MAG Twenty-four and the Eighteenth Fighter Group escorts the bombers.''

By 0600 hours, Guadalcanal had emptied itself of most of COMAIRSOL's fighter planes, 112 of them. Navy Corsairs and army Lightnings were now droning up The Slot, braving the thick overcast and rain squalls. The air units flew low and Mitchell hoped they could not miss the navy bombers because of the poor weather conditions over the Solomons.

Also by 0600 hours, the 97 planes from USS *Saratoga* and USS *Princeton* had left their carrier decks. Fortunately, the sea was calm northwest of Bougainville when the TF 38 reached its launch position, 57 miles northwest of Cape Torokina and 130 miles southeast of Rabaul.

By 0615 hours, after the Navy planes were far to the westward, Admiral Sherman grew worried. His TF 38 now had a mere squadron of Lightnings from COMAIRSOL on CAP to protect his carriers against possible Japanese air strikes. He was not sure that 16 P-38s would be enough to protect *Saratoga* and *Princeton*. Fortunately, a dense cloud bank had rolled over the TF 38 fleet and Japanese snoopers were not likely to find the carriers. Further, the Japanese did not expect any air strikes on Rabaul in this foul weather, especially from U.S. carrier planes.

At 0700 hours, Lt. Col. John Mitchell spotted the 71 planes from USS *Saratoga,* and

Mitchell called the AG 12 commander. "This is Army Red leader; we're going ahead for harbor and gun battery sweeps. Your escorts are on the way; right behind us."

"Okay, Army Red," Cmdr. Henry Caldwell answered.

The AG 12 commander watched the Lightnings zoom off ahead of his *Saratoga* air units. And, before the P-38s of the 347th Fighter Group were out of sight, Caldwell saw a new group of approaching planes. These were the P-38s of the 18th Fighter Group. Soon enough, Maj. Bob Westbrook called Henry Caldwell. "This is Army Blue leader; Army Blue leader. We'll escort you into Simpson Harbor. One of our squadrons will hang around you, and the other squadron will hang upstairs."

"Very good, Army Blue," Caldwell said.

The AG 12 commander settled in his cockpit as the 44th Squadron Lightnings jelled into diamond formations overhead, while the P-38s of the 70th Squadron settled alongside the navy Dauntlesses, Avengers, and Hellcats. Caldwell stared at the army planes curiously, for he had never dreamed he would see the day when the Army Air Force would be protecting the Navy Air Force.

A moment later, the Corsairs of MAG 24 arrived at the rendezvous area of 4 degrees by 153 degrees. Maj. Greg Boyington called the AG 23 leader, Lt. Cmdr. Harold Funk. "This is Baa Baa leader; Baa Baa leader. We'll be escorting you to Blanche Bay."

"Roger, Baa Baa."

"Baa Baa Squadron will maintain a high cover and Two-twenty one Squadron will hang alongside," Boyington said.

"I read you," Funk said.

Soon, the two squadrons of Corsair fighter planes assumed their escort positions around and atop the AG 23 Avengers and Corsairs from USS *Princeton*.

As the 209 U.S. planes droned towards Rabaul, tension worsened among the American airmen. Every pilot, gunner and radio man in the formation had heard about Rabaul and none of them relished the idea of assaulting the Japanese stronghold. The heavy ack ack and swarms of interceptors that U.S. flyers had always encountered there had equated Rabaul Bowl with a spider's web.

Neither the COMAIRSOL fighter pilots nor the TF 38 bomber crews had ever been to Rabaul. They did not know what to expect; nor did they know where the Japanese cruisers and destroyers might be anchored. IQ officers of COMAIRSOL had studied photos and maps of Rabaul for many hours after word came to attack the targets that up to now had been reserved for the army's 5th Air Force. The 5th had given information on Rabaul to COMAIRSOL, but the data had only heightened the concern of COMAIRSOL and TF 38 officers. The configurations of Simpson Harbor, Blanche Bay, and the outer roadsteads of the Gazelle Peninsula indicated that the Americans could expect a blanket of ack ack fire from an entire semi-circle of shoreline and mountain ridges. General Twining had warned Lieutenant Colonel Mitchell that his 347th Group needed to knock out those ack ack sites or the navy bombers could suffer severe losses.

The American air formations droned towards Rabaul, flying above the heavy overcast that had swept over the Bismarck Archipelago and the Solomons. The dense clouds did offer one advantage: the foul weather effectively hid the American air activity from the Japanese. Neither recon planes nor submarines had seen the huge American air formation approaching Rabaul and the leaders at Rabaul assumed that the unfavorable weather had ruled out any U.S. air missions.

By 0800 hours, Lt. Col. John Mitchell of the 347th Fighter Group saw the ring of mountains that enclosed Rabaul Bowl and he picked up his radio. "This is Army Red leader. IP in ten minutes; ten minutes. Army Red will attack harbor guns and land based AA positions." Then he called Commander Caldwell. "Commander, there's a southeast wind blowing right into the harbors towards those anchored ships. If the vessels get under weigh, they'll have to come straight east. I suggest that you come right across the Crater Peninsula to attack from the north. Check your maps."

"Yes, sir, colonel," Cmdr. Henry Caldwell said. "We'll follow you."

"Escorts will hang above you to take on interceptors," Mitchell said. He now called Westbrook. "Major, make sure you stay close to those navy bombers."

"Roger, colonel," Bob Westbrook answered.

Mitchell then called Boyington. "Hang close to those *Princeton* bombers."

"Will do, colonel," Boyington answered.

"All Dauntless and Avenger gunners stay alert, stay alert," Caldwell warned his TF 38 airmen. "We'll be approaching IP in five minutes; five minutes."

Then the American air formations swung into St. George's Channel.

At the same 0800 hours, on the shoreline of Keravia Bay, Cmdr. Yasumo Doi of the harbor command was walking along one of the dirt lanes, kicking small stones in his path. He had occasionally stared into Simpson Harbor where tankers were fueling Kurita's anchored cruisers and destroyers. Suddenly, he heard sirens wail across the huge Rabaul complex. Doi squinted up in the clear sky where some 70 Japanese fighter planes were on combat air patrol. Then, Doi heard the ignition of aircraft engines from another 100 fighter planes that had been on full alert at the navy and army airfields at Rabaul. Regardless of the weather conditions, after the air assault on November 2, General Imamura had insisted that aircraft remain on constant alert.

At Lakuani Field, Capt. Goro Furugori quickly amassed 20 pilots from the 22nd Sentai to man Tony fighter planes. At Vunakanau

Field, Cmdr. Minoru Genda called together 30 Zero pilots of the 26th Wing to man planes, while at Rapopo Drome Capt. Tokeo Shibata mustered 30 fighter pilots to man Zeros of the 4th Kokuta Wing.

Thirty Zeros from the 26th Wing under Lt. Takeo Tanimizu and 40 Zeros of the 4th Wing under Lieutenant Nishizawa and Lieutenant Iwamoto were already airborne on CAP. Eleventh Air Fleet headquarters quickly called the three air leaders.

"Enemy aircraft approaching from the north! Enemy aircraft with many escorts. Air patrols will intercept at once! At once!"

"We will attack immediately," Lieutenant Nishizawa answered. He then called other pilots on CAP. "We will climb high, to twenty thousand meters, and attack from above. Be sure to attack in three aircraft V's."

The Japanese aircraft veered 45 degrees, climbed high over the Vulcan hills, and prepared to meet the oncoming American planes. Meanwhile, the pilots below climbed into the cockpits of their fighter planes, while gun crews leaped into the pit areas of the antiaircraft weapons.

While the air units at Rabaul acted quickly in this emergency, the ships in the harbor could not escape the sudden approaching American planes. Fuel hoses were still pumping oil into warships when the air sirens wailed. The tankers quickly rolled in these hoses, while ship commanders issued sharp, loud orders to weigh anchor at once. The vessels were not likely to reach St. George's Channel for better maneuvering room before the Americans attacked.

At his headquarters in Rabaul township, Gen. Hitoshi Imamura scowled. Why didn't the recon planes that continually patrolled the sea detect these hordes of enemy planes before the aircraft reached Rabaul? Was Imamura to suffer the same disappointment he had three days ago? Would he agonize through another hour of destruction to once more delay a counterinvasion of Bougainville? Imamura cursed. What could one expect from the incompetent Imperial Navy? The Emily reconnaissance planes had failed again, as the navy had always failed. The 8th Area Forces commander only hoped that this time the Japanese fighter pilots would stop these aerial interlopers.

At his own bungalow, Adm. Tomishuge Samejima rushed to his porch to squint up at the sky. He saw his own Japanese aircraft jell before zooming northward and he then watched the frantic activity in Simpson Harbor and Blanche Bay. Cruisers, destroyers, and marus were emitting thick curls of smoke from their stacks as engine crews fired up boilers to speed out of the harbor. Samejima stared upward again, hoping to catch sight of the American planes, but he had not yet seen any.

Adm. Junichi Kusaka, meanwhile, reacted quickly to the air raid sirens. He called all his air unit commanders: those at Rapopo,

Vunakanau, and even the army field at Lakunai.

"Get aircraft out at once. At once!" he told the executive officers at each field. "We must stop these interlopers this time. They must not cause the damage and death they did a few days ago."

"Pilots are leaving the airfields now, honorable Kusaka," one of the officers answered the 11th Air Fleet commander.

"Good, good," Kusaka said. Then he looked at his aide. "What of the units on combat air patrol?"

"All three squadrons are now flying to the northward to engage the enemy aircraft," the aide said. "They will make every effort to destroy the American bombers before they reach the harbors."

"Let us hope so," Kusaka said.

But the 11th Air Fleet commander was apprehensive. He feared his airmen would fail again today; that he would suffer a replay of that miserable November 2 afternoon.

## Chapter Fourteen

The Zeros on CAP under Lieutenant Nishizawa and Lieutenant Tanimizu rose higher and waited for the American planes to break formation to make their runs. The Japanese pilots could then gang up on individual U.S. aircraft. However, the Americans would not accommodate the Japanese. Lt. Col. John Mitchell warned both the fighter pilots and carrier pilots to keep together.

"Stay tight! Maintain formation. Remember, Three-fortieth Squadron pilots will follow me to hit Simpson Harbor, Three-forty-first will attack the land batteries along the shoreline, and Three-forty-second Squadron will attack ships in Blanche Bay."

The three squadrons of Lightnings from the 347th Fighter Group roared into Rabaul from St. George's Channel. Mitchell took the 340th directly west over Blanche Bay to strafe the ships in Simpson Harbor. Captain Shubin veered his 341st Squadron south over Cape Gazelle to hit the AA batteries along the shoreline, and the trailing 342nd Squadron came in to hit the ships in Blanche Bay.

By now, the horde of vessels in both harbors had begun skimming desperately about the water, trying to escape into St. George's Channel for more room. They flitted about the harbors frantically, with little time to unleash accurate AA fire at the American P-38s. In turn, Lieutenant Colonel Mitchell and the pilots of the 340th Squadron raked the ships in Simpson Harbor with heavy fusillades of .50 caliber strafing fire from the six guns on each Lightning. The P-38s skimmed over the harbor in three waves and by the time the 4th Flight had made its run, antiaircraft gunners aboard the destroyers and cruisers in Simpson Harbor had scampered to safety from the blistering fire.

Almost simultaneously, Capt. Murray Shubin droned over Cape Gazelle with the 16 P-38s of the 341st Squadron. "Stay tight! Stay tight!" Shubin warned his pilots. "Those Nips upstairs will jump any stragglers. After we make our runs, we'll try to hit some of those Zekes trying to take off."

Shubin and his pilots sprayed the shoreline antiaircraft batteries of Rabaul Bowl: Blanche Bay, Kesavia Bay, and Simpson Harbor. They unleashed heavy fire on the AA gun pits, destroying nearly a dozen of them before they zoomed high, clearing the Vulcan Crater and then circling back to hit Japanese planes on the airfields.

Finally, the 342nd Squadron unleashed heavy

strafing fire on the vessels in Blanche Bay, the ships of the Torokina Interception Fleet that had already suffered losses during the Battle of Empress Augusta Bay against Adm. Tip Merrill's TF 39. Once more, Japanese sailors scattered in panic in the face of the withering .50 caliber strafing fire. By the time the last 342nd Squadron pilot had arced away from Blanche Bay, dozens of Japanese sailors had been killed, wounded, or chased from their gun pits.

Confusion prevailed inside Rabaul Bowl by the time the three P-38 squadrons of the 347th Fighter Group left the harbors and shoreline. Before the Japanese reorganized themselves to muster some measure of defense against the aerial assailants, the bombers and fighter bombers of the U.S. TF 38 carrier fleet zoomed low to carry out their attacks on the array of ships.

While the Lightnings of the 18th Fighter Group hung upstairs to meet Japanese interceptors, Cmdr. Henry Caldwell roared towards Simpson Harbor with his Dauntlesses from USS *Saratoga*. "In pairs! In pairs! As soon as you make your dives, pull up and get the hell out."

Caldwell led his dive bombers into the scampering array of ships: cruisers, destroyers, and marus of the 2nd Fleet. In the harbor, Adm. Matsuji Ijuin was aboard a launch boat that was putting across the water to flagship *Maya*. The first quartet of whistling American bombs almost lifted the boat out of the water, killing two Japanese sailors and wounding the others, including Admiral Ijuin. The Desron 27 commander then floundered in the water, the second time in a few days, to watch the aerial attack in awe.

One 500 pounder dropped right into the stack of flag cruiser *Maya* and exploded in the engine room, warping parts of the superstructure amidship and leaving the cruiser in a pall of fire and smoke. Although the direct hit did not sink the 2nd Fleet flagship, the Japanese would need five months to repair the heavy cruiser. From the bridge of *Maya,* Adm. Takeo Kurita cried frantically into a radio phone.

"Damage control! You must contain fires!"

The horror on Kurita's face was a marked contrast to the smug confidence he had shown yesterday when he arrived in Rabaul from Truk.

Even as Kurata issued orders aboard *Maya,* fellow cruiser *Takeo* caught two bomb hits on the starboard aft that opened a pair of holes below the water line. Heavy starboard flooding sent the cruiser into a ten degree list.

And still the Dauntlesses came on. Heavy cruiser *Atago* suffered three near misses that wrecked two storage compartments and warped the rudder so that the ship could only sail in circles. More bombs hit maru transports in Simpson Harbor, flooding one maru, setting fire to another, and wrecking the engine room of a third transport.

Now came Lt. Cmdr. Bob Farrington with his 16 Avengers from USS *Saratoga.* He skimmed low over the harbor, despite the AA fire from some of the ships. Two torpedoes from Farrington and his wingman skimmed towards light cruiser *Noshiro*. The Japanese warship avoided one torpedo, but the second slammed into the cruiser's forward quarter and exploded with a numbing concussion in the bow. The cruiser then took on tons of water and before repair crews sealed the flooding, *Noshiro* listed to ten degrees on the forward. Her bow was a total wreck and she was no longer fit for battle.

"Stay tight! Stay tight!" Lieutenant Commander Farrington implored his Avenger pilots. "As soon as you let go your fish, bank out of here and climb fast."

"Aye, sir," somebody answered.

As the ships in Simpson Harbor continued to zigzag in the attempt to escape the American planes, other Avenger pilots from *Saratoga*'s AG 12 also scored. A torpedo slammed into one of the 2nd Fleet's freighters. The ship exploded in a shuddering blast that sent fire and smoke spiralling skyward. Another torpdeo hit a second maru, a transport, and shattered the ship's bow.

Then came Jim Newell with the *Saratoga*'s Corsair fighter-bombers. Newell scored a bomb hit on heavy cruiser *Mogami* and the bomb exploded in a magazine. The concussion tore away half of the cruiser's superstructure, while killing and wounding more than 100 Japanese sailors. Ironically, *Mogami* had been recently returned to combat after heavy damage in the Battle of Midway over a year ago. Now, her decks were in shambles and she would once more return to the Kure Naval Yard in Japan for repairs.

Other airmen from Newell's Corsair division scored on destroyer *Fujinami* with whistling bombs that tore holes on the starboard. The destroyer settled deep in the water before repair crews sealed all flooding to keep *Fujinami* afloat. The destroyer was finished for any further combat.

As the aircraft from USS *Saratoga* lacerated the 2nd Fleet in Simpson Harbor, the Avengers and Corsairs from USS *Princeton* hit the scattering ships of the Torokina Interception Fleet in Blanche Bay. Harold Funk, the AG 23 commander, called his fellow pilots. "We're going in first on bomb runs. The Avengers will follow with torpedo runs. Stay tight! Tight! If you don't, those Nip interceptors upstairs will come on us like hungry wolves."

Funk led the *Princeton*'s Corsairs into the Torokina Fleet cruisers. Funk dropped two 500 pound bombs on light cruiser *Agano*. One bomb missed, but the other struck the forward area and exploded, ripping a huge hole in the deck and twisting the forward gun turret. Before *Agano* repair crews could deal with this damage, a second 500 pounder from a Corsair struck the midsection of the light cruiser, penetrated the deck, and exploded in one of the engine rooms. The cruiser quickly slowed to a limping five knots.

More bombs from the Corsairs near missed both heavy cruiser *Myoko* and heavy cruiser *Haguro*. Neither ship was in danger of sinking, but damage to their superstructures would keep Japanese crews busy for at least two or three weeks. Neither vessel would be going on combat sorties for some time.

Then came the Avengers from *Princeton*'s AG 23. Lt. Henry Miller, leading the torpedo bombers, singled out destroyer *Wakatsuki*. He called his wingman. "I'll take her on the forward; you take her on the aft."

"Okay, lieutenant."

Down came the two Avengers, almost at water level. The helmsman aboard *Wakatsuki* tried desperately to avoid the two torpedo bombers that plopped two fish into Blanche Bay. The destroyer could not escape both of them. One torpedo slammed into the starboard bow of the Japanese warship and exploded in a ball of fire and smoke. The explosion tore a hole in the hull and destroyed the #1 gun turret. Flames and smoke then enveloped the entire forward area of the suddenly listing ship. The vessel skittered about the harbor completely out of control before ramming into a maru transport that was also trying to escape Blanche Bay.

Before the Avenger pilots from AG 23 left the bay, the American airmen put a torpedo into another Japanese transport. The torpedo hit amidship and exploded in a rattling concussion that almost cut the ship in half. The vessel quickly sank, taking dozens of soldiers and sailors with her.

Only ten minutes after the assault began, nearly a score of flaming, smoking, or even sinking ships lay in Simpson Harbor and Blanche Bay. Although only one of the ships would actually sink, the Americans had damaged well over a dozen others—just what Halsey wanted. Six of the heavy cruisers were out of commission, as were two light cruisers and two destroyers. Further, six maru transports and a freighter were out of action, with one of the transports down. Adm. Takeo Kurita would not take his fleet to Bougainville.

The success of the American airmen from USS *Saratoga* and USS *Princeton* had been possible because of the P-38 and Corsair escort pilots from COMAIRSOL. Even as the 347th Group pilots made their strafing runs against the harbor and shoreline antiaircraft guns, the pilots of the 18th Fighter Group and from MAG 24 had waded into the Japanese Zeros on CAP. Maj. Bob Westbrook of the 18th Fighter Group's 44th Squadron cried into his radio:

"We'll take those Zeros to the west. In pairs; hit them before they can dive on those *Saratoga* bombers."

"Lead the way, major," Capt. Tom Lamphier of the 70th Squadron answered.

Then, the 32 fighter pilots from the 18th Group roared into the Zero fighter planes of the 4th Wing. In moments, rattling machine gun fire, whooshing 20mm cannon and 37mm cannon shells, and the whine of aircraft engines echoed across the sky over Rabaul Bowl. The two Japanese aces, Lt. Hiroshi Nishizawa and Lt. Tetsuzo Iwamoto, held their own against the Americans, but most of the other 4th Wing pilots could not deal with the superior P-38 fighter planes or the capable U.S. pilots.

Maj. Bob Westbrook and his wingman attacked a V of Zeros and before the Japanese planes veered away, the two Americans got all three planes with heavy .50 caliber machine gun fire and whooshing 37mm cannon shells. One Zero exploded in midair, another lost a wing before skittering into the sea, and the third lost its tail before cartwheeling to oblivion in the New Britain jungles.

Capt. Tom Lamphier caught two Zeros in a single pass. He opened on the first with heavy machine gun fire that shattered the cockpit and killed the Japanese pilot. And before Lamphier completed his run, he hit a second Zero with two 37mm shells that blew the Japanese fighter plane apart. The fragments fell into St. George's Channel. Other 18th Fighter Group pilots also scored, knocking down a dozen more of the Japanese planes from the 4th Kokutai Wing.

In minutes, 17 Zeros, nearly half of the 4th Wing's CAP complement, had fallen to the Americans. In turn, the Japanese pilots had only scored four kills against the U.S. fighter pilots. Nishizawa got two P-38s when he caught the right wing of one P-38 with thumping 20mm shells and sent the Lightning plunging into the jungle. He got his second kill with a barrage of .30 caliber machine gun fire that shattered both engines of the U.S. plane before the P-38 tumbled into St. George's Channel. Lieutenant Iwamoto, meanwhile, caught a P-38 just as the Lightning made a pass on a Zero and started to climb upward. Iwamoto sprayed the aircraft with .30 caliber wing fire that ripped apart the cockpit and killed the pilot.

Only a dozen of the 40 Zeros on CAP broke through the 18th Fighter Group screen to attack the American planes from USS *Saratoga*. One Zero pilot got a Dauntless just as the dive bomber released bombs. The Dauntless caught three 20mm shells that destroyed the engine and dropped the plane into the harbor. A second Zero pilot got an Avenger from AG 12 when thumping 20mm shells tore away the engine and right wing before the torpedo bomber splashed into the harbor, killing all aboard.

In addition, two Dauntless suffered damage, including that of Cmdr. Henry Caldwell. Eight Zeros had pounced on Caldwell's dive bomber. The heavy Japanese fire punched more than 200 holes in the sturdy American plane. The fire killed Caldwell's photographer, A/1C Paul Barneau and seriously wounded the gunner, AOM Kenneth Bratton. But, astonishingly, Barneau and Bratton had downed three of the Zeros before Caldwell himself damaged two more Japanese planes with his forward guns, and he chased off the rest. Caldwell would bring the shattered Dauntless back to *Saratoga* without flaps, radio, or ailerons, but he would successfully land the plane on the carrier deck. All three men aboard the plane would win Silver Stars, Barneau's posthumously.

Meanwhile, MAG 24 pilots waded into the 30 Zeros of the 26th Wing under Lt. Takeo Tanimizu. Within a few minutes, the two marine Corsair squadrons under Pappy Boyington and Jim Swett cut to pieces the Japanese interceptors. The marine pilots knocked 17 of the Zeros out of the sky. Boyington himself got two planes with rattling machine gun fire and bursting cannon fire. Capt. Jim Swett also downed a pair of Zeros from the 26th Kokutai Wing. Other Baa Baa pilots of VMF 214 and Whitetail pilots of VMF 221 also scored. After more than half of the 26th Wing planes on CAP went down in a disastrous few minutes, the other Japanese pilots scattered to avoid the same fate.

Lieutenant Tanimizu had been the sole Japanese pilot to score when he knocked down one of the Corsairs from VMF 221. Tanimizu caught the U.S. plane after the American pilot had just made a pass against a Zero. The *Junyo* ace shattered the tail of the Corsair before the American plane tumbled into the sea.

Further, several Japanese Zeros did break through the Corsair formations to pounce on the *Princeton* carrier planes that were attacking ships in Blanche Bay. The AG 23 formations lost one Avenger and two Corsair fighter-bombers, while suffering damage to three more aircraft.

These American losses were little consolation to the Japanese for the heavy beating against Rabaul air units and the extensive damage against Japanese ships in the harbor.

And the Americans were not yet finished. By the time other Japanese aircraft started taking off from their runways to intercept the American planes, Lt. Col. John Mitchell and his 347th Fighter Group pilots had completed the runs over AA positions, circled back, and came in low over the Rabaul airfields. With rattling machine gun fire and thumping 37mm shells, the three squadrons of P-38s shot up planes of the 4th Wing, 26th Wing, and 22nd Sentai still on the ground.

Mitchell and the 340th Squadron pilots struck Tobero Drome where they blew up two Zeros of the 4th Wing at the head of the runway, thus thwarting the takeoff of other planes. Similarly, Capt. Murray Shubin and the pilots of the 341st Squadron shot up several planes of the 26th Wing at Vunakanau Drome. The U.S. pilots set the aircraft afire, left them wrecked on the runway, and stopped any Zeros from taking off. Finally, the 342nd Squadron destroyed a half dozen planes or more at Lakunai Field, although a few Tony fighter planes from the 22nd Sentai did manage to get off.

The Japanese efforts had been too little and too late.

A half hour after the attack began on Rabaul, smoke and flames had engulfed the harbors and airfields of the Japanese base. Imamura, Samejima, and Kurita all looked in awe at the devastation inside Rabaul Bowl. The American air assaults on this November 4 morning had dashed all hopes of sending Kurita to Bougainville with a powerful surface fleet and ground troop reinforcements.

As the American airmen droned back to their carriers or to their land bases, the pilots and crews of the TF 38 carrier planes expressed both admiration and thanks to the marine and army pilots of COMAIRSOL who had protected them during the harbor strikes. For the first time in the Pacific war, air units of all three U.S. military services had worked together in a common effort, an operation that had resulted in astounding success. For the loss of five bombers and five fighter planes, far less than expected, the Americans had destroyed 29 Japanese planes in the air and 18 more on the ground. They had also immobilized the Rabaul airfields and the powerful Japanese 2nd Fleet.

When news reached Truk of this ravaging raid on Rabaul, Adm. Mineichi Koga expressed shock. He concluded that Rabaul was no longer a safe anchorage for his heavy ships. He ordered Takeo Kurita to weigh anchor at once with his cruisers—damaged or otherwise—and return to Truk.

Conversely, Gen. Ennis Whitehead of 5th Air Force, expressed delight when he heard of the successful carrier strike on Rabaul. Whitehead could not count on the U.S. Navy to aid 5th Air Force in the reduction of Rabaul. And, in fact, the ADVON 5th Air Force commander sent out 27 B-24s and 67 P-38s on the very afternoon of November 5 to hit Rabaul again. The 5th Air Force planes smashed wharves, supply dumps, and repair facilities to supplement the TF 38 destruction.

If the Americans had not finished off the Japanese stronghold, they had certainly left Rabaul shattered.

On the same afternoon of November 5, the Japanese attempted to strike back with 18 bombers against the two carriers of TF 38. But the bombers from Rabaul's 4th Wing under Capt. Tokeo Shibata did not even locate the carriers *Saratoga* and *Princeton*. They found only a half dozen small craft west of Bougainville. In the growing darkness of the late afternoon, Shibata mistook some LCI's and PT boats for transports and destroyers. The Japanese Vals sank one of the U.S. vessels, the LCI-70, whose gunners fought off no less than 14 of the Japanese dive bombers.

Cmdr. Benji Shimada also took off from the Shortlands with about a dozen Vals and a dozen Zeros, all that was left of the Yokoyama Wing in the northern Solomons. Shimada led the Vals and Lieutenant Commander Iwami led the Zero escorts.

"The dive bombers will attack the invasion beaches," Shimada said, "and the fighters will provide cover."

"Yes, commander," Iwami answered.

The Yokoyama Wing aircraft came into Empress Augusta Bay under some very low clouds and caught the Americans off guard. The Vals destroyed several tons of supplies and countless barrels of fuel on the beach areas before the Zeros under Iwami strafed the marine defense positions, killing a dozen Americans and wounding 30 or 40 more. Commander Shimada then got away clean with all of his aircraft in one of the only bright spots during the Bougainville campaign.

But the Japanese would score no more. By dawn of November 6, COMAIRSOL maintained continual CAP's over Empress Augusta Bay to stop further air attacks, while 5th Air Force and navy carrier planes continued to pound Rabaul during November: on the 6th, 9th, 11th, 13th, and 26th. By the end of the month, the 5th Air Force B-25s of the 3rd, 38th, and 345th Bomb Groups had finished off whatever ships were left in the harbors and what few planes had remained on the airfields.

In fact, as Col. John Henebry led his 3rd Group bombers back to New Guinea after the November 26 air raid, a wide grin creased his face. "Well," he told his co-pilot, "Rabaul has now become a milk run."

"It seems that way, sir," the co-pilot answered.

True, neither the 3rd Group nor any other B-25 group had lost a single plane on the raid; nor did any of the escorting fighter groups lose any aircraft. In reality, by November 26, Admiral Koga had not only pulled most of his ships out of Rabaul, but also the 26th Kokutai Wing—or what was left of it. Both Commander Genda and Lieutenant Tanimizu were glad to return to Truk.

As for the 4th Wing and 22nd Sentai, they continued to lose more of their aircraft during the November air raids on Rabaul, losing them either in the air to American fighter pilots or on the ground to American bombers.

Minoro Genda and Takeo Tanimizu would survive the war. Genda would open a sporting goods shop in Tokyo and Tanimizu would rise to the rank of captain in the Japanese Air Defense Force in post World War II. The Devil Nishizawa would die in an unfortunate crash in the Philippines in 1944 when his plane got hit by lightning during a thunder storn. Iwamoto would score 210 victories by war's end to become the leading ace in the Pacific. He survived the war, but he died of septicemia in 1955 at the age of 38. Captain Furugori continued to lead Japanese army air units until he was killed in action in the Philippines in November, 1944.

Among the Americans, Gregory Pappy Boyington got shot down over Rabaul in January of 1944 to spend the rest of the war as a prisoner. Boyington had then had his ups and downs after the war and he had even tried to run for Congress—unsuccessfully. He became wealthy though, with his famous Baa Baa Black Sheep book. The heroic Bob Westbrook of the 18th

Fighter Group was shot down by gunfire over the Philippines in November of 1944. When his plane crashed, his comrades tried to find him, but they could not. The man who had won a Silver Star, DFC, DSC, Air Medal, and many clusters to these medals was never heard from again and presumed dead. The handsome Charles MacDonald of the 475th Fighter Group survived the war and remained in the U.S. Air Force after World War II. He retired from service in 1966 after a distinguished career.

Col. John Henebry continued to lead the 3rd Bomb Group until he returned to the States in 1944. Henebry had become the king of Pacific attack bomber pilots in a unit, the Grim Reapers, that were kings of attack bomber groups. He survived the war, remained in the U.S. Air Force and then retired in 1968 to his home in Plainfield, Illinois. In his distinguished combat career, he had personally accounted for the destruction of 440 Japanese planes and 104,000 tons of shipping during 118 combat missions. No airmen in World War II, from any side, had even come close to this score.

Shortly after the November 5, 1943 raid on Rabaul, the 23rd Japanese Infantry Regiment marched through 40 miles of jungle to attack the Americans at Empress Augusta Bay. But, the U.S. marines wiped out the 23rd Regiment almost to the man. After this disaster, the Japanese made no more attempts to send troops overland from Buin or Kahili to attack the U.S. marine combat troops.

By November 15, the navy seabees had completed an airstrip on Bougainville and American planes moved up from Guadalcanal. Now, the COMAIRSOL aircraft pounded to a pulp the remaining Japanese troops in the northern Solomons. By the end of November, Captain Shimada abandoned the Shortlands and took his few remaining men and planes back to Rabaul to become part of the 4th Kokutai Wing.

By Christmas of 1943, Gen. Hitoshi Imamura, the disappointed 8th Area Forces commander at Rabaul, conceded the utter failure of Operation I-110 and the loss of Bougainville. He shifted his efforts from the Solomons to New Guinea where he expected the Americans to make new moves up the coast. Besides sending combat troops to New Guinea, he sent the 4th Kokutai Wing to Wewak to defend upper New Guinea.

"We succeeded with Operation Cartwheel," Gen. Ennis Whitehead said later, "because we had neutralized Rabaul after several weeks of steady air attacks. The November second raid by the Fifth Air Force and the November fifth raid by the U.S. carrier planes were the major blows in this series of air strikes. With the reduction of Rabaul, the Japanese were forced to write off Bougainville and the Solomons themselves."

"Air power did such a job on Rabaul," Colonel Henebry told an AP correspondent in December of 1944, "that we didn't need to invade and occupy the Gazelle Peninsula on our drive back to the Philippines."

From his headquarters in Rabaul, even in early 1944, Gen. Hitoshi Imamura still talked bombastically. "We had lost the Solomons and we had suffered severely at Rabaul. But our enemies will never set foot in the Philippines."

Operation Cartwheel had succeeded as totally as the Japanese I-110 operation had failed so totally. Within a year, the Americans would indeed return to the Philippines. General Imamura, however, would not see this event. On July 17, 1944, totally despondent over continued Japanse military misfortunes, the 8th Area Forces commander committed suicide in his bungalow at the now isolated, by-passed Japanese base of Rabaul.

# RING AROUND RABAUL

## American Participants

COMSOPAC (Command South Pacific) Admiral
William Halsey, Noumea, New Caledonia
TF 31—III Amphibious Transport Force—Admiral Len F. Reifsnider
3rd Marine Division—General Al H. Turnage
TF 39 cruiser-destroyer fleet—Admiral Stanton
"Tip" Merrill
T 33 — COMAIRSOL (Command Air Solomons)—
General Nathan Twining, Guadalcanal
MAG 24 (Marine Air Group) Colonel Richard
Mangrum
VMF 212—Major Gregory Boyington
VMF 221—Captain James Swett
Also VMTB 242 and VMSB 232
18th Fighter Group—(Army Air Force) Colonel
Aaron Tyer
44th Squadron—Major Robert Westbrook
70th Squadron—Captain Tom Lamphier
347th Fighter Group—Lt. Col. John Mitchell
Also: 307th Bomb Group, 5th Bomb Group,
42nd Bomb Group, and 18 Squadron RNZAF
TF 38 (U.S. carrier Fleet)—Admiral Fred Sherman
AG 12 USS *Saratoga*—Cmdr. Henry Caldwell
AG 23 USS *Princeton*—Lt. Cmdr. Harold Funk

COMSWPAC (Command Southwest Pacific) General Douglas MacArthur, Brisbane, Australia

U.S. Army 5th Air Force—ADVON commander, General Ennis Whitehead, Port Moresby, New Guinea 3rd Bomb Group (Grim Reapers)—Colonel John Henebry
  13th Squadron—Colonel Henebry
  8th Squadron—Major Ray Wilkins
  90th Squadron—Major Lee Walker
  38th Bomb Group (Sunsetters) Colonel Larry Tanberg
  345th Bomb Group (Air Apaches) Colonel Clinton True
  475th Fighter Group (Satan's Angles) Lt. Colonel Charles MacDonald
  Also: 43rd Bomb Group, 90th Bomb Group, 8th Fighter Group, 35th Fighter Group, 49th Fighter Group, 4th Recon Squadron

## Japanese Participants

8th Area Forces—General Hitoshi Imamura, headquarters at Rabaul
Japanese Combined Fleet—Admiral Mineichi Koga, headquarters at Truk

Fleet units:
  Southeastern Fleet, Rabaul, Admiral Tomushige Samejima
  Torokina Interception Fleet, Rabaul, Admiral Sentaro Omori
  3rd Mobile Fleet, Truk, Admiral Jisaburo Ozawa
  2nd Support Fleet, Truk, Admiral Takeo Kurita

11th Air Fleet—Admiral Junichi Kusaka—headquarters at Rabaul
  4th Kokutai Wing—Rabaul—Captain Tokeo Shibata
  22 Sentai Air Division-Rabaul—Captain Goro Furugori

26th Kokutai Wing—Rabaul—Cmdr. Minoru Genda

Yokoyama Wing, Shortland Island—Cmdr. Benji Shimada

Ground Units:
17th Army—Rabaul—General Haruyoshi Hyakutake
6th Infantry Division—Bougainville—General Noburu Sasaki

# Bibliography

Alcorn, John S., *The Jolly Rogers*, Historical Aviation Album, Temple City, Calif., 1981.

Constable, Trevor, and Toliver, Raymond, *Fighter Aces of the USA*, Aero Publishers, Fallbrook, Calif., 1979.

Caidin, Martin, and Saito, Fred, *Samurai*, Bantam Books, New York, 1978.

Craven, W.F., and Cate, J.L., Army Air Forces in World War II, *Vol. VI, The Pacific, Guadalcanal to Saipan*, Univ. of Chicago Press, Chicago, 1950.

Dull, Paul S., *The Imperial Japanese Navy*, Naval Institute Press, Annapolis, 1978.

Edmonds, Walter, *They Fought With What They Had*, Little, Brown and Co., Boston, 1951.

Fahey, James, *Pacific War Diary 1942-1945*, Houghton Mifflin, Boston, 1963.

Greenfield, Kent, *U.S. Army in World War II, Pictorial Record—War Against Japan*, Dept. of the Army, Washington, D.C., 1952.

Hess, William N., *Pacific Sweep*, Zebra Books, New York, 1974.

Jablonski, Edward, *Air War, Volume II*, Doubleday & Company, Garden City, N.Y., 1971.

Karig, Walter, and Kelly, Welbourne, *Battle Report, Vol. IV, Southwest Clean-up*, Rinehart and Co., New York, 1948.

Karig, Walter, and Purdon, Eric, *Battle Report, Vol. III: Pacific War: The Middle Phase*, Rinehart and Co., New York, 1947.

Kenney, George C., *General Kenney Reports*, Duell, Sloan & Pearce, New York, 1949.

Lord, Walter, *Lonely Vigil*, Chap. 3, "Forty Bombers Coming Your Way."

Maurer, Maurer, *Air Force Combat Units of World War II*, U.S. Gov't. Printing Office, Washington, D.C., 1961.

Maurer, Maurer, *Combat Squadrons of World War II*, U.S. Gov't. Printing Office, Washington, D.C., 1969.

Milner, Samuel, U.S. Army in World War II, Vol. 6, *Cartwheel: The Reduction of Rabaul*, Office of Military History, Dept. of the Army, Washington, D.C., 1952.

Morison, Samuel, History of U.S. Naval Operations in World War II, *Vol. VI—Breaking the Bismarck Barrier*, Little, Brown & Co., Boston, 1953.

Rust, Kenn C., *Fifth Air Force Story*, Historical Aviation Album, Temple City, Calif., 1973.

Sambito, Major William J., *A History of Marine Attack Squadron 232*, U.S. Marine Corps, Washington, D.C., 1978.

Steichen, Edward, *U.S. Navy War Photographs: Pearl Harbor to Tokyo Bay* (Official Navy Photos), Crown Publishers, New York, 1956.

Sunderman, Major James, *World War II in the Air: The Pacific*, Franklin Watts, New York, 1962.

## Archive Sources

**Alfred L. Simpson Air Force Research Center, Maxwell Field, Ala.**
Reel #B0043—History of the 3rd Bomb Group
Reel #B0065—History of the 18th Fighter Group
Reel #B0045—History of the 38th Bomb Group
Reel #B0047—History of the 475th Fighter Group
Reel #B00263—5th Air Force Combat Operations

**Naval Historical Center, Washington, D.C.**
American:
Reel #5051-1—1st Marine Amphibious Corps, Operation 21
ONI (Office of Naval Intelligence) Series
Combat narrative, Battle of Empress Augusta Bay
Operation summary of Bougainville campaign

COMAIRSOL daily intelligence summary, 2 November 1943 to 29 January 1944 USS *Saratoga* Operations Report, 5 November to 15 November 1943

The Halsey Report—"Campaign of the Pacific War"
Reel #A-14-43
MAG 24—War Diary, Bougainville campaign
COMAIRSOL Operation Plan #TI-43

Japanese:

ATIS Reports (Allied Translator and Interrogation Section) of Japanese records

JD 2—Gazelle Bay operations

JD 4 8th (Southeastern) Fleet operations

DJ 15—Crudiv 5 (Torokina Interception Fleet) operations

Japanese Monograph Records:

Monograph #48, Southeast Area naval operations

Monograph #50, 17th Army operations

Monograph #110, 8th Area Forces operations

USSSBS (U.S. Strategic Bombing Survey) interviews

#503—S. Fukodome (Combined Fleet staff officer)—"Allied campaigns against Rabaul"

#139—J. Najakima (4th Kokutai Wing executive officer)—"Solomons Campaigns"

#524—T. Ohmae (aide to Admiral Koga) "Southeast naval operations"

#495—Cmdr. M. Yamagach (Operations officer of Southeastern Fleet) "The Bougainville Campaign"

## THE SURVIVALIST SERIES
### by Jerry Ahern